Don't miss Celeste and Azrael's
first exciting adventure,

*Surrender the Dark*

Available from Pocket Books

# CONQUER THE DARK

## L.A. BANKS

POCKET BOOKS
New York  London  Toronto  Sydney  New Delhi

Pocket Books
A Division of Simon & Schuster, Inc.
1230 Avenue of the Americas
New York, NY 10020

This book is a work of fiction. Names, characters, places, and incidents either are products of the author's imagination or are used fictitiously. Any resemblance to actual events or locales or persons, living or dead, is entirely coincidental.

First Pocket Books paperback edition October 2011

POCKET and colophon are registered trademarks of Simon & Schuster, Inc.

For information about special discounts for bulk purchases, please contact Simon & Schuster Special Sales at 1-866-506-1949 or business@simonandschuster.com.

The Simon & Schuster Speakers Bureau can bring authors to your live event. For more information or to book an event contact the Simon & Schuster Speakers Bureau at 1-866-248-3049 or visit our website at www.simonspeakers.com.

Designed by Leydiana Rodríguez-Ovalles
Cover design by Lisa Litwack
Cover illustration by Gene Mollica

Manufactured in the United States of America

10  9  8  7  6  5  4  3  2  1

ISBN 978-1-4516-0884-7
ISBN 978-1-4516-0898-4 (ebook)

In memoriam

*Leslie Esdaile Banks, beloved mother, daughter, and friend. We were blessed to know her, and will miss her dearly. She loved her devoted fans and wrote for them with all of her heart.*

# CONQUER
## THE
## DARK

together in inseparable passion . . . they had discovered it was simply unavoidable.

Azrael had found his Remnant, Celeste; two of his brothers had found their Remnant mates in the months following the battle in Philadelphia. Bath Kol had Aziza with him, and although not a Remnant, she was no less a dear part to the group. Now those women were like the sisters Celeste had never had, and she was grateful for the wonderful addition to her life. Three women, like her, who now knew what it was to be swept up in a maelstrom of altered reality. That made for a close-knit sorority that had bonded over fear, war, tragedy, triumph, and divine intervention—and dished about it all. Celeste released a quiet sigh of pure contentment; she was blessed.

If only things could go on this way with her man, her angel, peaceful and happy, his brothers sated and re-laxed, their partners the first real female friends she'd ever known. The warehouse was a sanctuary on the banks of the Delaware River in Philly. But she knew that the clock was ticking. Learning to live in the moment was the only way to mentally survive. Maybe that was how Az made sense of it all, too? Being immortal had to have given him a philosophical perspective.

Rather than dwell on what couldn't last forever, she tucked away any unpleasant thoughts and watched Az-rael work through his methodical tai chi dance.

Deep in meditative prayer, serenity wafted from his very being as he opened his arms and slowly bent his knees, beginning his morning ritual. She could literally see the energy move through him in a thin, blue-white charge that began to cover his skin as his entire body became engaged in the graceful, ancient choreography. As if witnessing a celestial fan dance in which his majestic wings lifted and dusted the floor, creating music in the pauses and breaths and sweeps, she watched in abject reverence.

It was all so beautiful that emotion tightened her throat. She was supposed to be dead by now. Azrael had found her on the night she'd seen a demon take her ex-boyfriend's life, and she'd been hell-bent on also taking her own.

But with a touch, Azrael had pulled the drugs and alcohol out of her system. With patience he'd convinced her to stop running from him and that she hadn't had a psychotic break, hadn't lost her mind. Then he'd shown her that angels and demons truly existed and took her on the most hair-raising journey of her life.

Time was relative. Three short months ago she'd met an angel and everything she thought she knew about the so-called normal world had been shattered in an instant. Three short weeks ago she'd lost the last living relative that she cared about—her aunt Niecey—and yet because of Azrael, she'd been at peace about that. Now that she knew there was actually another side and that what she'd heard all her life hadn't been theoretical, it was easier to accept many of the losses, even the hard ones such as her mother and Aunt Niecey.

Tears rose to Celeste's eyes and then slowly burned away when she thought about all that Azrael had given her. He'd claimed that she'd saved him; but what she could never explain was that it was the other way around.

Before him, there was only fear and self-destruction. No one understood her gift, except her dear late auntie.

Only her aunt knew that Celeste could see way down deep into people's souls and feel what they felt. Only Aunt Niecey had borne witness to how the dark side had murdered her parents and thrust her into a world of poverty and addiction and madness that seemed to have no cure. Until Azrael had shown up, the only thing she'd known to do to stop the pain of seeing demons and so much frighteningly horrible weirdness was to drown it all in a bottle. Her so-called gift was so debilitating back then that it left her weak and vulnerable, unable to work, and with a psychiatric file as thick as a phone book. The ravages of poverty had taken their toll on her health and self-esteem. All along she'd thought it was her own fault, until Azrael came to show her that she'd been targeted for suffering by the dark side because of the coming work she was about to do.

Sudden joy filled her heart now as she watched him bend and turn, the cabled sinews stretching along his thick biceps and forearms . . . her gaze going to his massive but graceful hands that could caress ever so gently and heal, but that she'd also seen wield blades of death to behead demons. Surreal.

Oddly, that made her feel safe, after all she'd seen in her life. Yet, the warrior angels who'd been trapped on earth since their first big battle with the fallen, some twenty-six thousand years ago, had been waiting for her . . . waiting for her prayer and her willingness to sacrifice herself for them so that they could return to the Light, even if they'd violated divine edict and lain with the daughters of man while here.

And after twenty-six thousand years, all it took was the

right combination of her prayer as a member of the Remnant—a half-human, half-angel Light Nephilim with twelve strands of DNA hiding in her genetic code, to fuse with the Angel of Death's intention to liberate his trapped and suffering brethren from this density. Profound. She'd sent up the heartfelt request; Azrael had opened the portal to the Light. But there was only one taker, Jamaerah, a gentle spirit who could no longer endure his entrapment in the flesh. Once liberated back to the Light, he demonstrated to her how angels and positive spirits still helped from the etheric realm. The rest of the battle-hardened, Jack Daniel's–drinking, partying crew, who had thought all was lost and previously lamented not being able to return, had stayed when given the choice, deciding to ride or die with her and Azrael to the end.

That was the thing they'd taught her, too—just knowing one could leave if one wanted evaporated the illusion of being trapped. That paradigm shift was the freedom that the angels with dirty wings, her guys now, needed. She'd given them that and they loved her for it, calling her *the key*, since she'd unlocked their minds and commuted their sentences for violating the divine law not to lie with human women while on earth. In return, they'd given her unparalleled protection and knowledge. Many a night and well into the dawn they'd all sat up with her and her Remnant sisters debating the merits of the lessons learned by having everything angelic except immortality stripped from their beings.

To hear Bath Kol tell it, hellfire would have been easier. But they'd each agreed that, by being made manifest, by temporarily losing their wings and being plunged into the temptations of the flesh, they'd gained an empathy for humanity that just couldn't be fully perceived while in etheric form.

To experience heartbreak, suffering, physical pain, desire, rage, jealousy, lack, need—all of that had given them serious respect for the human condition. Now when they fought for humankind, they fought with a whole different level of regard for the beings that endured here even with demon oppression besetting their existence. After twenty-six thousand years here in the flesh, this special dirty-angel corps knew that humans weren't just weak cattle. They'd been outgunned and outmanned by evil, immortal forces way stronger than humans could ever hope to be. Yet many people still endured, held the line, helped their neighbors, sacrificed their lives for others, were honorable and loved and reached out to those less fortunate, despite the tidal wave of negative forces. *That* was courage under fire, to be sure.

And her angels said *that* had been what the Almighty had known and seen in the divine creation. It was also why to not serve humans was such a defiant act. To be righteous and perfect when one is all-powerful is not difficult; to do so when mortal and weak and hungry and afraid is heroic. Azrael told her that the Source of All That Is saw that striking quality in its creation and demanded the angels respect that. Most did, but some did not—hence the war that has raged on since the planets last aligned to open the veil between worlds.

For all that Azrael and the others gave her, the one thing none of them could bestow upon her was peace of mind as the date of the next alignment approached.

Celeste quietly sighed. The soft sweep of Azrael's wings and the gentle pat of his bare feet against the floor were soothing. Had his dance not been so profoundly beautiful, she would have closed her eyes and allowed the constant metronome-like rhythm to lull her back to sleep.

But there was no way to close her eyes on that splendor, just as there was no way to unknow all that she'd come to see and learn since he'd entered her life. Never in a million years could anyone have told her she'd be living with a battalion of angels in a retrofitted warehouse with the future of the planet hinging on one date: 12/21/12.

# Chapter 1

**B**ody glistening with a thin sheen of sweat from his exertion, Azrael opened his eyes and offered her a lazy smile. "Good morning."

"Back atcha," she replied, loving the easy rumble of his voice.

"How long have you been awake?"

"Ohhh, just about long enough to thoroughly enjoy the floor show," she murmured as he came to the side of the bed and sat near her.

"I didn't mean to wake you up." He leaned down and brushed her mouth with a light kiss, then pulled back to look at her.

"You didn't, and I wouldn't have minded if you had." She reached up and traced the line of his square jaw with the cup of her hand. Warmth from his body radiated out in a palpable blanket as he leaned in for another, deeper kiss.

No matter what he'd eaten, his kiss always tasted sweet like ambrosia. That lacquer always coated and masked everything else he'd consumed, even the insides of her mouth. By now she'd learned to judge his mood by the concentration of that wondrous flavor. This morning it was mild and delicate, telling her that he was thoroughly contented and relaxed. When he pulled back again, this time he found stray wisps of her hair to push behind her ear.

"Would you like some breakfast?"

She raised an eyebrow as her smile broadened. "I was just about to ask you that."

Her comment made him laugh. "Celeste . . . you are my ruination, you know that, right?"

"Yeah."

They both laughed as he pounced on her, but the play came to an abrupt halt the moment Bath Kol's angry voice shattered the calm. It was impossible to hear exactly what he was yelling about, but it was definitely a mood killer.

"I need to go check on my brother," Azrael said with a resigned sigh.

"Yeah, it was time to get up anyway," she replied, trying to shake off the disappointment.

Azrael slowly peeled his body away from hers, gave her a wistful glance, then got up. "Could be nothing, then again . . ."

"Could be everything," she said with a shrug, swinging her legs over the side of the bed. She yanked her hair up into a messy ponytail, found a scrunchie on the nightstand, and stood.

Azrael looked so forlorn as he crossed the room and hesitated by the door that it made her swallow a smile.

"I'll be right back, okay?"

"Don't worry about it. I'm gonna wash my face and brush my teeth, then rustle us up some grub. What do you want to eat?"

"It's not in the kitchen," he said, then let out a breath of frustration as another bellicose outburst drew his attention toward the door.

Celeste just shook her head and chuckled quietly as he exited, then searched in earnest for her pajama pants and slippers, as well as a sweater. In bed, she'd been nice and cozy. But the huge warehouse was drafty as all get-out in November. This place wasn't like the one Bath Kol had retrofitted in New York. There, before the dark side had ambushed them around the corner from his South Bronx club, Bath Kol and his Sentinels had been able to stay in that massive warehouse long enough to rig it with heat and electricity and collect all sorts of furniture and creature comforts from eras gone by.

However, now that their collective date with destiny was so close, and they now had the added complication of humans within the angel roost to protect, they had to stay on the move. Heat was provided by whichever angel body was in the room, pure energy wafting off him. Once he left, the bitter cold set in.

Celeste boxed her arms as she headed to the makeshift bathroom. Sure, it had been well cleaned and used the old plumbing system from when the factory warehouse had been opened years ago, but one had to conserve the water that was provided by a series of huge, leveraged drums, which also needed to be regularly replaced.

Plus, the abandoned building had no formal electricity

either. It wasn't as if she could just walk into a room and flip on a light or blow-dry her hair after a shower. If alone, she and the other humans in the building had to get as much done as one could during the daylight hours and use the ambient light coming in through the endless banks of windows.

But that didn't stop them from having illumination or cooking altogether, as long as one of the brothers with a little celestial juice was in the room. It was still inconvenient as hell, but not as inconvenient as being discovered by nervous humans or being ambushed by demon forces.

Therefore, she could live with the preferred option of survival, even if that meant taking over dilapidated industrial structures that were far enough away from dense human populations to avoid heavy collateral damage if a firefight broke out. And ever since the battle on the Delaware, the brothers had decided that they liked having a water source at their back door.

Every day one of them would go to the river and anoint it with a prayer, and instantly it became a blue-white death trap of holy water should demon forces try an incursion by sea. Their airspace was fiercely guarded by brothers taking shifts on the roof. No doubt they loved the old factories and warehouses that dotted the East Coast waterways because those structures gave them room to stretch their wings like giant birds of prey, and with a little angelic cloaking they could keep themselves occupied with all manner of sports while on the expansive roofs.

By land, they had the perimeter lit up with hallowed-ground prayer barriers. The unused floors beneath the couple upper floors they took over at the tops of the buildings for bedrooms and the common areas were well fortified, too. Massive elevators were perfect for their fleet of Harleys and crotch-rocket motorcycles. Table-tennis boards, foosball stands, and basketball hoops took up a large section of the common area, and they *loved* the Wii—literally playing all their games acrobatically on the fly. Wii video games and the realistic interactive games on the Xbox 360 blew their minds and brought them endless delight as they fought demons, bet on who was a better sharpshooter, better guitar player, talked trash, drank beer, and played cards.

That common room stayed lit night and day, as did the multiple refrigerators it contained, which nobody seemed to forget to lend their juice to—not because it kept the food edible for their human charges, but more likely because it kept the beers cold. But after twenty-six thousand years of battle on earth as Sentinels and Guardians, who could begrudge the guys a little fun?

However, the one thing they could not do was kill a human just because he or she discovered the whereabouts of their battalion's roost. If humans showed up, such as cops or building inspectors, the brothers had to deal with that intrusion fairly, humanely, even if the hassles that those people caused were enormous.

If a demon wanted in or wanted them out, the easiest thing to do would be to mind-stun some poor human law enforcement officer to investigate squatters and have them legally ousted. The angels' cloaking themselves to minimize that possibility was one thing, but changing a person's mind or simply expunging it for their own convenience violated the edict of allowing humans free will.

Yeah, they were going to have to move again soon. She could feel it in her bones. That was probably what had Bath Kol raising hell in the common area first thing in the morning. She could hear him and Isda at the center of a heated debate. It sounded as if the other brothers were taking neutral positions and simply watching.

Celeste splashed cold water on her face, wishing for a moment that Azrael were there to heat it up, then banished the thought. They all had more important things to do than to worry about water temps and creature comforts.

Quickly finishing her morning routine, she spit out her toothpaste and swished a gulp of clean water around in her mouth, spit again, then dashed down the football-field-length hall toward the common area.

The closer Celeste got to it, the louder the debate raged. As she entered the large, open area, Melissa was sitting across the room at the double-long picnic-style table with her head in her hands and her profusion of dark-blond curls hiding her almond-hued face. Tension riddled the Remnant sister's tight posture. Arguing and dissension jacked with Melissa's nervous system. Badly. Celeste frowned. Everybody knew that. Like all of them, Melissa had been through a lot, shuttled from her native Aborigine mother's outback hideaway to her Danish father's people in Demark. In between, the dark side had claimed much of Melissa's innocence and peace; the same way Magdalena's life had been no day at the beach, running from Ecuador to Colombia and subsequently falling into the wrong hands before Gavreel found her. But the way each woman processed stress was different. Melissa would allow it to implode within her and come off analytical and as though it didn't bother her, whereas Magdalena would blow a fuse. If the brothers didn't stop this crap, they were gonna make Celeste want to start smoking again.

When Maggie looked up, her intense, dark eyes said it all—*help*. The Remnant sister's exterior beauty and gorgeous face appeared serene and calm on the surface, but Maggie's eyes always conveyed her inner chaos. Even Queen Mother Aziza, a sensitive who had been with Bath Kol for years, seemed to have no effect on quelling the dispute. She sat ramrod straight, her back facing the table, her regal head held high and topped with purple-fabric-swathed dreadlocks. The middle-aged woman drew long, steadying breaths for calm, and her delicate, dark-walnut-hued back expanded and contracted slowly as though trying to filter the negative energy zinging around the common room. Then Aziza turned slowly, giving Celeste a meaningful glance as the male voices escalated.

Gavreel stood near the table close to his mate, Maggie, tension riddling his athletic, six-foot-two frame while blue-white energy caused his long, dark hair to slightly lift off his broad shoulders. Wearing a steely barrio-grit, the more angrily he glared at Bath Kol and Isda, the more distraught his Remnant became. But Paschar, who usually had the disposition of a yogi, with tranquil East Indian features and a melodic voice, constantly sent his gaze between his mate, Melissa, and the arguing angels, seeming ready to jump into the fray at any moment.

Nodding at Aziza, Celeste fully entered the wide-open space just in time to see Azrael jump between Bath Kol and Isda, who'd lunged at each other, wings spread for battle.

"Okay, guys. What's going on?" Celeste looked from Bath Kol to Isda with a frown. "All this first thing in the morning? Really?"

"There appears to be a dispute about whether we simply move this encampment and hunker down in the country, or travel abroad to locate an item that we may need in an upcoming battle." Azrael released a long, weary sigh. "No one wants to have to uproot our temporary homestead or to travel to potential international danger zones, but Bath Kol had a vision that very well may warrant the sudden change."

"I'm not going to Egypt! Dat's final, mon! Not like dis!" Isda shouted, spittle flying as his dreadlocks crackled with blue-white fury energy. "Have you been watching the news? You see how de whole Middle East just collapsed like a row of dominoes, mon? Egypt was just in a mad state of unrest, and if you haven't checked, it's not exac'ly tourist-friendly right now!"

The more upset Isda became, the thicker his Caribbean accent grew as he argued his point. "So I suggest you get a cup of coffee and sober up! Face it, BK, your visions have been fucked up for centuries, so now because you've *supposedly* been clear for a few months, you draggin' us on a suicide expedition with Remnants in tow? You must have bumped your damned head last night!"

"Me? Me! I've bumped *my* head?" Bath Kol shouted back, his face red and veins standing up in his neck.

Pressing his stone-cut chest against Azrael's outstretched hand, Bath Kol looked more like an irate Hells Angels biker about to kick off a bar brawl than an angel warrior of Light.

"There's nothing wrong with my visions these days, and I know what I saw in my meditations this morning, son!" Bath Kol looked at Azrael for moral support, then back to Isda, dragging his fingers though his spiked blond hair in frustration. "Just stay in your fucking lane! I have province over *prophecy*—you have province over nourishment—waaay different. So, if I want something to eat, I'll ask you what's on the house menu, but—"

"Tell me dat shit when you don't have a fifth of Jack Daniel's in your system, aw'ight!"

"Yo!" Azrael shouted, pushing both would-be combatants back. "Don't either one of you forget that I have province over angel *deaths*." He looked at Bath Kol and Isda hard as they sized each other up. "The language," Azrael said, pointing at the kitchen table where the women had gathered. "Not to mention, you all know better. Going at each other like that and lowering the vibrational frequency in here with cursing and anger is a sure way to get this joint overrun. So I suggest everybody just calm down!"

Isda walked away a bit, flexing the muscles in his majestic dark-chocolate chest, biceps, and shoulders, finally retracting his wings. Bath Kol kicked a stray kitchen chair out of his way and walked off a few paces, then turned and folded his arms over his barrel chest.

After a moment, Azrael rubbed his palms down his face. "That's better," Azrael muttered. "Arguing amongst ourselves is getting us nowhere. And if we need a tie-breaker, Paschar also has province over visions—"

"But not prophecy!" Bath Kol shouted, slapping his chest. "There's a difference!"

"You done?" Azrael waited until Bath Kol backed off, then sent his angry gaze around the room for a moment, challenging anyone to speak. Twenty-one angels looked at Azrael. The two combatants, Bath Kol and Isda, glared at each other across the room in a standoff. Gavreel and Paschar stood beside their Remnant mates with furrowed brows, clearly concerned. The remaining members of the Special Forces battalion that had chosen to stay on earth took up spectators' positions around the room.

Aziza, the only human sensitive in the group, glanced at Celeste again. Somehow Aziza's eyes beckoned Celeste to intervene again, but she wasn't sure what the psychic healer wanted her to say. Under normal circumstances, Aziza herself was able to calm her mate, Bath Kol. He trusted her as a human seer, and the one who'd labored over him and his men for years with healing ministrations to draw out toxins from their beleaguered systems. Her voice was normally like a balm to his shattered nervous system as she helped him balance his stressed-out chakras and restabilize his etheric body so that he could function in this density without so much emotional pain. But today, he clearly wasn't seeking her counsel, so Aziza apparently wanted Celeste to intervene through Azrael.

"Ask the locator then," Isda finally said, lifting his chin and jerking it toward Celeste. "Months back, she knew where to tell Paschar to find Mel and told Gavreel right about Maggie—that she wasn't in Colombia any longer but was on that flight coming into Miami. Celeste is more neutral than Paschar, who's just gonna side with BK to keep the peace."

"That is true about Celeste's locating skill," Aziza said in a calm tone as she studied Bath Kol for a moment and then looked at Celeste. Seeing the indignant tension in her lover's body language, Aziza stood and went to him. "Not because your visions are flawed, BK, or because Paschar will side with you just for the sake of harmony. But because in these last critical weeks, it's best that all clues get impartially corroborated."

Bath Kol lifted his chin but didn't push his lover away and instead slung a thick arm over Aziza's shoulders. "Fine. Ask her."

All eyes went to Celeste, and she glanced around the room, finally seeking silent counsel in Azrael's troubled gaze. "Ask me what?"

"If—"

"Let *Az* ask her," Isda yelled across the room, cutting Bath Kol off. "You know better!" Isda added, pointing at Bath Kol. "You ask a question in a certain way and you'll get *exactly* the answer you want. You ask it neutral, and you got a betta chance at da truth. I don't know about anybody else in here, but I, for one, want da truth."

Isda folded his arms, and Azrael, before proceeding, waited until Bath Kol held up both hands in front of his chest. Eyeing both Bath Kol and Isda with a warning glare not to further interrupt, Azrael walked forward and took up both of Celeste's hands.

"We need to know if you can get any impressions

about a very important piece of antiquity . . . something metal with sacred writings on it."

Celeste stared up into Azrael's eyes, then closed hers. Warmth from his hands and his aura spilled over her hands and traveled up her arms to envelop her entire body. Soon she could hear only her own breaths, then her own heartbeat, as everything around her faded away into the background. The center of her forehead began to tingle and soon felt even warmer than her burning hands, as did the top of her head. Slow-moving visual impressions flooded the dark space inside her lids until she could feel her lashes beginning to flutter. Quick, shallow breaths replaced her long, slow breathing. Then she saw it—a huge book . . . or . . . big metal pages.

Celeste opened her eyes with a gasp. "Like tablets?"

Azrael's hands squeezed hers gently. "Yes."

"Some are . . . green, like how copper turns on the roofs of buildings?"

"Yes," Azrael murmured, now bending to allow his forehead to touch hers.

Tingling warmth covered the places they touched and she relaxed into the sensation, almost beginning to feel as though she were floating. It made her close her eyes again, and when she did, more impressions flitted through her mind.

"Some are gold," she said in a soft voice. "But some are crystal . . . and there's a clear crystal mummy case with . . . gold bones?"

She opened her eyes and looked up at Azrael, thoroughly confused. "I don't get it."

"The metal library," Maggie said in a hesitant tone,

glancing around the group. "When I was in Ecuador with my grandfather, he said the Shuar tribe's shaman protected a metal library from outsiders. He only told me because he said I had a special secret destiny . . . It had the things Celeste spoke of. But white men came with an astronaut—an exploratory team that was pulled together by a famous guy from NASA, and all they found was a very old stone ring. They could never find the actual library or the entrance to it. Defeated, they left, but they came back again to Cueva de los Tayos still looking for the way in, never knowing that the true opening was under the Pastaza River, not aboveground. No one told them, though. It was sacred tribal knowledge."

"Yeah, the warrior brothers knew about the tablets and the protectors of the vault, but the dark side never got this close before, even with humans jacking around looking for it." Gavreel shook his head and rubbed his palm over the nape of his neck. "Seems like the closer we get to 2012, the closer the other side gets to their objectives, too."

Azrael nodded. "Their efforts to find the vault have obviously been renewed since we kicked their asses in Philadelphia. That's gotta be why they're on a mission searching for it now—before that last battle, they thought they could take us without needing the tablets, which are bound into one sacred book."

"Right, and what Maggie is talking about is the human Stan Hall's expedition," Gavreel said with a confirming nod toward Azrael. "That opening is at seventy-seven degrees, forty-seven minutes, and thirty-four seconds west, and one degree, fifty-six minutes, and zero seconds south."

"So if you know the location, mon, then why we all—"

"That joint was cleared out years ago, dude," Bath Kol said, shaking his head.

"It's true what BK says about that. They had to move the library out of South America. It was too hot, and non-authorized human exploration was getting too close." Gavreel looked around the group, gaining nods from all the other angels except Isda.

"So how you know, mon? You don't have visions like BK and ain't been over there yet."

Gavreel frowned and stood a little taller, clearly taking exception to the challenge. "I came into this manifestation with that continent and the representative ethnic groups from it in my DNA pattern, just like the rest of you came in bearing a pattern that ensured you were matched to the familial human tribe of your Remnant to better blend in with it. We also received the resident knowledge of the geographic region our Remnant was from." Gavreel paused, giving Isda a hard look. "So I can safely say that Maggie's grandfather was teaching her facts, not legends, brothers. The entrance to the massive underground network that was carved out by some of our brothers during the first war spans the continent and was indeed hidden underwater to keep the tablets from falling into the wrong hands . . . but, like BK said, that library was moved."

"Grandfather said even though it was underwater, it did not mean you would get wet," Melissa added softly. "An earthquake made a natural opening behind the river."

"That was the dark side, trying to break into the vault the Incas once guarded—until they got wiped out, then so many of the Shuar," Gavreel said, shaking his head. "But, yeah. The new opening along with more insistent human expeditions made the move inevitable."

"No one is disputing your knowledge," Azrael affirmed, glancing at Isda with a frown before returning his gaze to Gavreel and then the others. "We've had many protectors of the vault from the ancient Atlanteans, the Kemetians, Sumerian tribes, the Incas, the Mayans, Tibetans, the Aborigines, the Native Americans, and many of the Norse tribes, to name a few. Given that, why are my brothers arguing about the fact that the library has moved?" Azrael looked around the group again. "The facts are simple; the library has circled the globe—and has been hidden everywhere from Atlantis to Iceland."

"Which was my point," Isda said, vindicated. He gave Bath Kol an angry look but then focused his attention on Azrael. "It's been on the move true. But Kemet—Egypt— was the second place it was transferred after Atlantis went down. So why would it go back to the most obvious location of ancient ruins, huh? Why not the sacred temples of Thailand or some remote Fiji island?"

"What's on the tablets or in this big book they've been consolidated into that's so important?" Celeste asked, glancing around. "I got impressions, but I don't understand what this place is that housed it and why everyone is so wigged out."

"In Dreamtime," Melissa hedged, sending her comments in Celeste's direction, "my grandfather showed me a place far away that had thousands and thousands of metal books on massive slanted shelves. Some pieces were so heavy one man could not lift a book alone. Others were maybe forty to fifty pounds each, with tablets inserted within them like pages—single sheets of metal. Also there were all sorts of plants and seeds stored there for a rebirth of the mother, he said."

Melissa stared off toward the sunlit windows as though seeing the images unfold right before her eyes. "It was like a giant library, and he called it the Hall of Records . . . and a botanical ark in case the final battle left nothing but scorched earth."

"And while it was in my old homeland of Ecuador, many men were discredited and died with the secret in their hearts trying to find this repository of knowledge," Maggie said in a reverent tone. "There was also war in Ecuador . . . in 1997. I was just fourteen and we prepared to move to Colombia. Two years before that, Peru bombed an Ecuadorian military base. Things were escalating. My grandfather got sick and he said that evil forces were trying to find the library . . . and me. The next year, in 1998, the only man outside the tribe that knew about how to find it was shot in the street and he died. Even though my grandfather was very ill, we moved to Colombia anyway. I was fifteen. They said it was a robbery—the man who was shot. Grandfather called it an assassination. "

"It was, beloved," Aziza said, wrapping her arms around herself. Her voice drifted as she closed her eyes and her lids began to flutter. "Men who tried to tell the Western world were discredited. They even took Neil Armstrong there, the famous astronaut, as Maggie said. They found a ring, dated 1500 BC, but it was just a relic left behind during a hasty move." Aziza squeezed her eyes shut more tightly. "That was in 1976."

"The Bicentennial!" Celeste shouted, pulling away

from Azrael to pace in a circle. Information poured into her mind so quickly that it made her ears ring. "The timing of that first expedition attempt by an international team— led by a well-known explorer of the cosmos, freakin' Neil Armstrong, for crying out loud—syncs up with a milestone in American history . . . just like the first vision I had about *the event* occurring in Philadelphia. I saw a horrible battle, but didn't know what it meant at the time . . . and we all soon found out that we'd have to take a stand in Philly or die trying. And I'm still getting very strong impressions that something major is yet to happen here."

"Correct," Isda said with a smug glance toward Bath Kol. "Even da lady says it's still g'wan 'appen in Philly, mon."

"Okay, okay, I stand corrected," Bath Kol said, beginning to walk away. "My bad."

"No," Celeste said, rounding Bath Kol as everyone in the room strained their attention in her direction. "Whatever is in that library has to come here . . . or *will* come here. But that doesn't mean it can't originate from somewhere else."

"In the Bible it's very clear, ladies and gentlemen. Celeste is right. Says in the last days the only church that had found favor with the Light was the church of Philadelphia, which translates to the congregation or institutions here. It's in the Book," Bath Kol said in a slow, calmer tone. "Check it out in Revelation 3:7, if you guys are still into reading the old texts, dude. Philadelphia holds *the key* of David—he that opens and no man shuts. Need I say more? It's in the Book. Case closed. There's gonna be action in Philly. We can bank on that part. But what I'm trying to get you guys on board about is the fact that we have to head it off at the pass, and to do that we have to go back to the old country—Egypt."

"So, whatever these tablets are—in the form of one huge book—the dark side is going to bring them here, eventually, and that's not a good thing, right? We need to get the tablets first?" Celeste looked around the room and then back up to Bath Kol.

"Yeah, that's the problem in a nutshell, baby girl." Bath Kol smoothed his palm over his hair and walked away toward the refrigerator and opened it to get a beer, then looked at Azrael. "You wanna tell the little lady or should I?"

"The library," Azrael said slowly, crossing the room in a calm lope, "was written in precious metals and crystal—because it's not only permanent, it's also conductive. Precious and semiprecious stones were also used . . . diamonds, quartz, lapis, you name it, to keep certain frequencies within the chambers. That treasure made the library vulnerable to human incursion. Humans, who could be sent in to breach the protective prayer barriers, even when dark forces could not. Humans can walk over prayer lines. Humans can cross through areas that have white Light protection in ways a demon cannot. So demons lead humans to the areas where they need things extracted and where they cannot directly go in themselves. That's why it had to be hidden."

"But I don't understand," Celeste said, frowning and lifting her heavy ponytail up off her neck. "What was so deep in the library—in fact, why write it if there was worry it could fall into the wrong hands?"

Azrael let out a long sigh. "My brothers of the Light who got trapped here after the first big war with the fallen had to wait some twenty-six thousand years before the alignment happened again—the alignment that would open up the veil between worlds, per the Mayan calendar and the ancient Kemetic calendars, yes?"

"Yeah, yeah, I know that part," she said, growing impatient.

"We needed a way to regenerate our human armies that were battling the forces of evil with us. When the alignment ended and the portal shut down, only a few of us remained here in the flesh. Most were extracted home to fight the darkness from the etheric realms. Those left were Special Forces," Azrael added, giving a nod of respect toward Bath Kol and Isda. "Their mission was to search for the Remnant . . . beings like you that are the hybrid offspring of angels and humans. Actual physical intervention was necessary; not all of what had to be done could happen from the etheric realms.

"Dark Nephilim had to be slain, Remnants of the Light had to be protected while our trapped brothers like BK and Isda were also trying to hold the line with their etheric brothers and sisters—our side needed ground troops. We needed a way to raise significant human armies of the Light to assist when the time came. But that knowledge couldn't fall into the wrong hands. That's why it had to be secreted away."

Paschar nodded. "The demons had almost overrun the planet. The fallen were many more in numbers than we, as they had hundreds of thousands. To keep humankind from completely going dark, ofttimes, Celeste, we would raise a human army to fight side by side with our physical and etheric forces to beat back evil. It was always for a just cause and to save humanity."

Turning slowly, Paschar motioned to his body and then toward Melissa. "My Remnant that would have matched my tribe was lost. But because of you, I was able to locate Melissa nonetheless. The brothers that manifested as a Dane and as Aborigine did not get to her before I did, but that is no slight upon their valiant efforts. Searching for each of you to be born is literally like looking for a needle in a haystack without a locator. We had that as a challenge until you were brought to us, while also trying to beat back demon incursion upon humankind, and protecting the vault."

Azrael let out a hard breath and began to pace, raking his locks with his long fingers. "The problem is very complicated, Celeste. The sacred vault holds information only shared with the highest-level human priests and shamans, those whose souls were without question on the side of the Light. There needed to be a repository of information that would help keep humanity from falling into the Dark Ages, to help them remain advanced—just as in all the Golden Ages . . . and to be a legacy once we finally retreated from the planet."

Isda released a long whistle and folded his arms over his chest. "Well, you saw what 'appened to Europe when da Dark Ages hit 'em . . . damned bubonic plagues, witch hunts, barbaric medical practices, no social justice, people living in total human squalor . . . the Inquisition, burning people at the damned stake for believing in gravity and dat de earth was round—*insane* and all orchestrated by the dark side . . . when access to the vault was temporarily lost to high priests and priestesses of the old cultures. Kill the shaman, kill the knowledge, mon. Occasionally had a breakthrough, like Merlin, but by and large, the period was bad. Took a couple of centuries of human history to come back from those ashes, brother."

Bath Kol nodded. "There's information in the vault that some cultures might call magic, but it's just energy manipulation. Stuff like how to levitate heavy objects—a good thing to know if a demon battalion is on your ass or if you want to build a Stonehenge or pyramid to increase the positive energy flow in a region. We gave them star maps—astronomy, an understanding of the way the gravitational pull from heavenly bodies affects different personalities, what you call astrology . . . showed them the logic of mathematics in numerology. Then organized religion started trying to keep this info from the people, the dark side said it was the occult . . . outlawed the use of herbal cures, crystals, started relegating feminine energy—women—to the spiritual sidelines, man . . . it was a jacked-up public relations campaign by the darkness. Anyway, long story short, in there is info on how to cultivate crops, sacred geometry, sacred architecture—"

"Like Masonic principles?" Celeste said eagerly, cutting Bath Kol him off.

He shrugged with a half smile. "Yeah, something like that. But all Masonic mysticism comes from Egypt by way of the vault."

"The founding fathers of this country were Masons, and a lot of that sacred geometry is embedded in

Philadelphia architecture." Celeste looked at Bath Kol as he glanced at Azrael. "Maybe there's a clue here?"

"Right, little sis," Bath Kol said, taking her more seriously. "The Egyptians, otherwise known as Kemetians, were the first people since Atlantis to really absorb the vault and apply it to the fullest. The vault used to be hidden under the Sphinx when the Nile Valley was fertile and that big sucker was half-underwater, some twenty-six thou ago. Then it was necessary to move it deeper into the interior— we hid it in Songhai, then Mali, some of it in the repository of Timbuktu, but no place was as strong or impervious to invasion as Kemet was for all those years. From there the vault did a tour of duty in Asia and all the way up into the Himalayas in Tibet and over to Indus Kush—or India—as the dark side laid siege to the Nile Valley using Roman legions. China became a hotbed of turmoil, Persia was crazy, and the dark side took up residence in Babylon—so we got it over to the Americas, first with the Incas, then Mayans . . . some of the Hopi tribes, then over to Europe, and back out."

"There were so many secrets in the vault," Azrael said. "Countless technologies humans needed to know to protect themselves and the planetary environment."

"Better stated," Bath Kol pointed out, ironically gaining a nod from Isda. "If they were going to fight along with us, humans needed to know how to eat right in order to get and stay strong, how to instantly heal and regenerate from a mortal wound, how to infuse the human body with additional physical power to make the average Joe as strong as Hercules."

"So give me credit where credit is due," Isda said, frowning. "I'm not some short-order cook. That was a cheap shot, mon." Isda lifted his chin with pride. "I have province over nourishment, the thing you need to supercharge the cells of your body. That is why blight and famine are such crimes. The dark side does this, not the Light, and even so—there is enough food on this planet to feed every hungry soul what is clean and good . . . but greed is evil. It keeps food for profit from the starving."

"Okay, okay," Bath Kol said, waving his hand. "I'm sorry. But can we not lose focus, man?"

"Speak," Isda said impatiently, walking away to lean on the other end of the table.

Bath Kol released a breath of frustration, then turned back to the four women, focusing on Celeste. "Like where do you think martial arts came from, or the Zen meditations? Or all of the walk-over-hot-coals-and-still-be-chill stuff? There's a reason why we had to teach human warriors that, ladies. Like how is some dude gonna walk over hellfire when the demon armies spread a carpet of that down under our human legions, huh?"

When no one answered his rhetorical question, Bath Kol walked off a bit and sipped his beer. After he'd turned the bottle up to his mouth and taken a healthy swig, he winced and looked at the group again. "Just like we have to constantly update our knowledge of human culture, customs, and speech patterns to blend in, humans had to learn some of our cosmic gunslinging methods in order to survive the darkness. Main thing humans needed to know was how to raise the dead if you've got a hundred thousand slaughtered troops on the battlefield, a li'l somethin' interesting in the metal library, as humans call it."

For a few moments, no one spoke. No one moved. Then Celeste broke the silence with a simple question.

"So, if the dark side gets ahold of this library, the right section of it, they could literally raise the dead?"

Bath Kol nodded. "They could raise the dead along with every demon and fallen angel we've sent to the pit over the last twenty-six millennia if they get to the book in the library that holds those tablets."

# Chapter 2

Celeste moved to the table and sat down slowly, joined by Aziza. It took a moment for what Bath Kol had said to sink in, and Celeste needed to repeat it to be sure she'd heard right.

"So, you're saying that if we don't find this library—or at least that one book of tablets—and hide it, if the dark side gets it, they could raise an entire army of darkness?"

"No," Bath Kol said, now leaning against the sink. "The vault was relocated to Egypt because that was the last place they'd look for it again. That's called hiding in plain sight, darlin'. For a while we had it totally underwater, like off the coast of Japan—until the United States nuked them in WWII . . . and then we hid it in the Bermuda Triangle. But it sort of defeats the purpose of leaving a legacy for humankind to help them if they can't access it, so we brought it back to one of the original rotation sites. That's why the main vault is back in Egypt.

But we need to remove the book from the vault and stash it directly under our protection for safekeeping from now on. That's my argument."

"Then what's the problem?" Celeste glanced around the group.

"The one crystal book of tablets with the prayers on it that can get the job done is missing. Not to mention, the bad guys now have Imhotep's crystal sarcophagus with his gold-covered bones in it. *That's what I saw in my vision*." Bath Kol eyed Isda until Isda looked away.

"Imhotep was a genius," Bath Kol said, pressing on for Celeste, "and member of the Light Remnant, just like those other dudes in the Good Book that lived seven to eight hundred years. But since Imhotep came before them, his skeleton was dipped in gold to protect the DNA in his marrow and to make his Light energy in that DNA more conductive—enough so that with his bones and the prayers from the crystal tablet, recited on the winter solstice, which is the darkest day of the year on the planet, December twenty-first, the reanimation energy can be focused. That focused energy will allow the dead soldiers from battlefields past to be able to get up and fight again. Houston, we've got a problem if the dark side gets the crystal book of resurrection tablets to go with a Light Remnant's bones. Dark Remnants' bones can't reanimate and of course we've hidden the tombs of all of the Remnants of Light, but Imhotep is one of the most powerful they could have found."

Bath Kol turned to Isda and crossed his arms and lifted his chin. "And, again, that's the reason I was lobbying to head to Egypt, to find the book before the dark side does."

"But how did a freaking crystal tablet book get lost?" Celeste was out of her seat at the table on and her feet. "Seriously!"

"Human free will, ma. That's the risk of dealing with 'em. You think you know people, then something spooks 'em, or they think they're getting a better deal from the other side . . . a kid gets held hostage and they break, or they just plain get tricked, whatever. We try to keep tabs on 'em, but, hey, those of us down here can't be everywhere at once—and once some of our secrets fall into the wrong hands, if they block out etheric vision from the Light, just like we can block theirs coming from the dark, what can you do?" Isda said with a shrug, going to the refrigerator. "Anybody else want a brew while I'm over here? My stomach is too messed up now for breakfast this morning."

"Yeah," Azrael muttered, walking over toward Isda and extending a hand to accept a bottle. "Isda, I would have thought after twenty-six thou, you would be used to last-minute missions across the globe."

"The man has jokes." Isda popped his bottle cap and clinked his longneck beer against Azrael's. "You never get used to the drill . . . and remember, the last time we were travelin' light. No humans. No females. All immortals. And you ain't been here for that full monty, mon. I've got a right to be hoppin,' spittin', cussin' mad. You have no idea what it was like all this time in the temporal zone—and you've jus' been here three short months, found your Remnant on day one . . . unheard of. So give some of us battle-weary brothers a break, if we ain't exactly all gung-ho."

Azrael nodded. "Point taken."

"Thank you," Isda said in a churlish tone. "We can walk tru' da ether and be in Egypt before lunch. To travel wit dem is a hazard, mon. No offense. First we gotta get phony passports, get 'em tickets, get 'em tru' security and patted down and on a flight. Twelve, thirteen hours later they land. Then they gotta rest, gotta eat. Plus being female Remnants in a city of twenty million beings that are still in what you might as well call a civil war, some of whom are looking for what we're looking for, is not a good t'ing. So, I'm not hating or being melodramatic. All I was *trying* to tell BK is that we needed to send a reconnaissance team over there—and I was arguing about not going with the most precious cargo we've got in tow. But he says to leave them behind with a weaker security team is leaving them like sitting ducks for a snatch and grab—and I feel him on dat, too. It's a rock and-a-hard-place setup."

"When was the last time we had a visual on all the elements of the vault?" Azrael looked from Bath Kol to Isda and back.

Bath Kol rubbed the nape of his neck. "Okay, I admit it; I haven't been the brightest bulb in the pack, all right. My light was dimming until you came down here three months ago and found Celeste. That battle on the waterfront was a V my spirit needed."

Azrael released an impatient breath. "When was the last time?"

"A few years ago, when an old priest in Turkey had a vision. He took the crystal book of tablets out of Egypt when a bunch of bull kicked off in the Middle East. But I know somehow he or someone he confided in got it back there. I feel it in my bones, guys." Bath Kol rubbed his neck again. "The old man was cool, just like all our shamans and priests and priestesses in the past that we gave the gift of discernment to—he was clean, man. The old man saw a premonition of the dark side taking the sarcophagus, prayed so he could mentally shoot the image of the abduction he witnessed to our side to alert us, and then preempted them and hid it on hallowed ground. The old dude was incredible. He maneuvered getting both the book and the sacred sarcophagus moved to a safe place, even at his frail human age—and for a long time, it seems, no one was the wiser about his stealth moves."

"You say when bull kicked off in the Middle East?" Isda said incredulously. "What fucking era, mon? Excuse my French in fronta de ladies. A few years ago could be the 1960s, 1940s, or two thousand years ago!"

"The man said to watch your language," Bath Kol muttered, using his beer to point at Isda. "You know how the years run together down here, okay, so don't throw stones if you live in a glass house. Like you were always vigilant—never smoked a tree, never—"

"All right, gentlemen!" Azrael shouted, quelling the brewing dispute. "That's how this got out of control before. The point is, where is the old man now?"

"Father Krespy passed on . . . like in 1982. He was well into his eighties when he had the tablet, and then his young apprentice, an Egyptian Muslim who was working with the old priest as an interfaith protégé priest, Daoud Salahuddin, took it to keep it on the move. Again, why I said looking in Egypt is a sound strategy."

"BK, 1982 was just prior to the Harmonic Convergence," Aziza said with a horrified whisper. "Before the period shifted to the time of Light."

"Yeah, the dark side was hunting down everybody who had Light consciousness in their spirits around that time, making people sick, making them die suddenly, you name it. They knew that if they didn't cull our human ranks of Light-bearers, when the shift came, we'd be stronger and have better access to keep the human vibration high and positive. That's the last thing the dark side wanted, was for regular human Joes to be thinking, reasonable, humane individuals. They want war, ignorance, bigotry, fear, strife, yada yada yada. So knocking off good world leaders, community organizers, people in the trenches holding the Light, was their dealio. Always has been. But there was a definite uptick in the dark side's activities just before the Convergence."

"C'mon, man . . . that was like almost thirty years ago, and it didn't dawn on you to give us a heads-up?" Gavreel looked around the room and headed toward the refrigerator.

"You know, BK," Paschar said in a tight voice, "that's saying a lot to send the angel in charge of peace to get a beer because you've caused him to *lose it*."

"Nineteen eighty-two?" Gavreel said, then opened his beer and began to pace.

"Yeah, that's right about the time I started drinking," Bath Kol said, heading to the refrigerator for another beer. "You all have no idea what I see in my sleep and all day long."

Azrael closed his eyes and spoke in a low rumble. "Then how do we know it's not too late?"

"Because if they had it, they would have been back to kick our asses already," Celeste said slowly, sitting.

"It was cool," Bath Kol said, taking a swig from his bottle. "It was with a vetted apprentice who'd taken over for the old priest. How many times do you think the library has changed hands over twenty-six thousand years, brothers? Gimme a break. Humans last these days—what? like three score or seventy years or whatever? I forget. So caretakers change hands. Get over it. The point is, our guys up in the etheric realms sound the alarm through my visions if we're in imminent danger of a real threat. Most of the time, the terror level is on yellow," he added, looking at the women at the table.

After releasing an impatient breath, Bath Kohl rubbed the nape of his neck. "But this morning, I got a real warning at a red level basically—all right, folks? The dark side finally found the bones that were kept separately from the crystal book of tablets. They found Imhotep's bones after all these years. So, the last thing we have time for is arguing amongst ourselves. And I'm *the last* person who feels like doing sand and tombs at a hundred twenty degrees in the shade, okay? But it is what it is. We have to go to Egypt and dig for where the guys on our side may have hidden the book. It's out there in the desert in that hot, dusty, sandy, chaotic place going through a regime change. Hey, that's not my fault, just the facts—so don't shoot the messenger."

Celeste's Remnant sisters reached out their hands and squeezed hers, adding Aziza in the ring, all sharing nervous glances as they sat at the table. But just as Celeste was about to pull away, a blue-white charge slowly covered her fists, seeming to run through the length of the other women's outstretched arms.

"The thing that is so sick is the dark side has created a full-scale blackout of the entire region, jamming vision frequencies from our side." Bath Kol tossed his old bottle into a recycling bin with a crash and reached into the fridge to open a new cold one. "That interference covers North and East Africa all the way through the Middle East, and forget trying to see into the Holy Land at this point. We've got them blocked, they've got us blocked—the stalemate is so ridiculous that neither side can really see what's going on over there, which goes back to my original point of needing actual boots on the ground to get the intel we need."

"Daoud never left Cairo with it," Celeste murmured, then looked up at Azrael. "It's fuzzy, but I just don't think he left the area."

"Whoa, our locator can see past the dark side's barriers when she's joined by the power of three?" Bath Kol said in hushed awe. "Who freakin' knew? But it makes so much sense."

❖

*Just like that, their* fate had been sealed. She and the ladies were flying to Egypt. Cloaked angels would be guarding the plane in the air, an advance team would walk through the ether to prepare the way on the ground, and their individual protector mates would be at their sides for the interminable, twelve-hour, nonstop flight.

Celeste blew a stray curl up off her forehead as she grabbed a section of folded T-shirts from her drawer and brought them over to her small, carry-on suitcase. This was so not how she'd planned to spend her day.

Logistics had been decided by edict; when Azrael was stressed, he didn't do management by committee well. A small contingent of angel warriors would remain in Philly to scout out a new location. Their role was to thoroughly equip the new barracks with artillery, protective prayer barriers, as well as living necessities, while an advance guard led by Isda would walk point in Egypt, clearing the path for hotel accommodations, transportation connections, and any mundane human issues that could get in the way.

Meanwhile, cloaked angels would escort their Air Egypt flight the way F-16 fighter jets escorted Air Force One. Azrael, Gavreel, Paschar, and Bath Kol would sit beside the three Remnants and the one sensitive like federal air marshals guarding VIPs, all without regular humans ever being the wiser.

Celeste shook her head the more she thought about it. If average travelers only knew . . . The flight they were booked on was probably the safest flight heading to that region that had ever left the ground.

Still, that didn't stop her from worrying about what could happen once they touched down. She knew they had to find the crystal book. She knew they had to somehow secret it away. But that didn't explain what she and her three "special" sisters were specifically supposed to do.

How were they going to tip the balance and turn on the Light within humanity's growing darkness? Ignorance was so pervasive; the American airwaves were polluted by propaganda! No real news, no authentic journalism, was left; only talking heads that did the bidding of greedy corporations. One dark-souled billionaire alone had been allowed to buy up television stations, radio stations, newspapers, magazines, and even a movie studio. The havoc only one human being had wreaked on the national consciousness was staggering—all it took was one powerful person without a moral compass to hire talking heads who would do his bidding. From there it was all downhill; the public as sheep were basically led to their slaughter, spouting rhetoric and talking points that they regurgitated from charlatans without true understanding. Mob rule was created, civility was gone, and the dark side had won the public relations war.

So what *the hell* could *she* do? She was just one person.

"That's just it," Azrael said calmly, drawing her attention to the bedroom-suite door. "He is just one man aided by the forces of darkness."

"The guy who bought up seventy-five percent of the airwaves is *a billionaire*," she replied, always amazed at how Azrael appeared just when she needed his calm wisdom most, but was never intrusive about the open-mind link they now shared.

"Still, he is one man," Azrael repeated. "*One* human."

"One human with a *lot* of resources." She sighed and resumed packing.

"You are one woman with a lot of resources, aided by the forces of the Light."

She stared at Azrael.

"In the end-times, the last will be first and the first will be last." He held her gaze. "We are in the end-times, Celeste."

"But do you know how many minions they have duped

in that one propaganda empire alone? Like, if I wanted to get my words out to the masses, if I had something true to tell people, the propaganda machine would discredit me or wouldn't cover it. So how?"

"I don't know how yet. We've always been told to have faith and leave the details to the Source of All That Is." Azrael smiled. "So far, that's worked for me."

His easy acceptance made her smile, and he crossed the room to draw her into his arms. Leaning down to take her mouth, his slow kiss under any other circumstances would have made her relax. But its too sweet ambrosia lacquer told her that he was more stressed out than she was.

"What's wrong?" she asked quietly as she pulled back from their kiss and caressed the side of his face.

"Nothing," he murmured, then hugged her tightly.

"I thought angels weren't supposed to lie," she whispered into his ear.

"It's not a lie, nothing is actually wrong."

"You're splitting hairs and dancing with words—not technically lying, but avoiding telling me what's bothering you."

He released a heavy exhale. "I just know this mission will be extremely challenging for my brothers, emotionally—even though they'd never admit it in a thousand years—and I grieve for them."

"Talk to me," she said gently as she drew back and gazed deeply into his eyes. "This has to do with Isda and Bath Kol, doesn't it?"

Azrael nodded and released another weary sigh. "After the war, maybe five hundred years in, their battalion broke the prime edict and lay with the daughters of man . . . this was in Atlantis and Lumeria. Our warrior brothers along with their fallen demon colleagues immediately beset the human populations, spawning the Titans and dark Remnants that our Light forces had to rout out. Both angels and demons procreated with humans, even though our angel brothers *knew* this was not allowed. But time and battle fatigue . . ."

Celeste nodded and drew him into a hug. "That's how people like me got made?"

"Yes," he murmured, kissing her temple. "Remnants of Light were scattered throughout the human race, and those hidden recessive genes carrying twelve strands of DNA were buried deep within the populations, only to emerge like you."

Azrael pulled back and looked at her, tracing the edge of her jaw with his thumb. "After what I have experienced with you, there is no judgment in my spirit toward my brothers about how that happened. But in that day, the Law was the Law. And just as the fallens' offspring created great misery and havoc, my brothers' offspring created great civilizations . . . some were the first pharaohs, some elected to go dark and become great Roman conquerors. That was why there was the Law, because humans have free will and choice here on the earth plane. That choice was unpredictable. Some went dark, even those made by my brothers in the Light. This region that we are about to visit is like walking over a grave."

When Celeste frowned, Azrael briefly closed his eyes and spoke in a low, somber voice. "My brothers have buried lovers, wives, sons, and daughters in the Nile Valley, Celeste.

When Isda first incarnated here, he was a warrior. Then he broke the Law and was banished from home to forever be a Sentinel. He never turned dark, but when he was informed that his Remnant, a descendant of one of his closest allies, was born, he tracked her through the modern Sudan all the way to Uganda, out through the Caribbean, only to learn that she'd perished. She would have been the daughter of one of his closest angel battalion brothers, generations removed. Thus Isda is a warrior who has lived through the greatness of the African interior empires to watch it fall to colonization, then turn in on itself in civil war. He saw the horrors of the slave trade, fought in the Caribbean to lead uprisings against that. My brother's spirit is exhausted. And now we have asked him to return to where he remembers the streets and temples paved in gold and with advances to civilization . . . to what it has surely become now. His heart shatters. That is why he protests so bitterly—he is no coward, just battle-weary."

"Oh . . . Az . . ."

"Celeste, being immortal is a double-edged blade. A gift, and in a human body of flesh, also a curse. You live through it all, and see it all, but then you get to remember it all and feel it all, too."

Guilt swept through her as she reflected on how oblivious she'd been to their pain. What she couldn't bring herself to verbalize to Azrael was that a part of her had thought it would actually be easy for them to return to old battlegrounds to scout out possible hiding spots, just because they were familiar with the terrain. In hindsight she now realized how foolish a concept that had been.

"I'm so sorry," she murmured, now staring up at him,

unblinking. "I never thought of it in those terms, or even thought about how hard it must be for the original warriors that got trapped here to go back to the old empires. I just thought . . . I don't know—like they'd know where everything was because they'd been there before."

"How could you know?" Azrael said as he held her face in his hands. "Being immortal is almost incomprehensible to the human mind, just as we didn't truly understand the pain, risk, desire, and sacrifice involved in living within the frail structure of a human body. While in etheric form and in the heat of battle, we were invincible. That is why the Source gave us this lesson and left the best of the forces here for so long to experience it all . . . a necessary thing to develop mercy, empathy, and good judgment, as well as to cultivate respect. We have definitely gained respect."

"Maybe . . . I don't know, Az, maybe Isda should stay here, if going back will be so hard for him?"

"No. He has to face it. Egypt, or Kemet, will spare no man. It was the first great civilization and they were all there . . . they will all have insights. Bath Kol will have to revisit what Alexander the Great, a direct descendant of his, wrought there against Isda's people. All of them will feel it. All of them will walk through temples or familiar areas that they haven't returned to in thousands of years . . . and their souls will cry out. But they will also be able to feel critical directions through that pain."

Celeste placed her hands on Azrael's wrists as he cupped her face, then slowly covered his palms to thread her fingers between his. "What over there will make your soul cry out?"

He pulled her against him and spoke into her hair. "Nothing. I was lucky. When I fought, I was etheric and powerful and then extracted home as the Angel of Death—deemed too valuable at that time to leave for the lesson. I've only been incarnate the three short months that I was sent to locate you. And in those three short months I have most assuredly learned to respect the power of the flesh." He rubbed her back and rested his forehead against the crown of her head, making his confession in a low rumble. "Until I learned loss and pain and want, I was so arrogant, Celeste. Only because of your heartfelt prayer to the Source on my and my brothers' behalf was the Law repealed, and only because you are not fully human did I slip through the door of judgment on a mere technicality or I'd be in jeopardy of being banished like they'd been— made a Sentinel to roam the earth for all time . . . because God only knows that once I met you and bonded with you, not falling in love with you was impossible. Not being allowed to join with you created a want . . . an ache like I've never experienced in all of existence. But then you prayed for us all, asked for mercy, and as has been promised by the Source of All That Is, mercy was not denied."

He released a shuddering breath and kissed her temple with force. "Don't you understand that is why my brothers so adore you, Celeste? Your forgiveness and lack of judgment allow them to be human, to live and love and not be near perfect as long as their spirits stay in the Light, all without being denied access to returning home. Warriors that have known centuries of banishment can now go home, but chose to stay here and fight in the flesh because of you."

For a while they just stood there absorbing the magnitude of his words, her spirit and skin soaking in the warmth of his. She thought of Jamaerah, the angel of manifestation, who had seemed to her like a beautiful teenager, a lover of music and art . . . and whose heart was breaking because he could not love, yet could never go home simply because he'd lain with someone he'd once cherished long ago. His sad, melodic guitar had stirred her conscience that fateful morning they'd met when she'd witnessed him tearfully playing a Carlos Santana ballad, "Put Your Lights On." She would never forget it.

Maybe it was because the others were so battle-toughened that she hadn't as readily seen their pain. But she hadn't truly considered how deeply conflicted the others had to be. Jamaerah had been the only one that had taken up Azrael's offer to go into the crystal column of Light to return home to heal. That had also made her not understand how deep their wounds were. But she suspected after they walked across the sands of their past, others might elect to leave the earth plane to return home just as Jamaerah did.

Not knowing what to say, she simply tightened their embrace, pulling Azrael closer against her as she rubbed his back with broad palm strokes. He'd once told her that her touch was healing, and she prayed with all her might that it was now.

"It's going to be all right, baby," she murmured against his chest, not knowing how in the world it would be. "I promise."

# Chapter 3

*Under any other circumstances*, their small group would have been flagged by Homeland Security. They were traveling to Africa with tickets purchased the same day as the flight, with only carry-on luggage? And with a bunch of dudes with five-o'clock shadow, a couple of them standing six-two, six-three, six-four, and all looking like military commandos, just by their sheer size, and with foreign-looking women in tow? Get serious.

Only angelic intervention had allowed them to run the gauntlet of heightened airport security, but the guys took the pat-down rather than the body scanner, not sure if the wings in their shoulder cavities might show up.

On the whole, if it weren't for their connections with the Source, getting a flight to Egypt for eight people leaving the same day, with couples able to sit next to each other at that, would have been impossible. But by 6:00 p.m., the four couples had made it through the onerous security screening and were in line as their boarding zones were called.

Azrael squeezed Celeste's hand and kept his gaze slowly roving the restless crowd. She noticed that the other brothers were doing the same, as though expecting a supernatural gang war to break out at any second.

Babies were crying, women in traditional garb, with youngsters and packages destined for family abroad, jostled them. Impatient tourists huffed and puffed, while businessmen looked at their expensive watches and eyed the gate agent to get a move on for first-class passengers. The line snaked forward and Celeste's attention fractured all over the place wondering who could be a human in cahoots with the dark. Full paranoia set in as she monitored the brothers' tension, not sure of its source.

When the gate agent asked for her ticket, Celeste almost jumped out of her skin. Clearly the wait to get on the evening flight had worn her nerves down to a nub.

"You okay?" Azrael murmured discreetly once they were in the Jetway.

"Yeah," she said, glancing around.

"You see something, you say something," he said in a low rumble just for her ears.

"All right," she whispered, "but you guys are freaking me out!"

"In the Egyptian Museum in Cairo? Really. And to think it survived a local uprising because human protesters barred the doors to protect their own national treasures. How perfect." Asmodeus threw his head back and laughed hard, causing his rich, dark-brown mane to flow over his broad shoulders. "All this *fucking* time? The demons never cease to amaze me!"

Flawless and handsome, save for the nasty holy-water burn that marred his left cheek, Asmodeus's tall, muscular body gave birth to raven-hued wings as Forcas nodded and ripped open the dusty storeroom crate. Antiquity surrounded them but their focus was singular.

"Asmodeus—"

"Nathaniel," he corrected. "Only my modern name, lest you invoke it around those who would know me from the old world."

"My apologies," Forcas said with a sweeping bow, causing a cascade of platinum tresses to momentarily curtain his alabaster face and intense, icy-gray eyes. "But do take great care, milord."

Going to the opened crate, Asmodeus quickly discarded the packing hay and stared down with reverence at the golden bones ensconced in a clear coffin. After a moment he reached out toward the crystal sarcophagus, but then drew back.

"It would not be like Krespy or Salahuddin to have left this to chance. I am sure it is booby-trapped for the darkness."

Forcas nodded and remained silent, but tossed the crowbar he'd just held on to the top of the crystal encasement. The second the metal object connected with it, a blue-white light surrounded the sarcophagus, turning the crowbar first red- and then white-hot.

"That was just from me holding the bar and sending

my energy signature into it. Had that been one of us . . ." Forcas brushed off his black leather coat and adjusted his sleeves.

"Get a human," Asmodeus ordered, fangs slowly lengthening in his mouth as his mood turned dark. He stared at Forcas now with coal-black eyes, no whites to surround his expanded irises. "Then make the bastard struggle and bleed on the sarcophagus. Innocent human blood and tears always break the prayer-barrier charge."

"From there, milord?"

"Bring it to the desert under your province of invisibility. I have an army to heal. Once my inner circle is raised again, we can go about the business of finding the missing tablet to raise an army."

Forcas smiled and nodded and looked out past the rows of cases, zeroing in on the closest human energy he could find. "I think the guard, Salim, wants a smoke. I think Salim is so anxious that he'll come back here to take it, rather than go outside on the lawn where he normally goes. Maybe his manager is hassling him, maybe he needs to hide away back here. What do you think, Nathaniel?"

Nathaniel laughed and walked deeper into the metal shelving, becoming a thin mist of dark smoke.

*Azrael looked down at* Celeste as she drew in slow, easy breaths. She created a wonderful warm spot against his side. After hours of watching old movies with Arabic subtitles, she'd finally stopped fighting her need to sleep. The entire flight had settled down, even the cabin crew was seated and lightly snoozing. Everyone except him and his brothers.

Each man was lost within his own thoughts but alert. Azrael tried to envision what it would have been like to actually live through that span of history his brothers had endured. Try as he might, he couldn't conceive of what it must have felt like to see the first cornerstone of the first pyramid laid, or to watch entire civilizations vanish . . . or perish.

Survivor's guilt lacerated him. He'd been one of the lucky ones, like Gavreel, to have been called back before the alignment ended. He didn't have to incarnate and experience the agony of the earth plane for millennia. He'd had to deal with it for only a few months. The Angel of Death and the Angel of Peace had been called back in unison, because death and peace were inseparable and could not be sacrificed as a resource then.

The others would remember the thousands of years of agony they'd suffered while trapped on earth, and naturally that reality would leave a bitter taste in his brothers' mouths, even if they tried not to show it. This mission would take them all back to the beginning, and the key would be to make sure the team didn't turn on itself.

But as much pain as he'd experienced in human form, he'd also experienced ecstasy that he didn't know existed. It began with her touch, the radiating warmth she'd sent into his back when he'd first arrived and she'd tried to hug away his pain. His wings had been shorn from his body upon entry to earth, and Celeste had seen the thick, raised scars at his shoulders and thought someone had abused him. That had made her weep inside her soul for him, made her graceful fingers play over the injured tissue as her spirit cried out against the injustice.

Somehow that had ignited the dormant strands of DNA within her, lighting each one and fusing them with the angel code within his. In return he'd siphoned all the poisons out of her system and nourished her back to health, which only strengthened her Light. From there she became a sweet addiction. Just touching her skin while holding her hand literally got him high on the etheric energy that pulsed between them . . . and built the desire to join with her to a frenzied ache that had no rival.

No, he could never pass judgment on his brothers, nor any beings that joined physically and fused souls for the sake of love. Perhaps that had been the one thing to save them both, that he loved her so deeply and she'd returned that to him—her heart innocent of the depths of that emotion until they'd met, he a virgin to the entire experience, yet adept in how to please her by hearing the requests murmured by her every cell.

With her warmth coating him and her inner Light lazily threading through his, he could feel renewed desire begin to stir. The blue-white cords of her energy laced with the slowly pulsing silver-gold threads in his and dueled just under the surface of their skins. He could see it if he concentrated hard enough, just as he could see the light auras of mortals and predict their health. But her light tangling with his in a barely visible, sensual dance had been maddening at first.

After months of being almost unable to keep his hands off her, finally their energy synced up enough to allow them a calmer coexistence. The flame was now a constant, steady, but manageable burn between them. Sometimes just a caress was enough to sate them, or a kiss, or, as now, just a gentle embrace. She no longer got him inebriated as before, but her touch had definitely changed his system and added to his power. The sum total of her being bonded with his created a synergy, a force of nature to be reckoned with, and the dark side had learned that the hard way.

When he'd first crashed to earth, his back was bloodied and scarred where his wings had once been—shorn off for a lesson in humility. He was broken and flight hobbled. It had been the first time he'd ever seen himself as marred. But she saw completion, she saw him whole, and through her eyes he began to envision himself as that until he was. His wings had returned and he'd been able to literally pull his blades of death through the ether into his hands in the material, physical realm. Fury, belief, a call to his brother Jamaerah on the other side, and sheer white Light energy driven by the need to protect his beloved had put the twin handheld battle-axes made of titanium reinforced by Light into both palms to once again take demon heads.

She'd given him a cause more profound than the one he'd had before, a personal aspect to this battle that took his death-dealing against the darkness to an inspired new level. All of this ignited by the selfless love of one woman. All of this due to learning what it was to ache for a human being, to revere and respect what they meant to each other.

As he watched her sleep, he was reminded just how fragile a human's life was compared to his and his brothers'. Her existence was as fleeting as a mayfly's in comparison to an immortal's, just a frenzied gulp of life that ebbed all too soon.

Azrael glanced down at Celeste again and gently kissed the top of her head, wishing that he could drift away into the abyss of peace for a few hours, yet accepting how impossible that would be from now on.

*The urge for a* cigarette slammed against Salim so hard that it made his hands shake. The Egyptian Museum guard glanced around and slowly eased his way to the back storeroom and slipped inside it. If he went out back or out front, his supervisor would see him and there'd be consequences. It didn't matter about the edict regarding smoking inside. He'd be careful and no one would know it was him.

A wan stream of mote-filled sunlight filtered through the high, dusty windows. Rows of cataloged pieces lined the shelves as he moved to the very back to where old crates and refuse that had yet to be sorted were stored.

Leaning against a crate that was pulled out into the aisle, he extracted a pack of Camels from his khaki uniform chest pocket and dug into his pants pocket for a box of matches. Without proper ventilation and the day in full blast, sweat trickled down his temple as he brought a butt to his lips in the insufferable heat.

But an icy chill made him look up from the flame and

glance around. He quickly put it out and hid his unlit cigarette and matches. A draft like that maybe meant someone had come in from a back exit. If it was a coworker, fine. But if it was a supervisor—*shit*.

He moved away from the crate quietly, turned the corner, and a huge foreigner blocked his path.

"No! No!" he said with a frown, pointing at the blond, who just smiled at him. "You go out!" *He hated tourists.* The bastards were always wandering into areas they shouldn't be! But at least it wasn't a supervisor.

"I say you go!" he repeated, becoming more agitated as the blond man extracted a fresh pack of Camels from his long, black coat.

"No, no, no! You cannot smoke here! You must go!"

The blond coolly regarded him and defiantly placed a cigarette between his lips, then struck something that Salim couldn't see between his fingers and lit the butt anyway. As angry as that made him, he was also entrapped by the scent and sight of the luxurious smoke that wafted toward him. Never had the urge to smoke been so powerful. Just smelling the burning tobacco made him briefly close his eyes and lick his lips. Sweat made his shirt cling to his body, and unable to resist any longer, he snatched his pack out of his pocket.

Quickly fumbling with the half-crushed pack, he pulled out a cigarette and hastily put it between his lips and lit it. He dragged so hard that he started coughing on the initial inhale, but then dragged on it again, hands shaking. The ecstasy that filled him on each drag brought tears to his eyes, and he didn't care that this stranger saw him break the rules.

"Every man deserves a last smoke before he dies," the stranger murmured.

The comment made Salim stare at the unarmed man as though he were mad. But just as Salim was about to take a step forward to challenge him, something grabbed him from behind. A hand covered his mouth; whatever held him had a viselike grip. Twisting and turning, he struggled to break free. A burning cigarette lay on the floor, his pack strewn, matches scattered, and still the foreigner smoked, regarding him with a smile.

"You have a choice—you always have a choice. Touch the contents of the crate of your own free will or have a supervisor find out you've been smoking back here with all this hay."

Another, deeper voice said from behind him, "How much antiquity is in this museum? I heard that if a person were to spend one minute looking at each piece that was housed here, it would take them a full year."

The blond before him smiled wider, revealing eerily long teeth. "There's more in the British Museum, and in France and in Italy, than here, but I think if your supervisor came and saw this smoldering on the floor, you'd lose your job."

"Touch it," the deep voice whispered, giving Salim gooseflesh from fear.

He nodded quickly, not sure of the odd game the European tourists were playing with him, but they frightened him and he just wanted to get away from their sick folly.

The force released him and he spun to see who had held him. A tall man with deeply tanned skin, brown hair, and strangely dark eyes smiled, then nodded toward the crate beside them.

"I will touch this, then you go," the guard said, summoning courage to speak. "This is not for tourists."

"When you're done, we will go," the darker of the two men said.

Salim reached out and placed his hand on the crystal top of what had to be a coffin. But as soon as he did, a black charge that looked like a dark current welded his hand to the surface. When he tried to draw away, it yanked him in hard, slamming his cheek against the top of the crate. The current was coming from the blond foreigner's hands.

"It was his free will," the blond said calmly as Salim struggled and fought against the building pressure.

"Indeed it was," the other foreigner replied with a smirk as Salim's ears and nose began to bleed. "A human sacrifice does the trick every time."

Soon the guard could taste the warm, salty ooze of his own blood in his mouth as he heaved and thrashed against the crystal surface, unable to scream. Then with a loud crack, the blond snapped his fingers and the pressure suddenly stopped. Salim sank to the floor, exhausted, but to his horror, what seemed like hundreds of tiny gargoyles scuttled between the shelving and crates toward him. Razor-sharp claws extended and mouths filled with twisted, yellow fangs, the gray, little beasts dashed in his direction as he began screaming and pushed himself up to run.

In seconds they were on him. His wails went unnoticed as the demons dragged his body up onto the sarcophagus, biting, scratching, goring him, sloshing his blood everywhere until it covered the crystal case. Soon everything went quiet. His screams were no more. His body lay desecrated, a bloody mass on top of the ancient coffin.

"Leave the guard. He has served his purpose. Now that the Light's booby trap has been properly dispelled, bring this to Giza where no one can see," Asmodeus said, then he walked down the aisle and disappeared.

*In the distance, the* skyline of Cairo wavered in the desert heat, a mirage like a thin charm bracelet sparkling against the sun. Three enormous pyramids now seemed smaller than a man's hand from where they stood. Demons dropped a crate and instantly began tearing away its wood frame. As soon as they'd cleared the debris, Asmodeus summoned a black serpent from the depths of the sand and used its body to draw a pentagram around a blood-drenched crystal case.

Without the sacred tablet, he faced a necromancer's nightmare. To raise the fallen, he'd have to call up each of the slain by name—a tedious task that would require time and knowledge that he didn't possess. Fury and frustration united within him as he stared at how the sun still glinted against unstained sections of the crystal coffin. The Light still had the advantage, but not for long.

For now, he would call up Appollyon, the destroyer, who'd ruthlessly been slain by Azrael with a battle-ax in his back, right between the wings. Then there was Bune, whose fighting form was the three-headed dragon. Pure treachery had lured Bune into an explosive trap. Just as

Lahash, his dark angel brother of judgment day, had been tricked into an aerial battle over the Delaware River and subsequently broiled to death in holy water.

Asmodeus rubbed the side of his scarred face, remembering how Azrael had emerged from the river wet and covered with holy water, so that when they'd lunged at each other and connected, the vile substance had burned like battery acid. Then there was that bastard Isda, who'd beheaded the lovely Onoskelis, protectress of perversion, just as Azrael had beheaded Malpas, the raven. Then to add insult to injury, Azrael's Remnant bitch had blown off Pharzup's face.

"Calm yourself or you will not be able to perform the incantation even to raise the five dark warriors we lost," Rahab murmured into Asmodeus's ear as she appeared behind him from within a sand dervish.

"You have caught me in a very violent mood, Rahab. Do not toy with me."

She leaned in and kissed the side of his neck and massaged his massive shoulders, her long, blue-black hair billowing around them both in the rough desert wind. "My name means 'violence,' remember, my love. And as you know, I rarely toy with anything—that is Onoskelis's province, not mine."

He turned around and kissed her savagely.

"Tell me, when you pull off this coup, what do you want beside power?"

Asmodeus smiled at her. "I want to be second-in-command to the Dark Lord with all the accoutrements of that office. It beats where I had been, in a Warrior angel regime, undistinguished. Never again."

"Is that all you want?" she murmured, her eyes beginning to narrow.

"No. It is the first thing, so that I can have everything else."

"And you've been promised such a title?"

His smile broadened. "I have been having private negotiations that have borne fruit. Failure is not an option."

This time when he kissed her hard, he drew blood. She wiped her mouth sensually with the back of her hand.

"Then by all means," Rahab said with a fanged smile, "I should get to work."

*Celeste woke up with* a quiet gasp that made several adjacent passengers stir. But just as quickly, a protective arm tightened around her.

"What's the matter?"

Slightly disoriented, she wiped her eyes and looked up at Azrael. "I felt like I couldn't breathe for a moment. Felt trapped. I can't explain it. Like I was closed in and I could still see light around me, but there were dark streaks and dust and grime, like on a really dirty windshield."

Sitting forward a bit, she lifted her ponytail and drew down the airline blanket, then suddenly shrugged out of Azrael's hold. "I'm sorry, it's just that I feel so hot all of a sudden."

He felt her head and then the side of her neck. "You're burning up, Celeste."

He was out of his seat in a shot, heading for the back of the plane. She was too weak to move and simply slumped against the window. When he returned, he sat half in the seat, facing her and offering her a bottle of water. After several sips she slumped back against her seat and sighed.

"Tell me I'm not coming down with the flu or something crazy before *this* trip," she said.

"No," he said in a concerned tone. "I don't think it's the flu."

# Chapter 4

*C*eleste closed her eyes and took in slow breaths through her nose to stave off a sudden bout of nausea as the plane began its rapid descent to Cairo International. The pilot's announcement that the Great Pyramids at Giza could be seen from the left bank of windows on the plane only made her squeeze her eyes shut more tightly as her stomach roiled. A light squeeze of Azrael's hand somewhat quelled the discomfort, but when she opened her eyes, every passenger appeared to her as a swirling mass of light energy.

"Breathe through it," he murmured, and wiped her damp brow with a kiss.

She nodded, knowing that there wasn't the privacy to have a deeper conversation about her strange waking sensations, but he'd heard her distress nonetheless. This time when she opened her eyes, the passengers and crew had returned to normal, but she noticed Gavreel and

Paschar attending to her sisters. Okay, so it wasn't just her. Aziza was rubbing her temples as though staving off a migraine.

Azrael clasped her palm and brought the back of her hand against his lips. The second he did that, she felt adrenaline riddling his system, so much so that it put a slightly metallic taste in the back of her mouth.

"Kiss me," she murmured as the flight dipped again.

For a moment he just stared at her, then he complied. But it wasn't the light peck that she was expecting to test for ambrosia lacquer on his tongue. He held the sides of her face, gently at first, brought his face close to hers, then suddenly took her mouth with so much force that it frightened her.

When she pulled back, he looked away, hands trembling. They sat back in their seats mute, and eventually she glanced around as other passengers looked away, embarrassed at the sudden display. But his brothers were sitting back, eyes closed, breathing slowly, gripping their armrests, practically sparking. What the . . .

"This region is a vortex," Azrael murmured in a gravelly rumble. "I had not anticipated this. We will discuss it later."

"All right," she replied, taking him at his word.

None of the brothers looked good. Gavreel had clearly lost his sense of peace, Paschar was just as undone, and Bath Kol seemed to be on the verge of an asthma attack. Beads of perspiration had formed on Azrael's brow, and his once-dry T-shirt and sweater were damp. He looked to be about ten seconds away from stripping the offending articles over his head to release his magnificent wings.

She watched a muscle in his jaw pulse as static electricity began to climb through his long dreadlocks. Thinking fast, she grabbed his hand and held it hard. "Ground through me."

He nodded, almost gasping, but instead swallowed the sound so hard that it made his Adam's apple bob in his throat. "I need to release them so badly, Celeste, it hurts," he whispered, then allowed his head to drop back with his eyes closed.

He was referring to his wings. Other passengers hadn't heard his comment and just assumed he had flying anxiety when the opposite was true. The desire was so thick within him to be out on the thermals, flying beside his brothers into a battle, that it was making his shoulders thicken.

Speaking to him in a hissed warning, she clenched his hand against her heart. "Listen to me, Az—you cannot have a wardrobe malfunction on this flight. We clear? It cannot happen, no matter what."

Past the point of speech, he just fervently nodded and glanced out the window, then turned away from it as though someone had slapped him.

"We just dropped in altitude from thirty thousand feet to ten, the entry point of aerial assault, the sweet ten, just above the clouds with a sight line to the ground forces."

Flat-palming Azrael's heaving chest as a stewardess neared, Celeste shook her head. "Az, I'm serious, man."

"Is everything all right?" the stewardess asked, looking concerned. "Sir, do you need some water?"

"He's fine," Celeste said, glaring at Azrael. "Just has trouble with landings after a long flight."

"Oh, yes, understood. Plenty of people hate takeoffs and landings, but we'll be on the ground soon."

Celeste waited until the woman had passed them to go strap herself into the jump seat in the back.

"Azrael, I don't know what's—"

His kiss was feral and punishing as his hands threaded through her hair. He pulled her against him and spoke in a hot rush against her ear. "This vortex is one of three in the motherland of humanity. The Nile Valley waters flow from south to north like no other river in the world, up from the Garden of Eden to give birth to where mankind settled east of Eden." His voice was a harsh, sensual rush that sent a shudder of want through her. "The power here, where the original Tree of Knowledge grew . . . the air is electric, it is where we all came in . . . where the vibrations enter our cells and magnify everything—then with the sun and the sacred geometry created here . . . the Giza plateau is a landing strip . . . it's . . . it's . . ."

"Okay, okay, sit back and breathe through it," she said quietly as the landing gear of the plane disengaged from the body of the aircraft.

Pushing him against the seat, she watched him wince as the plane bounced into a touchdown and then raised its flaps. It almost seemed as if Azrael and his brothers had identified with the aircraft, their bodies straining with the jumbo jet as it came to a slow, rolling stop.

Winded from the emotional drama of it all, she sat back and took in several breaths herself. What the hell had just happened?

Nausea had been the precursor to her last highly eventful ten minutes of the flight, not any kind of cosmic power surge. She had initially felt something ominous and dark when she'd awakened, not the euphoria of battle that Azrael and the others had just experienced. But now was not the time to debrief all that. She just wondered how the unseen angels flanking the plane's wing positions had taken all of this, or were they part of the reason the interior group was having a collective meltdown? Whatever the cause, she was definitely worried about how the testosterone rush was going to effect them once they stepped foot on actual Egyptian soil.

Impatience grated her as the double-row, passenger-packed flight taxied to the Jetway. Then there was the nerve-fraying wait as people jangled with luggage and small, wailing children. Celeste counted to ten, just wanting to get off the freakin' plane, trying her best not to lose it. Screaming at people to just move out of the way would solve nothing, and knowing that there really were angels and a Higher Power, did she truly want to yell at disabled, elderly people who clogged the aisle or a mom with four little kids and no help?

Summoning calm, she waited in the most civil mode possible, hoping that four battle-ready angels didn't just clear the aisle like first responders might in a blaze. They were more stressed out than she was, and when she saw Gavreel—the frickin' Angel of Peace—wipe his palms down his face as a lady with a bunch of packages took her sweet old time keeping it moving, she *knew* something was in the air. Maggie looked to be three seconds from slapping the annoying diva in the aisle, and Aziza was body-blocking Bath Kol. Finally he snapped.

"People have been on this flight for almost thirteen

damned hours, hon—step into the aisle and let people out who do not have all the shit you have! All right! Can you do that?"

Aziza closed her eyes as the stricken woman scooted into the seating area and glared at Bath Kol.

"Thank you," he muttered. "I'm just sayin'."

Sarcastic applause came from the rear of the plane, which was probably the only reason Aziza didn't die of mortification. But Bath Kol's outburst broke the bottle-neck and freedom was in sight.

Almost running out of the aircraft, customs forms in hand, they barely acknowledged the crew's standard debark farewell. The second they crossed the threshold, they left the shelter of perfect temperature modulation to a hundred-degree blast of Egyptian reality in the Jetway. Immediately Celeste caught Azrael under his elbow as he staggered, walking zigzag almost as if he were drunk. Inside the cooled building, he improved slightly and endured the paperwork processing like a root canal without Novocain. Within the hour, their small troupe had made it to the front of the airport, freedom within their grasp.

Leaning against a building column, Isda greeted them with a wide smile.

"You feel the power hit here, mon?"

Bath Kol pounded his fist followed by the others.

Isda glanced around. "How you ladies doing?"

"I just need to get out of here and breathe real air," Celeste said, feeling her stomach begin to get queasy again.

"No worries. Got a small minibus parked out front—got people who know some people watching it and giving me a few minutes parked illegally to break da law." He laughed at his own joke and slapped Azrael's backpack. "Need me to carry that for you, mon? You know, I have to eat my words and give BK his due. As much as I hated coming back here, I still have a *lot* of good memories of this place, and I'm just glad the main protests are over so we can maneuver a little bit, feel me? The loves of my life were here. Whew. I got your bags, mon, seriously."

"No, I'm good," Azrael said, his breathing labored they neared the door.

"You don't look good, mon. Look like the vortex is kicking your natural ass."

"I said I was all right!" Azrael said way louder than was necessary.

"Hey, I'm in the Light, bro. Remember?" Isda said, chuckling, and seeming to delight in his brother's distress. "I tol' you this wasn't no place for no punk, right? Told you the energy was old and hard and was a wicked old bitch that didn't care."

"Shut up, man. Where's the van?" Azrael rumbled.

"Right over there," Isda said with a wide grin, unfazed.

Bath Kol gave Isda a hard look. "Brother, you're manic. This is the memory high before you crash and burn, and you're getting on everybody's last nerve. You're gonna go up real fast and come down real hard, because your DNA is linked to this region—so *chill*."

"Whatever," Isda flipped back, rolling his eyes as he walked ahead of them. "Kiss my ass. I'm happy. Get over it if you're not."

A trickle of perspiration rolled down Celeste's back and between her breasts as a blast of unseasonal Egyptian heat, sweltering for that time of year, suddenly accosted her the moment the airport doors opened. Isda pointed at a white Toyota minivan that looked as if it could seat twenty passengers, but was dubious in the air-conditioning department. However, the reliability of the rickety vehicle was a much lower priority than the increased tension she noticed among the brothers.

As they walked across the pavement and their footfalls connected with actual concrete, each of them slowed his gait, their lids closing in what seemed like slow motion as a thick, blue-white spill of energy bubbled up to cover their feet and climb up their bodies. The sight stole her breath and stopped her in her tracks.

Isda glanced over his shoulder at her. "They'll be all right. Gwan fuck 'em up for a few hours, tho."

She hurried forward with the other mortals in the group at Isda's insistence and climbed into the van as he chided his overwhelmed brethren.

"You comin' or what, mon? Standing on a street corner in Cairo ain't no place for a lady, or ain't you get the memo?"

His admonishment seemed to break the trance as a muezzin call went out over the city. The long, mournful wail enveloped the group, producing a serenity that had previously eluded them. Like large hunting dogs, the brothers closed their eyes and tilted their heads, quelled by the sound, and then they moved as a unit toward the van.

"All respect to the Mu'aqqibat—our protector brothers in the Light, angel forces of the Quran, while we inhabit this land . . . hear our prayer and keep our mortal charges from death until its decreed time by Allah," Isda said as the brothers piled into the van.

"Amen," Azrael said with a nod of approval.

"Ashé," Aziza murmured as each man got settled.

"Well said, bro, we can use all the help we can get," Gavreel said with a hard sigh as he flopped down next to Magdalena.

Paschar just slid into the seat next to his charge and took up Melissa's hand and kissed it hard.

Barely after closing the door, Isda shifted the clutch and thrust the vehicle into the most insane traffic Celeste had ever seen. Aside from the demons, she could definitely understand why Isda had prayed for the safety of the mortals among them. In a city of 20 million people and unfathomable congestion that would make New York's Manhattan traffic seem like the Autobahn, every driver in Cairo clearly believed that *he* had the right of way. Screw you if you were a pedestrian, too.

But as disorienting as everything was, the visual wonder lying before her could not be ignored. The collision of worlds in Cairo left her speechless. Here East met West, great opulence contrasted with staggering poverty. Gorgeous domes built in ancient times stood next to modern office buildings that gleamed with twentieth-century glass, while burned-out buildings and unfinished constructions provided sanctuary for stray dogs and pigeons. And beyond the most outrageous skyline of chaos loomed the pyramids—right downtown one could look up and see one of the Seven Wonders of the World.

Celeste fought not to press her nose to the window and finally lost the battle, wishing that she could just jump out of the van to stand on the curb and open her arms and spin around in the atmosphere of it all. Yet as they passed the Eygptian Museum, something dark made her recoil from the window. She was distracted from the fleeting feeling by the way the brothers spread their palms against the glass, lighting it up with so much crackling energy that she feared it might shatter. That no one on the streets could see it still mystified her.

"Look," Isda said over his shoulder. "Here's the deal. We check in at Le Meridien Pyramids. The advance squad already has your room keys, money changed—you'll find a stash in the safe. I'll give each man the code to his box. I've duct-taped a nine under the inside drawer in your suite. In the back of this van is da heavy shit—RPGs, shells, semi-automatics. We got the holy-water bombs—the case in your room is for more than drinking, got it? All shells are hollow-point, hallowed-earth-packed. You've got forty-five minutes to knock the travel dirt off, change into something that can hide a weapon, and be back downstairs in the ground-floor restaurant. We'll eat for the mortals' sake, load up on water, then we head out to Giza. Some bull went down near there, I can feel it tweaking me nerves, mon, and I want our locator on it. Cool?"

The warriors in the van nodded as Celeste shared glances with Aziza, Melissa, and Maggie. It would be so not good to be caught in an Arab country, in Africa, with *what*, semiautomatics and terrorist-type ammo? She pushed it out of her mind as Isda pulled up to the luxury hotel and she stared at the pyramids that nearly cast a shadow over it.

"See you in forty-five," Isda repeated.

"In forty-five," Azrael said, pounding Isda's fist on the way out.

They hadn't walked six feet toward the door when one of the brothers from the house handed them their keys. Azrael looked back at the van that pulled off and repeated the number that Isda had zinged to him via telepathy.

"Forty forty-five."

"I got it," Celeste said, adjusting her purse on her shoulder and then pushing her way through the door.

Ice-cold air blasted her in the face, so frigid it almost gave her a headache. She glanced around at the opulent lobby, which was filled with European and Asian tourists who had obviously just emerged from the multiple tour buses parked outside. Even after the civil unrest, people clearly still wanted to see Egypt for themselves. The chaos was a blessing; it gave the troupe additional cover to just stroll through the pharaoh-themed lobby.

Black-lacquered throne chairs, glass tables that had gold pyramid bases, and lotus-flower-print rugs of crimson and gold gave the hotel almost a Vegas level of casino glitz. Gold-painted sphinx statues served as planters for giant palms, elephant grass, and ferns. Even the elevators were outfitted with green, marbled, carved hieroglyphics and scenes of queens and pharaohs gently touching fingertips.

By the time they arrived at their room down the long corridor, she was slack-jawed. Never in her life had she traveled beyond the Jersey shore, and to think she had to wait until the world was on the verge of Armageddon to see this made her shake her head.

After Azrael put the key in the door and went in first to do a security sweep, she timidly followed him in and just gaped. Their room faced the actual pyramids. Above a king-size bed with white-on-white, Egyptian-cotton, high-thread-count sheets and a goose-down duvet was a gold papyrus of Nefertiti and King Akhenaton. Black vases filled with ferns stood on either side of the bed nightstands. The bathroom was outfitted with green marble and gold fixtures; a glass shower that had hieroglyphics carved into the wall and a bidet sat beside the weirdest toilet she ever saw. Its strange plunger system was hard to figure out—the purpose of a long metal apparatus by the side of it she couldn't immediately fathom, and then instead of a handle to flush, a metal lever was in the middle of where the water bowl would normally be.

Now she understood Azrael's confusion when he first came to earth. She just stared at the contraption as he flipped on the light, checked behind the shower curtain, then made the rounds deeper into the room.

A huge flat-screen TV was positioned on the dresser, and gold-and-black satin armchairs that looked like the thrones of Ramses bookended a glass breakfast table. But her attention remained on the window and the pyramids and the small balcony just beyond the table.

"Is this to your agreement?" Azrael asked, finally dropping her bag and his backpack on the floor by the massive armoire.

"I've never seen anything like this, in all honesty," she said in a quiet rush. They were supposed to be battling demons . . . really? Why couldn't this have been five years ago when all she'd need to bring was a bathing suit, sunscreen, and a good camera?

"Then you approve?"

"Very much so."

He looked out at the pyramids and then back at her. "How are you feeling?"

"Better," she said with a sigh of relief. "You?"

"Conflicted." He looked out at the pyramids and then at her again.

She frowned. "I hope you feel better. Isda said it would pass . . . whatever this energy adjustment is."

"I suspect he is correct." Azrael picked up his backpack, dropped it twice, and set it on the dresser to begin searching for clean clothes and toiletries. After a moment, still seeming rattled, he headed toward the dresser. "The weapon. I almost—"

"Yo." She quickly crossed the room, stepping between him and the drawer and blocking the dresser with her butt. "Why don't you get a shower, drink some water, and chill out before you mess around and shoot yourself—or me."

"Is it that bad . . . and obvious?"

She looked up at him with a smile. "Uh, yeah."

"Then I guess there's no need for pretense," he said in a low rumble, and he bent and kissed her.

"We only have forty-five minutes," she whispered into his mouth, lightly biting his bottom lip.

"Then we shouldn't tarry," he murmured, deepening the kiss.

Pure ambrosia, stronger than it had ever before tasted, covered her palate, making her gasp. Suddenly it felt as if the substance had entered her bloodstream to release every endorphin within her. Moaning into her mouth, he stripped his shirt over his head and then gasped as his wings tore though his back with such force that blood splattered the rug behind him.

Searing skin met hers as he yanked her light sweater over her head and stripped her pants down her legs, never allowing his mouth to break contact with some part of her body while she kicked out of her shoes. His jeans and sneakers literally disintegrated off him, but the fire he'd lit against her skin was what drew her gasp.

Hands beneath each lobe of her ass, he lifted her up, taking her mouth, his tongue dueling with hers as he carried her to the bed to deposit her on it like a silent offering. Feathers covered the floor as he knelt at the edge of the duvet, plumes lost from his wings' violent ejection tumbling across the carpet from the forced air. As he bowed his head between her thighs, she saw just how badly he'd suffered during the flight.

A rivulet of blood ran down the center of his back, staining his gorgeous plumage crimson where it had emerged from his shoulders. To ease his agony, she found the sweet spot between his wings, her hand stroking it until he threw his head back and cried out, so overwhelmed that tears had risen to consecrate his thick, black lashes.

But this time as his mouth found her skin, it suckled the Light within her to the surface to leak from her pores in a blue-white wash of energy that covered them both until she feared she'd drown in pleasure.

He tended to her bud as if he were attending mass, slowly, reverently, and with purpose. Allowing her no escape, his tongue traced each petal and found favor in it, dipping into her until she confessed her pleasure upon escalating cries, his name embedded in the refrain.

Fisting his locks in both hands, she made him stop

and take her breasts and then her mouth, murmuring, "Please," until he finally heard her prayer. She couldn't take it, this new intensity of joining with him. Her heart was on the verge of seizure when she took his mouth, tears streaming, and demanded with a deft slide against his pelvis that he enter her.

He thrust so hard within her that it made her sit up and hug him as one strong arm captured her waist and he flat-palmed the bed for balance. From beneath his tightly closed lids she could see a thin line of neon blue-white light that followed the edges of his dark lashes. He seemed immobilized by pleasure for a moment, then something within him gave way as his fist slowly closed on the duvet, and his wings beat the air in time with his thrusts.

The nightstand lamps fell, furniture moved in increments, and the drapes billowed at the disturbance of the air. The steady drone of his twelve-foot wingspan threatened mirrors, wall art, as he dropped his hold on the bedding to splay his hand against her back as her hair was caught in the maelstrom he created in the room.

"Cel . . . este . . . Oh . . . Cel . . . este . . ."

He sobbed her name as though calling out for someone lost in the midst of a storm, then returned again and again to her body with hard thrusts as if he were trying to anchor her to him forever.

Burning, blue-white-charged sweat ran down his chest, over the eight contracting bricks in his abdomen to course over her belly and across her thighs. All she could do was hold on and slip into that pool of Light pleasure so deep that each inhalation sounded like a gasp of a drowning woman, and every exhalation was framed by her deep moan. She could now feel his voice through his shaft inside her as he matched her voice pattern like a revival call and response, every deep-baritone stanza sending shock waves in rings up her canal until she could literally feel the vibration of his voice explode within her womb. That's when she lost the rhythm and the last vestiges of control as she wept and he rode her harder.

It had never before been like this; something was different about this time. He bit his lip until it bled, his face was wet from tears, and then he released a subsonic moan that literally put a crack in the television screen and the window behind them. If he hadn't pressed her against his body as he lifted them a foot above the bed, she might have swallowed her tongue when the first pleasure seizure struck.

The powerful sensation made her arms and legs go limp as molten heat filled her, climbing up her torso to squeeze her heart. Holding her head in one wide-spread palm and her upper back with the other, he repeatedly convulsed against her, heaving seed and pleasure from his body into hers. Then he dropped.

They hit the bed with a thud, him bracing himself with his hands at her sides to save her from his full weight. Panting, gulping air, he spoke to her in bursts after a moment, his biceps straining to hold his own weight.

"Oh, God, Celeste . . . forgive me, baby. I lost control . . . I think I might have really messed up."

For a moment she couldn't answer him as reality began to set in. "What if you like really did . . . and I wind up pregnant? What's gonna happen? Is that a rule that could get us a lightning bolt?" She peered at him and bit her lip when he closed his eyes.

"It won't get *you* a lightning bolt . . . *me*, perhaps." He tried to smile, but it wasn't his normally confident one.

"I don't guess this is something we can pray about?"

Again he closed his eyes. "One can always pray for forgiveness . . . oh, man . . ."

"Tell me it's gonna be all right."

He nodded. "It's gonna be all right."

Silence enveloped them as she settled against his stone-hewn chest trying not to panic. All she could do was caress his sides as he wrapped her in his wings.

# Chapter 5

*She looked up at* Azrael and then over to the clock that was now turned on its side on the floor. By Isda's edict, they were supposed to be in the restaurant in fifteen minutes. She so couldn't deal with any vast cosmic misstep they might have just made. It was too late anyway—and if this was the end of the world, what a way to go out.

Maybe it was the overall stress or the insane levels of endorphins that now flooded her system, but suddenly she laughed as she held the sides of his face. She closed her eyes as the laughter turned into crying.

"It's going to be all right," he said.

She shook her head. "No, it's not, Az," she said, both laughing and crying. "Oh, my God . . ."

"Yeah," he said, then kissed her forehead, glancing around the partially destroyed room. His serious expression gave way to slow laughter. "Well, at least I feel better. How about you?"

For a moment she just stared at him as he retracted his wings and rolled off her. He slung a thick forearm over his eyes and sighed as his laughter ebbed. "This is soooo not in the book."

"Ya think?" She sat up slowly and glanced around the suite. "We can only hope management hasn't been called."

He sat up slowly. "Well, at least I can fix the room." He waved an arm and the chairs righted themselves, the cracks in the TV and window vanished, and the clock jumped back up on the table as the pictures on the wall straightened. Azrael glanced up and then looked at his hand.

"Well, I guess that's a good sign," she said, shaking her head and trying to get her hair to fluff down. "Can you fix this while you're at it?"

"I was just joking around," he said nervously. "You've never seen me do that. Kill demons, yes. That's my specialty—but manifesting, moving matter . . . not so much."

The two stared at each other for a moment.

"That's a good thing, right?" she said quietly.

"Given where we are and what we're supposed to do, one can only hope."

*Celeste kept her gaze* lowered as they rejoined the group in the restaurant. They were a half hour late to the table and her legs were still wobbly. When Azrael muttered a greeting and sat down hard like an unsteady old man, Bath Kol almost spit out his beer. Aziza kicked him under the table. Celeste looked at her sisters sheepishly, and they all glanced back at her with understanding. Just their complicit smiles made her feel better.

"So, now the gang's all here," Isda said in a peevish tone. "At least let the 'oman eat something before we head out to the desert."

"I'm not really that hungry," Celeste said, hoping to avoid any further embarrassment. She could grab an apple or whatever, for all she cared.

But Isda shook his head. "Your electrolytes are all off and you need some carbs so your sugar doesn't drop enough to make you pass out. The heat out there ain't no joke . . . and if you would be so kind as to hydrate her, Azrael. I do believe I left everybody water in the room."

Azrael just nodded and opened a menu. Melissa winked at Celeste and continued grazing on her salad. But Celeste did notice that Paschar was still touching his mate a lot, rubbing her back and sitting well into her seating area. She felt for the poor man. On the other hand, Gavreel was cleaning a plate of hummus and falafel, wiping it with fluffy whole-wheat pita bread. Judging by the litter by his place setting, he was a very peaceful individual now.

Celeste smiled as she placed her order and listened to Azrael order nearly half the menu. Anything that wasn't meat was fair game, and he'd already grabbed a roll. All worry about carbs and organic fare had obviously flown out of the window in this land where such luxuries seemed unheard of now. The guys had clearly adopted the policy to go local and clean out their systems later. Even Aziza had to relent. It was that or starve.

A newly revolutionized Egypt didn't have chichi organic restaurants, supermarkets, or five-star hotels that could keep up the posture of luxury these days without extreme effort.

Once the waitress left, Isda released a huff of breath. "Okay, folks, here's what ground intel has found out so far." Isda leaned in closer. "The Egyptian Museum is closed, mon. No big surprise about that, right?"

"What?" Celeste whispered as she glanced around the table.

"Beyond the protests, low staff levels, and all the hullabaloo, there was a so-called incident there yesterday morning, right about the time you all got on the flight. But they gwan open it up like tomorrow after they mop up and the authorities get done—too much tourist business to be lost . . . what little is trickling in. Everything is still spotty, you know. Things kinda open when they want to now. There's no schedule. But they gotta open the main tourist attractions, even if they only got a third of the buses coming in than they did before."

"Mop up?" Azrael said quietly, leaning in.

Gavreel stopped eating and leaned in next to him. "Found a body gutted and drained in the storeroom."

"Might have something to do with us, might not," Paschar said. "But the timing is really suspicious."

Bath Kol nodded. "Right now, that poor bastard's family is catching liquid hell. Because of the way he was killed, nervous authorities are saying Al Qaeda might have turned on him, he could have been a terrorist or in the crime scene here. You know how shit gets spun when there's no answers and the dark side is involved, bro. Just the way they say he was butchered put that event on my radar."

"I definitely felt something weird when we passed the museum," Celeste admitted quietly. "It was dark."

Isda folded his arms over his chest. "Den I say we eat up and get our girl out into the desert."

*Her body felt like* a wet noodle, and after being with Azrael, taking a hot shower, then eating, the last thing she felt like doing was going on a potentially hazardous quest. If she could have curled up into a little ball of humanity and gone to sleep for a couple of hours, she would have been a happy camper. But that just wasn't in the cards.

An impromptu ladies' room meeting when they all hit the lobby was just what her spirit needed. Aziza was the one to sense it first and called for it as only the Queen Mother of the group could.

"Gentlemen, we will be back," Aziza announced in a nonnegotiable tone. "The conditions on the road will be spotty at best, I'm sure. And after all this water we've forced down, we need to make one last run before getting into the van."

Without fanfare or giving the brothers options to protest the delay, she lifted her head and walked in front of the three younger women, who quickly followed. None of them said a word until they'd cleared and shut the outer ladies' room door. Maggie checked the stalls as though about to do a bank heist. Melissa grabbed Celeste by the arm, and Aziza said a quick prayer to seal the room against bad vibes.

"What is *wrong* with them?" Melissa asked in a quiet rush, staring at Celeste and then the others. "And make it quick before some tourist wants in here with us and we can't talk."

"Girl, I don't know," Celeste admitted. "It's like they are feeding off the energy from this region. Azrael said it's a vortex, where they all first came in for the initial battle with the fallen. So the brothers are hype."

"More than hype, they're also horny as shit," Maggie said, wiping her brow with an exaggerated smile.

Celeste started laughing. "Uh, yeah . . ."

"It's the energy firing up their kundalinis," Aziza said with a wide grin.

The women burst out laughing, then quickly covered their mouths.

"That is a way to put it, 'Ziza," Maggie said, giggling hard.

"No, I'm serious. Kundalini energy is chi, spinal energy, chakra source energy—oh, never mind," Aziza replied, unable to hold back her quiet brand of melodic laughter.

"But if they're so, uh . . . out of control," Melissa said, her smile beginning to fade, "what if they really lose control?"

All smiles faded as they stared at Melissa.

"I'm just saying that because Paschar was afraid that he couldn't pull it together to focus on not being out of control . . . and you know regular human contraception doesn't work on these guys—their seed just burns right through it. Full intent not to procreate has to be their will, and so I told him I didn't want to get a lightning bolt thrown his way and that made him back off me. I know we're now able to sleep with them without dooming them to eternity on earth, but I don't think the whole procreation edict or ban on having hybrid children by Heaven was ever lifted, do you?"

Beginning to pace, Melissa's normally analytical calm fractured right before their eyes. "It's like my whole life is changed in a snap. We've all be swept up into this altered reality where none of us know the rules, if we're breaking the rules or—"

"Making it up as we go along," Maggie said, nodding emphatically. "Would have helped if somebody told us stuff before it happened. I feel like my life got hijacked sometimes, then at the same time I'm so thankful that it did, given the downward spiral I was on, but it's all so bizarre and unsettling and miraculous and just weird."

"That's why I told Paschar no. I wasn't sure and he was acting really crazy, and I wasn't sure what that meant." Melissa glanced around the group. "Was that right or wrong? See what I mean? How do we know?"

"Beloveds, none of us knows what the right thing is. I have lain with BK as a pure human when we solidly knew the rules meant that would doom him . . . and every year that passes, I look older and he stays the same. Fate can be loving and nurturing toward our growth, and yet it can also be a demanding and cruel bitch when it comes to the fragile human ego. Yin and yang of it all, I suppose. I'm still learning and coping, young sisters. None of us is perfect or gets it right all the time." Aziza released a rare forlorn sigh. "But we do the best we can. When we know better, sometimes we do better. Yes?"

"I suppose," Melissa murmured. "I guess that's why something down deep told me to back Paschar off for now."

Celeste closed her eyes. "I didn't have that much will-power in me . . . shit."

"Ditto," Maggie said, and just shook her head. "I can't say no to that man. Gavreel makes my knees turn into jelly. What can I tell you?"

"But what I'm saying," Celeste whispered in a horri-fied rush, "is that I mighta really messed up—correction, *we* mighta messed up, big-time. There was *no control* hap-pening in our room, trust me."

"Well, how in the hell are you supposed to have will-power against the frickin' Angel of Death? Give yourself a break," Maggie said, wringing her hands, then going to Celeste to hug her. "I mean, Paschar has vision, so maybe he saw down the road a bit and could, you know, like temper his behavior because of seeing the future or what-ever . . . and Gavreel . . . well, he *is* peace—so while he took liberties that I gladly enjoyed, he wasn't out of his mind completely. At least I don't think he was. But the fact is, the control part isn't on you. So don't blame your-self; it is what it is, or was what it was."

Celeste groaned as she allowed her forehead to rest on Maggie's shoulder and the other women came to her to rub her back. Maggie's advice was always so blunt and so ac-curate that you couldn't avoid its impact, whereas Melissa gnashed the facts to death. Then Aziza would come in to say her piece so philosophically that her words sometimes made people not worry about stuff they should really have been insanely worried about. One could be too mellow when action was called for. But in a circumstance like this, what the hell action was there to take except freaking out?

"Girl, you are so not making me feel better right now," Celeste said into Maggie's shoulder. "But I love you anyway."

"We love you, too, honey—but what you gonna do?" Maggie shrugged. "It's done now and there's no going back."

Celeste released another groan. "I know."

"Maybe Azrael can un-intend or something?"

Melissa's attempt at problem solving only made Celeste's shoulders slump more.

"Would you be serious?" Maggie fussed.

"Well, who knows what all these guys can do? They don't even seem to know the full range of their powers down here yet. I'm just saying it could be worth a try and a conversation with the man."

"I really don't think that's something you'd ask an angel to do, Mel." Maggie shook her head and Celeste could feel Maggie's entire body become rigid as she responded to Melissa.

"Okaaaay, I'm sorry. Don't get bent. I'm just trying to come up with practical solutions before lightning bolts start flying from the sky at our van," Melissa replied, sounding genuinely hurt.

"Do you hear yourself? Stop scaring her," Maggie said, her voice beginning to escalate.

"Maybe it wasn't that bad," Aziza hedged, then placed a calm hand on each of the arguing women's arms, dispelling the negativity through touch.

"Oh, it was bad," Celeste countered, and let out a

frustrated sigh as she squeezed her eyes shut more tightly. "His wings came out so hard he splattered the carpet with blood, then turned over tables and chairs and rearranged furniture with wind turbulence."

"Holy shit," Melissa said, covering her mouth.

Aziza gathered Celeste away from Maggie's hug and turned Celeste around to face her. Placing her hands squarely on her shoulders Aziza spoke with dignified calm. "We are not going to give way to panic, fear, or worry. We are going to cross that bridge when we come to it. What happened might not exactly be in the divine law, but then again, who knows, given all the changes and new circumstances that have come out of all our unions and prayers. So let's move forward on a positive vibe and take each day as it comes. Besides, we have bigger concerns right now. Let's stay focused, okay?"

Even though the thought of returning to the mission produced its own brand of stress, just hearing Aziza's wise counsel made Celeste's shoulders relax. Everything that had happened in the hotel room might just have been a stress reliever, now that she really thought about it. Maybe Azrael hadn't lost the ultimate control and was just battle hyped. After all, as her sister said, he was the frickin' Angel of Death and therefore probably took the whole battle thing more deeply into his bones than the others. Maybe. That was the pretty lie she was going to tell herself to help keep from freaking out.

Meanwhile, each woman's hug added an additional sealing balm to Aziza's and soon they were all ready to smile again.

"Okay, we've been gone long enough," Melissa warned.

"A few minutes more and they'll know we're talking about them and might get suspicious."

It was the simple truth and enough to make them begin to quickly file out toward the lobby. But Celeste had to chuckle as Maggie held her back a bit with a mischievous grin.

"Knocked the furniture over from wind turbulence? Really?"

"If you say a word . . ." Celeste shushed her and dragged her out of the restroom trying hard not to laugh.

Emotions running high and needing downtime to recover from the flight, Celeste said a futile prayer that plans had changed and everyone could take a much-needed nap. Knowing that wasn't going to happen, she trudged past the lobby with the group and steeled herself for the blast of heat that almost knocked her over when the hotel front doors opened.

Her body longed for the soft duvet and cool temperatures inside. Just a few hours and she'd be ready to go wherever they insisted. Instead she found herself back in the small white van on a mission. Thankfully the trek by vehicle was only fifteen minutes from the hotel, and a wide-open landscape soon emerged from the horizon. A hundred-yard parking lot preceded the monuments, as did a formal park ticket-stand entrance barricade with rest-stop-style toilets. However, they didn't have to stop. Isda and his advance team had taken care of acquiring the nearly-impossible-to-get-pyramid entrance passes.

"You need to stop yawning and give me a little credit, mon," Isda fussed over his shoulder toward Azrael and Gavreel. "You know how hard it is to get into the big pyramid? People stand in line at five o'clock in the morning to be sure they can, and by dis time of day, sold out."

"Thank you, man," Azrael said in a mellow tone, stifling another yawn.

"In your debt, bro," Gavreel said, leaning his head back on the seat and closing his eyes. "For real."

"Yeah, whatever," Isda muttered as he pulled their small vehicle into a space by behemoth tour buses and lines and lines of parked vehicles. "*Dis*-mount!"

"Ya think this whole leadership-in-the-land-he-knows-best thing is really going to brotherman's head?" Bath Kol muttered to Azrael as he passed him. "Just sayin'."

Azrael held up a hand, seeming too exhausted even to contemplate the matter.

But as soon as every warriors' feet touched the sand, Celeste watched them snap to attention, their senses keen, their eyes roving the terrain.

"Is everything all right?" Melissa asked, touching Paschar's arm.

He shook his head. "Not at al, Mel."

Celeste hugged herself as they followed Isda, feeling the unease creep into her bones with every footstep.

Camel drivers stood swatting flies and hawking rides right next to arts-and-crafts vendors who claimed everything was handmade, but looked as if it had been manufactured in China. Aggressive youngsters plied everything from mini-maps to small plastic pyramids and light-up Tutankhamen lens.

"Ladies, stay next to your guardian," Isda said under his breath, circling back to protect his group. "Here ain't like the States. If you're female and unescorted, you're fair game for whatever, feel me? If you get separated from your man, just claim to be the wife of one of the other brothers. Here, they got more than one wife and may even try to buy you from your mate for, like, twenty camels or some shit. Cool?"

"Are you serious?" Maggie looked around the faces in the huddled group.

"Very," Aziza confirmed. "So stay close."

"Especially when we go over by the camels," Isda added.

"Whoa, whoa, whoa," Celeste said, gesturing wildly with her hands. "Why in the world would we need to travel on some huge, smelly beasts that from where I stand have crap all over the ground near them?"

"My question *exactly*," Maggie said, folding her arms.

"Because if we are going deep into the desert, a camel is necessary." Isda looked around the group. "They won't let cars go to where we need to check out. We brought the ticket to get back here. Maybe we can divine something or get a vibe inside the big boy when we get back, but for now, we ride and we stop when Celeste says stop." He handed Azrael a camera. "So act like a tourist and stop beefin'. You ought to be really chill by now anyway."

Maggie glanced at Celeste, whose cheeks were rosy with embarrassment. Celeste set her sight on the camels ahead and pursed her lips. Not a word, she would not say another word for now. Azrael and Gav swallowed smiles, gave Isda the nod, and Bath Kol chuckled as the group moved forward. Only Paschar lagged back a bit, constantly stroking Melissa's back as they walked.

They hadn't gone ten paces when they were barraged

by eager vendors. Azrael just shook his head, calmly declining, and he and Isda keeping the group moving. But the children's bleating pleas broke Celeste's heart. That's how Melissa and Maggie got caught. A small boy and his sister offered pencils, then maps, then trinket after trinket, and suddenly the two women had fallen behind. By the time the group turned around, they were surrounded by passionate bedouin men who had begun a healthy bartering among themselves for how much they'd pay in livestock for each woman.

"Be cool, man," Isda said as Azrael headed back toward them.

Azrael towered over the eager suitors, who were garbed in long, brown robes with their heads covered in thick, white twists of turban fabric.

"Are these your wife?" the taller of the two men asked with a pleasant smile. "I am prepared to make a generous offer."

Before Azrael could answer, the other man slapped his chest in a cheerful manner. "But I would take good care of them, even if I have less camels—I, Saddiq, am good at what I do!"

The men howled with laughter as Melissa and Maggie quickly got behind Azrael.

"You have two, you should share," the older man said. "You American?"

"Go help the man out," Bath Kol said to Isda, shaking his head. "You know Az hasn't been down here long enough to lie fast on his feet."

"True dat, mon," Isda replied, taking off in an easy lope.

"No, no, no. You cannot buy my brother's wives. I have already told him I would pay two hundred camels apiece for each one."

"Whooooaaa," the younger man said, bowing in front of Isda with respect. "If I had so much, I would pay that for any of them, especially her." He pointed toward Celeste.

"Oh, no," Isda said with a smile as Azrael frowned and began walking back toward the group. "Mess with that one there and you might lose your life."

Both men took the comment in stride, holding up their hands and backing off laughing.

"First wife?" the older of the two called back.

"Only wife," Isda shouted back, and pointed at Azrael.

"Nefertari!" the young man shouted. "He is Ramses—like a bull!" The vendor did a little jig and laughed, much to the delight of his friend and the other vendors who hung back, smoking.

Isda shook his head as the group reconvened. "See what I mean?"

"I confess, I was not prepared for that onslaught," Azrael said, smiling at Isda.

"Uh, yeah," Bath Kol said, then raked his fingers through his sweat-damp hair. "But it is a hundred and twenty degrees out here, people, with not a butt crack of shade—so can we stop amusing the locals and do this thing?"

Isda resumed walking and chuckled. "Watch your step, ladies."

He didn't have to tell Celeste twice. Every two feet inside the perimeter of the camel rides section, which amounted to no more than a long, frayed rope tied to wooden stakes driven into the ground, the huge beasts had left a pile.

The closer they got to the animals, the more Celeste's eyes watered from their stench. Unfazed, the camels regarded them with defiant disdain while chewing their cuds and intermittently spitting like old men mawing tobacco on a Southern porch. The flies had declared open season on soft, foreign skin that had been sheathed in sweet lotions. Yet, for all of its repulsive aspects, somehow the situation was still pretty cool.

Mammoth pyramids that had been built so far back in history that it was hard to wrap her mind around them made Celeste feel as if she were suddenly frozen in time. Framing the monumental structures were the beasts of burden that had for millennia been making caravan treks with brightly embroidered blankets and square saddles covering their humps. Their modern-day drivers also looked as if they'd leapt out of a *Raiders of the Lost Ark* film, replete with long, white robes and black-and-white desert-sheikh headgear and bands, while park guards strolled by leisurely toking on Camel cigarettes and toting AK-47s.

Were it not for the modern-dressed tourists and buses, as well as the guards, the scene could just as well have been set five thousand years in the past. That didn't seem to be lost on anyone in the group as Isda loudly negotiated the rate for nine beasts of burden that would go off the beaten trail.

The camels looked tired after a wearisome day of tourists. But cash was king in the desert, as it was anywhere else. So with a switch and a lot of yelling, the expedition was arranged and each member of their group was guided toward a recalcitrant animal.

"Lean back," a camel driver shouted as Azrael mounted a large bull.

Celeste watched as the camel fussed, making a loud protest that sounded like a cross between a bear's growl, a Canada goose's honk, and a mule's bray. The animal obviously didn't appreciate Azrael's weight and let him know as it stood on wobbly legs, causing her and the others to gasp as the beast lurched, and for a second it looked as if Az would open his wings to avoid being pitched.

Who could have blamed him? It was such a natural reflex for the angels, and concealing those glorious appendages was like constantly having their arms tied behind their backs. But when it was her turn, she thought her heart would stop.

First of all, it was way different from being on a horse. A camel was twice as high, and the saddle was a weird, flat, rectangular contraption that fit snugly between one's legs. Second, the only way to mount a camel was if the beast was lying on the ground with its legs tucked beneath it, which meant it got up in stages. First it rocked to the front when it got its hind legs beneath itself, then it rocked backward as the front legs pushed up, creating a precarious seesaw motion for the rider.

There were no reins, just a knob at the front of the odd saddle to grip with all your might. The camels then loped in an odd sand shuffle that required one to flow with its rhythm. Sand or not, a fall off one of them guaranteed injury just from the height alone. Plus the cantankerous things used their long necks to turn back on the rider and nip, bite, or spit if they didn't like you.

A silent prayer bubbled up within her the farther

away they got from the monuments and the more hills and sand dunes they traversed. This part was not in the bright brochures posted in the airport and at the guest services desk.

But when the lead camel skidded to a braying halt and could not be pulled forward, Azrael dismounted with a one-handed vault and hit the sand. He held up a hand to signal the caravan to stop and for the camel driver to stop urging the freaked-out beast forward.

"Send them back," Azrael yelled above the wind that was kicking up.

Bath Kol dismounted with the other brothers as the camels began an open revolt, backing up and refusing to go forward.

"Over there!" Isda shouted above the now howling wind.

Celeste shielded her eyes against sand and debris, having to hold on with one hand as her animal rocked and pitched, trying to turn back to camp. But she saw it in the distance, the deep grooves of a pentagram etched in the sand that was quickly being covered over.

"We go back!" the lead driver shouted.

Isda drew away from the site and the brothers jogged back toward animals that now refused to lie down in the sand to be mounted. Bits of rock and stones bit into Celeste's skin, forcing all of them to use their forearms to shield their faces. But the camel drivers simply used the long, checkered headwraps to cover all but their eyes.

Azrael immediately ripped his shirt over his head, ran up to Celeste's camel, and handed it up to her for covering her face. Aziza unfurled her headwrap while trying to hold on to her mount, while Gavreel and Paschar gave up their shirts, too. However, that strategy, as chivalrous as it was, alerted the camel drivers that every man in the group was packing. Given that the desert seemed to function like the Wild, Wild West, that wasn't necessarily a bad thing. But it would be hard to explain to heavy-artillery-packing guards at the monuments when they got back.

As much as Celeste hated riding a camel and the smell of the sweaty beast, she found herself hunkered down close to its long neck; that is, until it snapped at her to get off him.

The way the animal swung around suddenly, the shifting sand, and her surprise toppled her. In a running leap that looked like an NFL, horizontal pigskin reach, Azrael caught her, buffering most of the fall as they hit the sand with a thud—but the moment their bodies touched the sand, a thousand scorpions belched from beneath them. The sand boiled with the venomous little creatures, potential death by a thousand stings scrambling up toward their bodies.

Azrael's wings were instantly out and he was in the air in seconds with her in his arms, pure reflex, as camels bleated and took off running with their freaked-out camel drivers screaming and fleeing behind them. Running hard against the gale-force wind, Gavreel, Paschar, and Bath Kol were forced to take to the air the moment they saw Aziza's camel's legs become engulfed by black serpents. Melissa's scream rent the air as something began pulling her and Maggie's mounts into the sand as if they had stepped into a bog. The poor animals thrashed, making them sink quicker as Paschar and Gavreel swooped in for aerial rescues while the sand turned red with the camels' blood.

"Get back to the van!" Isda yelled against the howling wind, both hands on a nine while hovering in the air.

"No!" Azrael shouted. "That will only draw the darkness toward the tourists!"

"I have to get that van, mon—given what's in it! You meet me over by the Sphinx and fly in low. Sandstorm is your cover, then walk out and find me!"

# Chapter 6

*Celeste kept her legs* wrapped around Azrael's waist and her face pressed against his neck, shielding her eyes from the stones and debris that pelted their bodies. With every wing stroke, she could feel him straining against the elements as the muscles in his chest, neck, and shoulders moved beneath his skin like steel cable, pulling and releasing the power of his flight.

He flew in the lead creating a V-formation that she knew had to lessen the air drag for the angels that flew in his wake. They were set up the same way migrating birds took to the air, each one's flight supporting the next individual's to better aid the entire flock, and they never left their own. But that meant as the strongest flier, Azrael took the brunt of the sand invasion that was so harsh it blotted out the unrelenting sun. Then, just like that, the storm was over.

Celeste looked up and over her shoulder. Angry sand

dervishes formed columns of funnel clouds back where they'd been attacked, but didn't follow them. Then she looked over Azrael's shoulder as he dropped them lower to whiz by the ground only thirty feet above it.

The majesty of the jaw-dropping structure before her fought for a place in her mind with the reality that they no longer had the storm as a cover. They were flying up to the back side of the Sphinx, the most magnificent structure she'd ever seen in her life. The Great Pyramids had stolen her breath, but this took her mind.

Tourists were climbing the rocks on a high ridge that allowed them to get up to shoulder level with the giant structure, but where it actually rested at the base was off-limits. There was no way they'd fly in and not be seen—especially since most people there had both cameras and binoculars.

Then before the thought could even form, Azrael let go of her with one hand. Her scream pierced her skeleton as she grabbed hold of him more tightly. Was he insane? They were barreling forward at seventy to eighty miles an hour and he let go? But then just as quickly, he stretched out his hand and a calm, blue-white wash of atmosphere surrounded them. All ambient noise was gone. She could no longer hear the wind rushing by her ears. All she could hear was the steady drone of his wings beating the air.

She looked up, but his focus was forward, his brows were knit, and his eyes were blue-white and glowing with unspent rage. She looked back as they rounded the face of the Sphinx and gaped at the aerial view of it with the pyramids framing it. That's when she wondered how anyone couldn't believe in something greater than normal humanity. One piece of antiquity, carved from what looked like a single piece of granite, stones ten to twelve feet high, twice her height, placed so exactly, so perfectly—with complex chambers inside the structure— not only did the pyramids rival the tallest skyscrapers in the modern world, but to this day still no one knew how they were created.

As she held on to an angel, her angel, she knew angels had to have touched this African civilization. Perhaps they were indeed mistaken for gods with a little *g,* or even aliens that flew in from the sky, but if this is what they'd lent to the development of human culture on the planet, there was a strong argument for giving them reverence.

To her panic, Azrael suddenly folded in his wings and dive-bombed toward their target with his arms held in tightly against his body. The wind whizzed past her as he spiraled like a bullet toward the outskirts of the parking lot where Isda's lone van sat idling. The others behind them followed suit, and she could hear multiple screams echoing to join hers, creating a Doppler effect. Then just like that, Azrael opened his wings as if they were giant parachutes, beating in toward her to hold him upright as he came to a running landing.

Isda threw open the van door. Azrael dropped her quickly and pulled her forward by a hand to enter the vehicle. Bath Kol was the last in and slammed the door, holding on to the seat backs with his head hung low, breathing hard as Isda peeled off.

"I gotta stop smoking," Bath Kol said, sweat dripping off his face. "But do you mind telling me, what *the fuck* was that?"

The other brothers gulped air and opened bottles of water, momentarily unable to speak after their recent exertion.

"The reverse of hallowed ground," Celeste said, accepting a water that Azrael handed her.

"What?" Isda glanced over his shoulder as they passed the pyramids.

"Look," she said, pointing out the window and wishing the air-conditioning worked a lot better. "Nobody is freaked out, nobody saw a thing, and whatever was after us didn't pursue us there. Those pyramids used to be tombs—right? where they laid the pharaohs. So no doubt they were well prayed over and consecrated. But further out where we were . . . well, hey. And whatever was after us came at us just like I imagine stuff from our side would go after an agent of darkness that treaded on hallowed ground."

"Lady's got a very logical point," Isda said. He kept his eyes on the road and then made a sudden U-turn.

"Yo!" Gavreel shouted, and Bath Kol toppled into an open seat. "Where you going, hombre?"

"Back to the greatest temple in the world," Isda said in a somber tone. "We can't just ride all over the freakin' desert. We need vision, insight, a place to hear through the veil better—especially since our boy here seems like he's getting stronger." Isda glanced up into the rearview mirror. "A sight-and-sound cloak for a small flying squadron, Az? You couldn't do that in the States, mon."

Azrael nodded. "I don't know what's happening to me here, man."

"Yeah, well, put your shirts on and let's go find out."

*This time when they* ran the vendor gauntlet, the expressions on each warrior's face seemed to keep back all but the little children. Azrael just dropped a handful of bills and kept walking, eyes now normal brown, but expression as resolute as the stone before them. The line before them was short at this hour, and guards waved their hands as though to motion that the park was about to close. But Isda held up a wad of cash, and that seemed to solve the overtime dilemma.

"Nubian, Nubian brother, come, come your family," one gate worker said with a wide smile glinting within his sun-burnished face.

"We want to wait until the other tourists are out," Azrael replied, adding to Isda's cash offering.

"No problems, no problems," the worker said, gaining consensus from the other workers that now huddled around.

In the distance Celeste saw a dispute arising in the camel drivers' area. Their drivers had just returned, missing four animals, and were waving their hands wildly.

Celeste discreetly motioned with her chin toward the ruckus that was unfolding near the camels. Azrael nodded and began walking toward them.

"Yo, mon, where you going?" Isda asked, catching up to Azrael in three fast steps and then holding him by the biceps.

Bath Kol was right on Isda's heels.

"To pay them for the unfortunate loss of their livestock . . . and to help them remember things a little differently," Azrael replied calmly.

Bath Kol and Isda glanced at each other as Celeste joined in the small, private huddle away from the exhibit-entrance guards.

"You think that's a good idea, Az? Like, the *last* thing we need to do is draw attention that we're back." She looked around Azrael and then up at him.

"The lady has a serious point, mon."

Bath Kol nodded. "Especially since we're not really supposed to be manipulating humans and all that jazz."

"We are also not supposed to allow them to suffer. These men are poor. The loss of a beast of burden means the loss of their livelihood in a very unforgiving landscape. The camels might not even be theirs or paid for, and if that's the case, their bosses could exact the toll of thievery upon them in an Arab nation, which could be severe for something they did not do. Their stories would never be believed, and who knows if the mere mention of it could get them stoned or worse. Our edict was to do no harm to mankind. Just our tripping over a supernatural land mine did harm. It must be corrected."

Azrael lifted his chin and strode away. Bath Kol shrugged and rubbed the hot nape of his neck and then squinted up at the sun. "Hey, you know how he is when he gets like this. There's no talking to the man."

Just like that, it was settled. The threesome trudged back to stand with the others at the opening of the vast tomb, all eyes on Azrael as the guards smoked cigarettes and sized up the women in the small group. Upon Azrael's approach, men ran and arms waved as a group leader chastised the fleeing camel drivers. He threw a cigarette butt on the ground, then several other men who hadn't witnessed the event dragged the screaming men to stand before Azrael.

The stricken guards began to stand, then suddenly the screaming men stood calmly and then laughed as Azrael pulled out a large bankroll from his pocket—one he hadn't had before. No one had to tell her that some angelic sleight of hand was going on. She and her sisters shared a knowing look. Resources were being manifested from the ether to fill pockets; minds were being calmed—all happening quietly right before her eyes.

Shoulders in that group relaxed. Men laughed. Guards lowered weapons and spoke to each other in a language she couldn't understand, but their body language told her everything she needed to know. The leader of the camel drivers' area accepted the bills and held some out for the previously shaken men, who hugged Azrael. Apparently he'd well overpaid for their losses.

After ten tense minutes of negotiations, Azrael returned to the group just as the last of the tourists were being flushed from the Great Pyramid. Eager to please the wealthy American who was flashing lots of cash, the guards scrambled to accommodate Azrael's request that his party be the only ones allowed in.

"Wait, wait, Diddy," one said. "I clear for you, okay?"

"I'll make sure no one comes behind you," another said proudly, saluting Azrael. "You play this football . . . basketball?"

Azrael smiled and shook his head. "No, man."

"You movie star—or like a music man . . . rap star?"

Isda burst out laughing. "Naw, dude can't carry a tune."

Seeming confused but deciding it wasn't in their best interest to continue asking questions, the guards dropped the queries and went through the structure, leaving a couple to handle the payoff details. After several long, hot minutes they emerged, sweating and smiling.

"It's all good, boss," the first out of the structure exclaimed.

"I take pictures?" another offered, clearly wanting to get in on the payday.

Azrael handed each man Egyptian currency what was worth a hundred US dollars. "No pictures, no guards—private."

The guards looked at each other sheepishly. One looked away as the leader came in close to Azrael.

"You cannot desecrate the monument with the ladies . . . not even for money."

"No!" Azrael said, holding up his hands in front of his chest. "Just prayer."

"Ohhhhh! You had me worried. You have no idea what people try to do within the great walls here!" The man looked embarrassed and wiped his forehead. "But prayer is not really allowed either, except for the right gift, how and when a man prays . . ." He shrugged and glanced around at his buddies, who were all smiles.

Azrael nodded and peeled off several more bills. "A tithe?"

The man nodded. "It is right to share, my friend."

"Can we go in now?" Bath Kol muttered.

"Yes, yes, but be careful—the way is steep and you are tall. Go low, low, bend and watch your heads."

This time Isda took the lead as they entered the dark; Azrael brought up the rear. Two brothers were in front, two in back, with one as a security checkpoint in the center between the women. Instant claustrophobia assailed Celeste as they bent in the tight, stone confines and began what amounted to a ten-story trek straight up, holding small handrails, bent over to walk beneath the four-and-a-half-foot-high ceiling. The steps, such as they were, amounted to slats placed close together and not deep enough for a modern foot to fit. If she was having trouble, she couldn't imagine how the guys, who stood well over six feet tall with shoes sizes and body mass twice hers, were faring.

No ventilation and insufferable heat added to dusty conditions that caused wheezing even if one wasn't asthmatic. But for sure, this space was sacred and was meant for the original purpose it served—to bury a king. It was not meant to be a theme-park exhibit, but that's what it had been turned into for the sake of tourism, and yet who could blame the local government for finally being the last to cash in on their own national treasures after, according to Isda, they'd been grave-robbed for centuries?

Then, most remarkably, when her legs were just about ready to give out, the tunnel opened up into a large stone room that was ten feet or more in height with a vacant stone coffin in its center. Angel brothers gathered around the coffin, with her and her sisters interspersed between them. Her nerves were wire taut as she looked at the way they'd slowly come in and the only one way they could get out. She breathed through a panic attack and fisted her hands at her sides. If scorpions or snakes or anything insane bubbled forth from the walls, they were trapped. Everyone seemed to be thinking the same thing, and they all looked at Isda for guidance as he lowered his head in a moment of silent prayer.

But when he opened his eyes, they shimmered with tears, and his inner light had begun to flicker behind his pupils. Bath Kol was the first to catch it, and he glanced at Paschar, who offered a discreet nod. Azrael backed the women in the group up just a bit, and Gavreel edged closer to Isda.

"You all right, man?" Gavreel said in a peace-inducing tone.

"Am . . . I . . . all right, the man asks?" Isda shook his head and chuckled sadly. "How can I be all right?"

"Okay, this was a bad idea. Let Az take the ladies out of here," Bath Kol said, heading for the open doorway. "We can do this divination with me, you, and Paschar— we get the vision, then we'll be out."

"How *the hell* can a man be all right, seeing this?" Isda suddenly shouted, his emotions exploding violently. He punched the wall, causing a chunk of stone to fall from it as his wings spread, ripping his T-shirt. "They took the bodies! Mummies are our ancestors—they took the bodies of our children! They have them on a road show all over the world! This place used to be green, mon! It was fertile, beautiful, and now—look at it! They have pissed in the monuments and smoked cigarette butts on these graves— and you ask me if I'm all right?"

Gavreel tackled Isda with help from Paschar.

"I ain't neva gwan be all right!" Isda raved as his brothers thrust him against the wall. "They ground up thousands of mummies, rich mortals did that, and they snorted them in secret societies! Defiled corpses and graves! Built developments over the goddamned Valley of the Kings! They're selling camel rides through the pharaoh's backyard. Heaven help me, I will lay siege to this land! I swear it on me immortal existence—I neva wanted to come back and see it. My heart cannot take it, mon—now after all we built, all we did and taught, now they got my boy!"

Isda finally grabbed Gavreel around the shoulders and sobbed. "Dat is who they took out there in the desert and defiled his sarcophagus with innocent human blood in a pentagram! Imhotep—they made up lies about one of the greatest geniuses in all history—my son! Do you hear me, Azrael, Angel of Death, my legion brother, you make dis shit right!"

"Listen to me, man," Azrael said, peeling Gavreel away from Isda and holding Isda firmly by the shoulders. "We're gonna find the body."

Isda nodded, his chest heaving. "You promise me."

"I promise you," Azrael said, then hugged him hard. "But you cannot lay siege to these humans."

"They're invaders! They aren't the original Nubian people. These are—"

*"Humans,"* Azrael said in a no-nonsense tone. "You know how this works . . . battles, wars, invasions, the ebb and flow—"

"Aided by evil," Isda shouted, pushing Azrael off him.

"Yes," Azrael said, nodding.

"They brought down one of the most magnificent empires."

"Yes," Azrael said quietly. "And choices made within that empire also helped."

"Imhotep was a part of the Golden Age. My boy had nothing to do with dat travesty."

"No, he did not," Azrael said in a calm tone, going to Isda slowly as one would approach a wounded lion. "And we will recover his sarcophagus and clean off the filth they covered him with."

Isda's eyes glittered in the semidarkness. "They made up movies about him as evil. They have children afraid of his name. They—"

"I know, brother," Azrael murmured. "We may not be able to correct all of that in one mission, but we can find him and return him to rest."

Isda nodded. "That's all I ask. I don't have much beyond that left anymore." Two huge tears rolled down Isda's cheeks as he allowed his back to slump against the stone wall. "I watched them all die. "Watched all of their inventions and brilliance get taken to other countries. Watched others be given credit for what my children discovered and developed here. They said the Greeks and Romans did it all, but it was my sons and daughters, and my grandchildren and great-grands." Isda closed his eyes and drew in a shuddering breath and then sniffed hard. "Then they put them in chains and after dat, mon . . . I couldn't come back here to see anymore. I would have murdered."

"You don't have to come back here anymore, brother," Azrael said, drawing Isda into a warrior's hug. "Do you want me to open up the column of light?"

Isda shook his head. "I don't want to go home until I can find his sarcophagus."

"Then, you tell us when it gets too intense. Some

battles you can sit out. After a tour of duty for twenty-six thousand, nobody can fault you."

"Thanks, man . . . I'm all right," Isda said as Azrael let him go. "It just fucked me up, is all. I felt all the energy on the walls, all the disrespect for what this place really was."

"Yeah, man. I hear you," Azrael said. "I feel it, too."

"Can I try?" Celeste said, coming close to the open king's chamber center stone.

Isda nodded and she waited, glancing around. "I need to get inside the space."

Isda wiped his face and went to the edge of the open stone enclosure. Walking around the edges of what looked like the long, rectangular trough, he nodded. "This wasn't Imhotep's, it was Cheops's."

"But if something evil happened in the shadow of this sacred ground . . ."

"Maybe let her try," Bath Kol said, imploring Isda without pushing him too hard.

Finally Isda nodded and held out his hand to Celeste to help her into the encasement that would have held a pharaoh's golden sarcophagus.

Each person in the room placed his or her hands on the edge of the granite enclosure while Celeste slowly lay down inside it. Not sure what compelled her, she folded her arms across her chest in the ancient mummy pose, her body moving of its own accord as she closed her eyes. Soon her lashes began to flutter and images began to take shape behind her lids. She could feel the surface of her skin begin to tingle, and suddenly she was weeping.

"Who is Dendera?" She sat up quickly with a gasp and wiped at her tears with dusty hands.

Isda looked at Celeste and then around at the group. "Dendera is a temple in the south," he said calmly, glancing around at the others as he began to pace. "A full day's journey by car and too dangerous to be going through da desert at night. If you drive, you need an armed escort against bandits who would take foreigners hostage for ransoms—along the way, you'll see . . . there's some burned-out tour buses . . . look like Mad Max and the Thunderdome was dere."

"Then, by all means, lets take the freakin' train," Bath Kol said, rubbing his neck. "Damn, why is everything here so complicated?"

"We'll follow your lead, Isda," Azrael said, helping Celeste out of the stone enclosure.

"Aw'ight, den," Isda said, closing his eyes.

"But the Valley of the Kings turned up nothing?" Gavreel glanced around the group and his gaze settled on Paschar for a moment.

"No," Isda said quietly. "When our advance team got here, that's the first place we looked. There are thousands of tombs in that limestone, mountainous region. We figured it would be a perfect place to hide a coffin. But with all the excavations still going on and the fact that the government actually built houses on top of the grave sites for miles—and people are digging in their basements striking gold and regularly selling antiquities on the black market, since that's worth more than the couple grand the government will give them for their homes . . . we pulsed the area. It was cold. Last place we even thought to look was the museum. Insane."

"It was the last place any of us would have looked," Azrael countered, clearly trying to make Isda feel better.

"Den it should have been the first place I looked, mon."

"It's all good, man," Gavreel said quietly. "Stop lacerating yourself. We're gonna work it out. So let's focus forward instead of backward. How do we get down to Dendera safely traveling with mortals?"

"Aw'ight," Isda said, drawing in his palm with his forefinger to show the direction they'd have to take from Cairo. "Gotta take the train way past Sakkara, Memphis, Beni Suef, Minia, past the rock tombs of Beni Hassan, even beyond Abydos, though not as far as Nag Hammadi. The route follows the Nile and we can get off at Qena, then catch a ferry over to Dendera." He raked his locks with his fingers and sighed. "You was feeling female energy, little sis, because dat temple in Dendera was dedicated to the goddess Hathor." He glanced around at his brother angels. "Our locator is on point."

# Chapter 7

*I*t was the shortest hotel stay in her life, and she deeply grieved leaving the sumptuous environs, especially when she saw the Cairo train station. It was not Amtrak's Northeast-corridor rails by any stretch of the imagination. As Celeste glanced around the dingy, passenger-swarmed station, it looked like something out of a low-budget, 1940s version of *The Orient Express*.

Every old cable TV movie she'd ever watched bloomed in her mind as she stood with the others impatiently waiting for the train. Haggling baggage handlers, old ladies swathed in traditional garb from head to toe with crates of livestock and children, arguing vendors selling cards and sweets for the ride and overcharging for water, made the platform a lively but also treacherous place. Several times her heart leapt into her mouth as small children with wares to sell darted between passengers, dangerously near the platform's edge. But somehow the little street urchins were as fleet afoot as mountain goats, navigating their way through hulking adults and luggage.

Standing at the far end of the platform, Celeste watched the enormous locomotive huff its way into the station. Desert sand clung to its battered gray-and-navy exterior. The group just looked at it, seeming impassive. Bath Kol stopped a darting child and purchased a pack of unfiltered Camels and a deck of playing cards with a sigh. However, clearly no one wanted to fuss about the change from the luxury hotel to the sleeper train, on account of potentially hurting Isda's feelings. It wasn't his fault that this was the fastest, safest way to travel.

A porter took their tickets on the platform and then led the way to a bank of five rooms along the inside of the larger sleeper car. The first thing that assailed her was the smell. Egypt didn't have a no-smoking policy *anywhere*, and old butts plus whatever smoke clung to the upholstery nearly made her gag. It didn't matter that she used to be a smoker herself; secondhand smoke stank to the high heavens, and when you added a layer of pine cleaner or industrial-scented air fresheners to the mix, it made her stomach lurch worse than the rickety train.

She was forced to get over it; they were gonna be on the train overnight, regardless. Each couple lined up as the porter eyed them and then opened their individual cabins. Windows were on the left, then a narrow hallway that permitted only one person to politely pass at a time was in the middle, and metal-outfitted rooms were on the right.

For a moment, Celeste just stared at the single-row seating that looked like a prison cot, or bus bench seat if she was being generous with the comparison.

"You never ride the train, miss?"

"No. It's my first time in a sleeper."

Celeste had replied and even shook her head, but the man still glanced up at Azrael as though waiting for an answer from him. She'd noticed that ever since they'd arrived in Egypt, no one ever asked her a question and accepted her response. Oddly, it seemed as though a man had to respond to validate the reply. This reaction wasn't just aimed toward her, she noticed. The locals seemed to treat all the women in their group that way. Hotel staff, restaurant waiters, exhibit guards, now the porter. Then, come to think of it, she hadn't seen a single local woman in a job since they'd arrived. Working women had been nonexistent in the airport once they got off the flight, they were nowhere to be found in the hotel, were completely absent in the train station except as passengers, and weren't at the monument sites, except those handing out toilet tissue in the ladies' bathroom. Bizarre.

The porter totally ignored Celeste and seemed to be quite willing to wait for Azrael to respond for her.

"No, she's never ridden a sleeper train before," Azrael finally said with a slight frown of annoyance. "How does this work?"

"Ah," the porter said, extracting a bunk ladder from behind the door.

Then in a series of magician-like flips, pulls, and flourishes, he secured a top bunk that was already made up with dubious-looking blankets and linens. Clicking it into place by lowering the bed out of the wall as if it were a foldaway ironing board, he added the ladder, then opened up the bottom bunk—she still wasn't sure how even after she'd witnessed it, then showed them where a sink that didn't work was hidden in the wall.

"Bathrooms are at either end of the car, the bar is three cars down, and I will be by in one hour with your dinner." The porter then showed them how to flip over their individual plastic dinner trays. "Meat or chicken or vegetarian?"

"Vegetarian," Azrael said, still marveling at the *Transformers*-like gadgetry of the sleeper car.

Celeste cleared her throat and motioned toward the waiting porter with her eyes.

"Oh, yes," Azrael said, going into his pocket for a tip, handing the man what Celeste estimated to be *way* too much by normal standards.

"Thank you, sir!" the happy porter exclaimed. "I will take good care of your entire family."

"You're welcome," Azrael said, but then stepped out into the hall as the others got settled in.

Azrael didn't have to say it, she could feel it. Everyone was worried about Isda. Sad glances passed among the group as each couple stood in front of their room in the narrow aisle and Isda stood in front of his alone with only an extralarge footlocker on roller wheels.

"Where's your wife with all of her dresses and shoes?" the gregarious porter said, obviously in a good mood now that he was well tipped by each previous angel brother he'd assisted.

"She died," Isda said in a flat tone.

"But you have two tickets," the man said, confused and seeming mortified by the gaffe. "And so much luggage."

"I'll take the top bunk; my luggage can go on the

bottom bunk." Isda leaned against the windows in the hallway as the porter hesitantly readied his room, staring at the floor.

"I am very sorry. I thought you were just teasing me and that maybe she had gone to the restroom," the stricken porter said, his voice a low murmur now. "But you are a young man. You should marry again and take many wives. This way you will not be sad for long. Have many sons. Many children are good. Then this life will be good."

"Been there, seen it, done it, and finished with it. I'm older than you think and really don't have it in me anymore," Isda said quietly, then entered his room, hoisted his footlocker onto the bottom bunk, and closed the door on the porter.

Bath Kol gave Azrael a nod. "This is the crash-and-burn part I was trying to tell him about in the airport, brother."

"Yeah, I know. I'll be back," Azrael said, looking over his shoulder into the room at Celeste.

"I'm fine," she murmured. "Go to him."

Bath Kol met Azrael in the hall. "Let me take first shift with him. They have a bar just three cars down. Aziza is cool and won't be able to stand the smoke in there—she's turning green from the smell in here alone. She's tired, wants to meditate and sleep anyway. All of this nonsense has frayed her nerves—you know the queen doesn't do violence or stress. So, I can go into the smoking car with our brother. Me and Is, hey, we go way back. I literally know where all the bodies are buried, and I never got to my Remnant in time, either. You kinda rub salt in his wound just by having Celeste—it ain't your fault, but it is what it is. Me, I'm philosophical. I've got queen, but, you know. Just fall back and give the man some space. I got this."

"You're sure?" Azrael landed a supportive hand on Bath Kol's shoulder.

"Positive," Bath Kol said with a nod, then headed toward Isda's room as the train began moving.

*So they've found their* way home," Asmodeus said, rubbing his jaw as bloodied scorpions swarmed his feet. He drew heavily on a hookah and allowed the smoky mixture of water-cooled tobacco and hashish to flow over his palate, savoring it as he inhaled and then released it through his nose.

He looked around at his newly reanimated warriors with disgust. The once-beheaded Malpas still had a visible scar around his throat and could not speak. His exquisite African features were now marred by a gruesome keloid scar that showed exactly where he'd been decapitated. He'd lost an arm that never came back. Where he'd been hit in the chest was a gaping sinkhole exposing burned, twisted viscera.

Onoskelis was also now mute from her beheading and wore a thick ornamental choker to hide the wicked scar. The once beautiful Lahash was now merely a withered, blackened skeleton from his full holy-water immersion. Bune's dragon heads were flesh-barren skeletons when he shape-shifted now, and his skin was slowly rotting off his bones from the shrapnel he'd taken in the ship explosion on the Delaware.

Pharzup's face, which had taken a shotgun blast

delivered by Celeste, was missing an eye and the left cheek and half a jawbone, and the injury made him constantly drool on himself.

But perhaps the most pitiable was the once-strong and Roman-god-like Appollyon, who, because of a blade to the sensitive-for-angel area between his wings, was grounded. His black wings were useless appendages that hung limply in an uneven dangle. The man had been hobbled by the Angel of Death. To see such beauty mangled in battle was pure sacrilege.

Asmodeus felt his fangs lengthening as dark fury consumed him. Only he and Rahab and Forcas had been left mostly whole. Forcas had regenerated from his multiple gunshot wounds; Rahab had escaped in time. Yet even Asmodeus still bore Azrael's mark on his once flawless face.

Quiet fury practically strangled Asmodeus as he studied the condition of his dark inner circle of the most valiant fallen. His warriors, like Lucifer, were to have been the most beautiful of all the angels—the best, the brightest, the strongest. Now they looked more like demons than dark angels. It was unacceptable. Abhorrent. Even his once flawlessly handsome face was burned and marred by his untimely contact with the Delaware River, which had been turned into holy water. Once he had the tablets, he would correct this abomination, too.

He stood and pushed away from the long banquet table and paced to the window to stare out at the Egyptian night sky. The feeding on the human that the demons had dragged in had not helped any of them, nor had the blood. He listened to the crimson fluid slowly drip off the table onto the hardwood floor. The sounds of his own battalion gorging had sickened him, and he couldn't watch them devour the disemboweled body with the injuries they'd sustained. Looking at them just made him think of his own disfigurement. Mirrors had been banished in the villa, but that didn't solve the problem in the way that finding the crystal tablet would.

Time was not on his side. They didn't have months to spend in this luxury Red Sea villa on the West Bank recovering. There wasn't time to waste consulting sorcerers, nor would it be advisable to risk petitioning the Dark Lord for his assistance at this late juncture in the campaign—which would mean admitting temporary defeat, which would also mean risking extermination or entering into a bargain that Asmodeus was unprepared for. He'd learned long ago that leverage was king in the dark realms.

"Milord," Rahab murmured, coming up behind him and offering him a goblet of blood. "We have been here for eons and will be so in victory after the next alignment. We have been written about in every book in every culture. This is only a temporary setback. Remember, we are the Lords of the Dead in the Book of the Jaguar Priests, the story of us that I like best. The thirteen and nine that descended from the stars, you leading twenty-one of us through the caves of blood, torture, bats, and jaguar bones."

"We cannot run away to Mayan country," Asmodeus said quietly, still gazing at the stars, not accepting her offered goblet of blood. "The fight is here, in the old country. Our enemies are here, the tablet is here. *Azrael* is here. The golden bones of Imhotep only helped us re-animate our fallen brethren because he was a healer of the Light. But they remain . . . as you see them. Severely compromised."

She glanced back at the swarming scarabs and scorpions that frothed under the table with small demons that fought for the raw scraps the injured warriors threw to the floor.

"Send the demons on a reconnaissance mission to find them tonight," she murmured huskily, leaning in to whisper her message privately into Asmodeus's ear. "Let them take the casualties and find out where our enemies are. They breed like rats. We do not. Live to fight another day. You are exhausted from the raising ritual, and perhaps also from the bitter disappointment that I feel crawling over your skin."

"And if I stayed here tonight, you would not propose that I rest, but that I would serve you by half fucking you to death," he said in a low, murderous tone, then grabbed her by the throat. "Now where would the wisdom be in that?"

She smiled and coolly regarded him and waited until he eased he grip and released her, then took a sip of blood from the goblet she'd initially brought for him. "I did not say that it was wise, but I guarantee that it would definitely make you feel better."

*Azrael pushed the top* bunk up to close it, then sat down hard on the bottom bunk next to Celeste. With both elbows on his knees, he hung his head and stared at the floor. Her hand rubbing his back made him close his eyes.

"I am no good at this," he admitted quietly. "I have no skill in this realm of healing humanlike emotions. In the ether, we do not have such gut-wrenching pain. When fighting as a warrior, there is just the battle, the demon killing—at least that was how it had been." He allowed his head to drop into his hands. "It is all so different now and good men are suffering . . . and I am powerless."

She leaned her cheek against his shoulder. "You are being taught the human condition, Azrael. This is the heart of it all. Knowing we are powerless over so much, and yet we hold great power over how we process our reaction to events. We can decide to live or decide to die from grief or heartbreak. We can decide to shut down or to move forward, even when we don't like the circumstances or the hand we've been dealt. We can choose to do the right thing, to be in the Light, even if everything around us is dark and scary and stronger than we are. We can choose to die for a righteous cause, rather than survive an unjust one. You taught me that. Keep talking to Isda when he's ready to hear you. If every brother holds him up and supports him through his dark night of the soul, he'll eventually come out on the other side of that tunnel whole and stronger for the experience."

Azrael slowly sat up and draped an arm over her shoulder. "You have the wisdom of the healing angels. The feminine energy of the higher realms, Celeste. I won't give up on my brother."

She kissed his cheek. "Good, because you didn't give up on me and I was a basket case when you met me."

He turned and looked at her. "You were a survivor. Demons had beset your human heart and human soul . . . and had so abused you."

"And I could have chosen to live or die, and the night you found me I was at the end of my rope. I had decided to die. Then you made me see what a gift I was throwing away. As hardened as I was to the message, you were relentless." She touched the side of his face and smiled softly. "Isda will hear you, just maybe not tonight. Patience."

"Now you sound like Gavreel."

"I take that as a compliment."

"It was meant as one," Azrael said, gently brushing her mouth with a kiss.

A light tap on the door made them both look up. Azrael stood and opened the door to see their smiling porter.

"I have brought dinner," he said brightly, and then, without asking them, reached in and flipped down their trays. "Eat and call me when you are done."

There wasn't enough room to turn around without bumping into each other, so Azrael simply sat and accepted the cellophane-covered trays that contained a 98 percent starch meal.

"Thank you, sir," Azrael said pleasantly, then raised an eyebrow as he stared at what had been left for them as their dinner.

White-flour rolls, cheap processed butter, some sort of highly processed chocolate and white-sugary-iced cupcake, processed mango drink, hard white rice, and a vegetable medley of zucchini and squash in tomato sauce, complete with a small wet nap and plastic tableware.

"I think we should give this back to him," Azrael said, inspecting the platter without removing the plastic and looking at it from all angles as if he were a forensic specialist. "Not that I am ungrateful, and I know there are people in the world who are starving, thus I will not waste it. But . . ."

"Yeah, I think we should stick to the organic fruit and nuts and water in your backpack, Az. I've still got snacks in my carry-on." She picked up the trays and edged around Azrael. "I'll return these. Let the porter blame it on the spoiled, fickle American chick," she added with a wink. "See what you can rustle up in the bags and I'll go see if anybody else wants to share what we've packed."

Azrael pulled his body in as much as he could as they did an awkward dance for her to climb over the open tray rests, him, and the bed. Then she shimmied out of the tiny cabin with both trays still balanced. He chuckled and she was glad that he'd smiled.

"I've got skills, brother," she said with a wink, then set off to find the porter.

He was at the end of the car dozing off in a little service room and appeared startled by her presence.

"Miss?" He stood, seeming embarrassed that she'd caught him sleeping. "You want a different dinner?"

"No, no, we're fine. We're just really more sleepy than hungry. It's been a long day . . . so we do not want to waste this—I mean, we haven't even touched it."

The man smiled and quickly accepted the dinners from her. "Are you sure? Because they count them, you know."

"Yes, I'm sure. You can have them."

"You are so generous, miss. Thank you." He glanced around and set the trays aside. "I will not knock on your door until tomorrow morning." He bowed and gave her a knowing smile. "You are a new wife, yes?"

Celeste laughed, finally catching his meaning, not having the heart to tell him that she wasn't exactly a wife yet. "I am new" was all she said, and that seemed to please the man even more.

"A new wife is a wonderful thing," he said, clasping his hands together. "*Sleep* well."

"Thank you . . . you, too," she said, leaving him to think whatever he wanted.

Celeste laughed to herself as she navigated the swaying corridor. As bone-weary as she was and as badly as she wanted a shower to wash camel funk, sarcophagus dust, and pyramid grime off her, the last thing she was thinking about was jumping Azrael's bones. True passion had already happened back at Le Meridien before demons had attacked them and drama occurred in the desert. Sheesh.

But thinking about that frenzied, intense lovemaking session, which had ended in Azrael's apology, made her hug herself as she walked back to the room. He'd said he *really* messed up—oh, God. If his intentions had gotten muddled and he hadn't firmly put it in his mind that he wasn't trying to make her pregnant as in the last few months . . . aw . . . man. And it wasn't as if she could be mad at the man. She wasn't exactly diligent herself, and that's what he'd told her it required, both parties setting their intentions not to have that happen.

They needed to talk about this more, but not on the

verge of the frickin' Armageddon—or the 2012 precursor to Armageddon, or whatever it was. Then again, if she wanted to be really philosophical about the matter, if they lost the big cosmic war, then it was all over and they had to kiss their asses good-bye anyway. A moot point. If they won . . . One thing for sure, worrying about it was not going to change the outcome, and at the moment, as Aziza had said, there were way bigger issues at hand.

"Gonna hit the ladies' room," she said as she passed their room.

"I found cashews, too," he said, not turning around, thoroughly engrossed in his foraging project. "And the sink in here is broken, just so you know."

She kept it moving and tried to relax, and did, as soon as she saw Maggie standing at the end of the car waiting on the bathroom.

Maggie was leaning against the window with both hands, staring out into the starry night. As Celeste approached, she looked up and pushed her dark hair over her shoulder.

"Did the porter tell you guys to turn off your car lights after you ate and to keep the blinds closed?"

"No, not yet," Celeste said, frowning.

"Yeah, well, he was talking to us when he dropped off our so-called dinner and kinda warned us about bandits and angry locals that sometimes *shoot at the train*." Maggie grabbed Celeste by both arms. "Do you hear me?"

"Are you serious?" Celeste just stared at Maggie for a moment. "Damn, that so reminds me of home."

After a couple of seconds, both women burst out laughing. The circumstances were so absurd that the sarcastic quip was the tension-buster they both needed.

"In Colombia, too—so what am I worried for?" Maggie waved Celeste away.

"Hey, as long as it's a twenty-two, then what? If they don't hit this train with an RPG shell, it's all good." Celeste shrugged and slumped against the wall.

Maggie shook her head. "It's all good," she repeated, sounding resigned as her laughter ebbed.

"You tell Mellie yet?"

Maggie smiled. "No, and a land mine won't disturb her right now . . . let love reign."

"In here? Really?" Celeste closed her eyes and laughed quietly. "I am so not hating, but damn."

"Apparently they missed their window back at the hotel because Paschar was following Isda's order to the letter to be downstairs in forty-five minutes. You know how he is, exacting . . . so, Paschar was really having a difficult time leveling off after the battle—that's why I came out here to put some water on my face," Maggie said with a wink. "They were bouncing our suitcases off the shelf. Gotta be standing up against the wall, but that's none of my business."

Celeste covered her mouth and laughed hard behind her hand. "Oh, my God . . . where's Gav?"

"In the bar with Isda and BK." Melissa giggled and bit her lip. "Did you ever expect your life to go like this?"

"Not in a million years, sis."

"Me either," Aziza said, exiting the bathroom and entering their conversation without missing a beat.

The older woman's normally calm mother-wisdom façade seemed beyond rattled. She clutched a handful of natural soap, a washcloth, lotion, natural hand sanitizer, wipes, and recycled toilet paper against her petite breasts.

"Here," she said, thrusting the toilet paper toward Maggie. "There's none in there, the soap is barbaric, and you cannot sit down in there—I forbid it. The bacteria in there is . . . is . . . there are no words. The food and filth are just beyond comprehension."

Celeste went to Aziza and hugged her. "Queen Mother, it's going to be all right."

"It's *not* going to be all right. I told BK things have inexorably changed. I need a shower to think. Clean air to breathe—this is recycled smoke. My chi is unbalanced here and my chakras are spinning in the wrong direction. This food *is poison*."

"Breathe, sister," Celeste said, still hugging Aziza as Maggie slipped into the bathroom with a wink. "We have wholesome food in our room to share with everyone."

"I was never supposed to be drawn into any of this," Aziza said, swallowing hard and finally melting against Celeste. "I had a life, friends, a spa, a routine. This nomad existence and army-barracks conditions with angels . . . I didn't sign up for this, not this time around. I was a priestess!"

When Aziza began to weep, her delicate shoulders shaking with each shuddering inhale, Celeste simply rubbed her back.

"You remember being here in another life, don't you?"

Aziza nodded slowly and released a heavy sigh. "I may be a full-blooded human, but my third eye is wide-open. I remember all my significant past lives—and they were all spent with BK. The one from here . . . it's sooo hard. In the king's chamber it all started coming back the more Isda became unglued. I remember that I got trapped in one of the temples as Romans razed it. I was trying to save sacred scrolls. BK was trying to get his men not to burn that one temple I was in, but in the mayhem of battle they did before he could stop them." She shrugged and pulled back to look at Celeste with kind, wise eyes. "Then I saw a red glow in the corner of the ceiling and set my attention there as the smoke rose. The next thing I remember was being a part of the rising smoke and flowing up and up and out. It didn't hurt; I was not in my body. I could see BK on the ground reaching toward me sobbing. And then I was gone."

Celeste folded Aziza's hands within her own to feel and absorb her sister's pain. Pangs of regret at not being able to save a sacred sight almost made Celeste cover her heart. Hurt and fury collided with true terror for one's own safety, and a long wail crawled up her spine, a wail that cried out for salvation from the horror of being over-run by foreign invasion. Then hopelessness set in, followed by resignation. The overwhelming sense of powerlessness put tears in Celeste's eyes.

"It was terrible," Aziza murmured.

Celeste hugged her. "I know and I am so sorry."

"Thank you," Aziza replied hoarsely. "But that was a long time ago."

Peace slowly reclaimed Aziza's countenance as she swallowed hard and wiped her cheeks with the backs of her graceful hands, her beautiful eyes sparkling now from the sudden cleansing. "This is a hard place for many of us to return to. You have a story here, too, sister. It just hasn't resonated within you to remind you of it yet. But thank you. I feel better and can probably sleep for a bit."

"If you need me," Celeste said, hugging her again, "I am there for you. I love you."

"I know that, and that's why I love you, too."

# Chapter 8

*Just having the opportunity* to put water on her face and wash her hands felt good, despite the deplorable conditions of the bathroom. True, as Aziza had said, a nice hot shower, a change of clothes, and a decent meal followed by some real sleep would have been the cherry on top—but given that they hadn't been eaten by hell-sent scorpions or serpents, everything was relative.

Celeste walked down the hall under the flickering train light looking out at the blue-black horizon. A part of her wished they could just go out and see what a sky looked like without city-light pollution.

When she entered their room, Azrael was lying on the bottom bunk on his side propped up on one elbow, sans T-shirt, sneakers, or socks, wearing only his black jeans and munching on an apple with a bag of open cashews and a bottle of water in front of him. His eyes were closed and his long locks spilled over his muscular chest and shoulders while he methodically chewed. Even under the worst conditions the man was breathtaking.

Not opening his eyes, he patted the side of the bed and slid over as much as was possible to give her a sliver of it to lie down on.

"Close the door and turn off the light," he said in a calm rumble.

"I smell like camel and—"

"As did I until I took off my shirt."

She laughed and shook her head. "Oh, I am so not taking off my shirt."

"Close the door and please turn off the light, Celeste," he repeated without opening his eyes.

"And you really shouldn't lie on there without a shirt and shoes on . . . there could be bedbugs."

He nodded. "If there were, they are gone now. I took care of it. Turn off the light."

She complied but pressed her back against the door listening to him crunch on his apple, looking at the royal-blue spill of energy flowing from him, over him, over the bed and onto the floor, almost afraid to step into the pool of it. "You know this is how Eve got in trouble, right? Just one bite and it was all over."

He laughed in a low, easy timbre that ran all through her. "Mythology, I assure you . . . like I told you before."

"Yeah, okay," she said, laughing softly, and then walked over to the small window and raised the shade. "It's so beautiful out there . . . I've never seen a totally dark sky with all those stars." She could understand how three wise men navigated the desert with the carpet of spangling majesty above them. "Imagine when the whole world looked like this."

"You should see it from above," Azrael said quietly. "Come lie with me, Celeste."

Unable to resist any longer, she slowly stripped her T-shirt over her head and left it on the suitcases, then stepped out of her socks and sneakers and went to him. She slid into the narrow bunk with him as he moved the cashews and water out of her way and then gave her his apple by draping one burning arm over her waist as he nuzzled her hair. The moment she took the fruit from him, he splayed a hot palm against her belly, almost causing her to gasp.

Melting into his deep warmth, she closed her eyes and bit into the succulent apple, sure that it had been made sweeter just because he'd been eating it.

"Let me know when you want anything else," he murmured against her hair.

"Not fair," she whispered, releasing all resistance against him.

"I was talking about cashews or water," he said, chuckling.

She playfully elbowed him, and that only made him laugh harder. "I swear sometimes you get on my nerves, man." She bit the apple hard and chewed it loudly.

"You're welcome."

"Humph. Back atcha." She took another bite as he dropped a bag of cashews in front of her and set the bottle of water within her reach.

"Thank you," she said more pleasantly, then turned a bit to kiss his shoulder. When she felt his breath hitch, she smiled.

"Back atcha," he murmured, then kissed her shoulder, returning the favor.

"Okay, okay, stop—before we embarrass ourselves on this train."

"I would not be embarrassed."

She laughed softly and opened the water. "I would."

He sighed and began stroking a lazy pattern up and over the swell of her hip and back.

"You need to stop," she said, chuckling more deeply and warming to his touch.

"It's meditative."

"Ohhh . . . meditative. Uh-huh."

"Yes. Quite. In fact, as I was waiting for you to return, I realized that I needed to fully absorb from this region . . . just as I had when I first came to look for you. Remember my first day on earth and how you took me to the library so that I could process all the knowledge in that repository?"

"Yeah," she said more thoughtfully, recalling how he'd walked down the stacks touching shelves, drinking in information without ever having to read it, just as he had in the supermarket, analyzing food and absorbing nutrients. She hadn't realized that he could now absorb history and images from any region. His ability to synthesize earthbound data was definitely getting stronger the longer he was on this plane.

Azrael nodded and sighed. "That is the only way I can understand Isda's pain, what happened here after we withdrew, specifically why the emotions of the team are running so high."

She snuggled deeper into his warmth and laid her head down on an outstretched arm, loving how his mind worked. Listening to him talk in bed while he was propped up on one elbow was like hearing the best bed-time story in the world. "Tell me what you learned today," she said in a soft murmur with her eyes closed, now able to also feel the gentle current of his energy that washed over her body, and suddenly realizing that he was cleaning the room and everything in it just for her.

Using white Light, he was manifesting that pristine angel condition, zapping potential bedbugs and bacte-ria, anything disgusting. He'd bestowed this subtle but profoundly caring gift upon her, in the same manner in which he and the brothers all cleaned their wings—just from the sheer intention of cleanliness. He'd done that to the room for her. It even smelled different, now that she paid attention.

"Oh ... Az ... thank you."

He kissed her shoulder again, his hand never losing its slow, constant metronome rhythm of gliding up and over her hip and back.

"I learned that women must have water," he said, smil-ing against her shoulder as he kissed it again. "I learned the reason why when mortals reincarnate, they forget the past lives, most times."

"Why?" She turned slightly to try to look at him, but gave up when it broke their warm seal. Snuggling back against him, she waited for the revelation.

"Because they are to bring the lesson forward but not all the entrapment. They must learn whatever that life-time had to teach them, encode that part deep in their psyche, but all the entrapment in anger, vengeance, guilt, shame, rage, hatred, vendettas ... those dark emotions are to pass away. If humans remembered everything, as soon as they came of age, they'd be on a path of war against their enemies. But, alas, sometimes they do remember . . . or because the lesson wasn't fully learned, they become re-entangled with their past pain or past persecutors. It is all so complex and out of the scope of what I was designed to accomplish as a mission. There are those of us on the other side who specialize in these matters. My goal was just to tap into a small segment of it to help me better understand how to help the team."

"Like Queen?"

Azrael nodded. "Yes. She was a priestess and had high knowledge from antiquity and was to bring all of that forward. But her new assignment, her new learning, would be how to live in the hustle and bustle of a metropolis like New York City and maintain those ideals from the temple."

"Well, she did that," Celeste replied, thinking about Aziza's wondrous all-natural spa and rejuvenation center in Brooklyn.

"Ah, but here on this train where she isn't able to get the resources she needs, she is very stressed. It is a humbling experience and important for her work going forward to understand why other mortals sometimes don't have the wherewithal to adopt her very strict rules and guidelines, even though she is correct."

Peace had replaced passion as she finished off the apple and nibbled on cashews, intermittently taking a sip of water.

"Wow . . . that's deep."

He nodded and released a warm, sweet current of

breath against her hair. "Her acute memory of being a priestess is making her very angry about the conditions of this train, when the lesson is for her to learn how to help people to transition to healthier lifestyles without the harsh judgment or criticism. If BK was not otherwise occupied helping Isda, I'm sure he would have cleaned their room and provided whatever she needed—but then he would have blocked the lesson. So, all things work for the greater good."

"You felt that all the way in here?"

"Absolutely. I was absorbing to learn and I felt her complete disgust."

Celeste smiled. "Then, uh, I take it you also felt what was going on in room number four."

He laughed in a slow, easy chuckle and kissed her shoulder. *"Absolutely."*

She laughed with him, teasing him as she ate a cashew slowly. "Then you also know *that's* not gonna happen up in here with no water, right?"

"Faith . . . *hope* . . . and charity, the greatest of all gifts is charity, Celeste."

"Oh, no, you are not working biblical rap on me?" She threw her head back and laughed harder, spilling nuts and water as he suddenly pulled her beneath him.

"I can make the sink work," he murmured with a wide smile.

She looked up at his handsome face, which was curtained in the dark by his long locks. Only moonlight and starlight shone through the window to blend with his blue energy flow.

"This is the land of the goddess, you know," he said

more seriously, then kissed her slowly. "Where in the beginning feminine energy was revered and respected. The Source does not discriminate—both were created equal and majestic. Balanced energies. You cannot have one without the other."

She touched the side of his face, still amused but losing some of her mirth the hotter he made her. "Yeah, but around here, the goddess is dead."

"No, she's not," he murmured, slowly kissing her neck. "Invaders tried to kill her, but they didn't succeed. I found one left from the old empire."

"I haven't seen Egypt treat women well," she said, warming to his game and losing her trend of thought as he kissed the cleft of her collarbone.

"Berber tribes . . . Arab invaders that brought warlike male energy after the Roman and Christian invaders had deposited that here. The original Egyptians, the Nubians," he murmured against the swell of her breasts, "thoroughly understood the value of the female principle . . . and I cannot imagine a world without that . . . now . . . that . . . I . . . know . . . how powerful . . . it is."

His breathing had changed and so had hers. She traced the hard ridges of his chest with the tips of her fingers, loving how the muscles in his abdomen contracted as she slid her fingers over them to unfasten his jeans.

"You're sure you can make the sink work?" she murmured, teasing him as she slowly lowered his zipper, then pushed his jeans down over his slim hips to begin a lazy stroking pattern up and over the swell of his tight, magnificent ass.

His captured her nipple in his mouth, suckling it

through the fabric for a moment before answering her, allowing that to be a part of his answer. "I can bring the Nile into this car, if that will aid your mercy," he said in a gravelly tone, then opened the center clasp of her bra to let her breasts bounce free.

The way he looked down at her and the heat that his kiss against her skin produced made her arch. She wanted his mouth and hands on her breasts so badly that she covered them with her own hands, unable to endure the ache the air against them produced. He got the message without her having to say a word and simply stripped off her jeans to discard them along with his on the floor.

"Just promise me you'll be quiet," she said on a heavy exhale as he blanketed her again, his shaft pulsing against her inner thighs.

"My word as my bond," he murmured, taking her mouth and then whispered hotly in her ear, "I will sound like the train."

"Your intent not to get me pregnant is intact, right?"

For a moment he just stared at her, then closed his eyes and finally nodded. "Yes. I believe so."

"That didn't sound very convincing."

Again he hesitated and then nodded. "I'm all right. I'm good."

"You sure?"

"Yeah."

Trusting him and needing him so badly it hurt, she squeezed her eyes shut and pressed her mouth against the side of his neck as his broad palm slid beneath her ass so he could enter her slowly. Thick, pulsing heat filled her in maddening increments, moving as he'd declared, with the slow rock of the train. Every thrust broke her inhales into short, quiet gasps of appreciation. Losing her mind, she wondered if it was too late to rescind her request to go slowly, soundlessly as she held the broad expanse of his back, knowing he wanted to release his wings so badly but wouldn't here in the tight confines . . . wondered if he would keep his word not to bring her humiliation, when that worry was quickly evaporating with his every stroke.

With her legs wrapped around his thighs, she lifted up on every pass to take more of him in each time. Finally his arms began to tremble and he dropped down to crush her, grabbing her ass hard, pulling her to him with sudden bursts of force, yet without changing the pace, breathing hard though his mouth with his head turned. The expression on his face was one of pure agony.

He was so incredibly close to the edge, and she was teetering on the brink of it right along with him. She could feel him straining not to shift gears, not to drop the hammer on his amazing body, to outstrip the train's lumbering speed, which would definitely out them. To help him, to help them both, on the next up-thrust she whipped her hips in a forceful circle while lifted off the creaking mattress. That didn't help.

He released a deep, quiet moan next to her ear, a sound so filled with agony that it almost made her start wildly bucking. Her circles and pulls had begun to drive him away from his rhythm. For a few insane seconds he'd lost it, had added an extra beat in the train's steady drone. Panting, he restored order; in quick, shallow sips of air, she destroyed it. Each time he pulled back on a thrust, she lifted harder and with more force to hasten his return without making the bed sound.

Suffering, for a moment he looked at the floor. Still semirational, she shook her head no. He closed his eyes and spread his knees. Still bent low beneath the top bunk, he took her mouth and with both arms wrapped around her hips, he lifted her onto him fast and hard the way they both needed him to now.

He swallowed her cry as the devastating orgasm hit, moaning low and forcefully back into her mouth as his body wracked in convulsing waves. Once the storm passed, he broke their kiss and slowly lowered her back down and collapsed on top of her.

"How did I do with keeping my promise?" he asked on a series of ragged exhales after a few moments.

"Phenomenal," she murmured, sprawled beneath him with her eyes closed. "Now you just gotta get that sink to work."

*Dawn kissed the horizon* at the same time he kissed her awake.

"I want to show you something," he murmured, drawing her out of bed. He led her to the window and stood behind her, pulling her back against his chest as he enfolded her in his arms and kissed the crown of her head. "The start of a new day in the motherland."

A spectacular pageant unfolded before her eyes against the vast horizon of golden sand. Heat waves shimmered up from the ground, making the large, gold-orange orb that seemed to be lifting out of the sand itself appear to be a mirage. Rose-orange splashes of color mixed with dark-blue streaks crisscrossed the sky as though a frenzied angel hand had unleashed a pastel paint palette against it. As the sun rose to take over the sky, it burned away the pinks and blues to dominate the heavens.

Azrael hugged her tighter and sighed into her hair. She covered his arms with hers and leaned into his warm embrace and closed her eyes.

"It's so beautiful."

He nodded. "Worth protecting for a thousand more millennia." He kissed her neck, nuzzling it. "I love you, Celeste. I only want to see this world or the sun rise in it with you here."

"I love you, too." She hugged his arms against her more tightly. She couldn't address the rest of what he'd said. It was a dangerous concept for an angel to consider, not wanting to be immortal just because she was mortal. She would age and die. She knew that was troubling him as she turned in his hold and stared up into his sad, contemplative eyes.

"One day at a time . . . the Serenity Prayer."

He nodded and kissed her gently. "I know why the ancient mortals built in stone here after encountering us," he murmured. "It was to leave themselves behind for us." He traced her cheek and her eyebrows and the bridge of her nose with trembling fingers as though memorizing her face with every cell in his touch. "If all I had left of you was a temple, Celeste, one with your beauty enshrined on the walls, I would bring incense and fruit and flowers there on a regular pilgrimage, too."

She hugged him, not wanting to even think so far

into the future. The concept that one day she'd have to leave him brought tears to her eyes and she quickly banished it. She and her sisters had quietly ruminated about aging and dying while their lovers remained unchanged, had wept together about it, stressed about it in their private female vent sessions, but she didn't want to go there now.

"I'll always be with you, no matter what. I promise."

"I'm supposed to tell you that," he said with a sad smile, pushing her backward to look at her. "I'm your angel, but somehow you seem to be mine."

He was getting stronger here, better able to quickly manifest the things they needed, better able to make instant assessments the more he absorbed information from the very land itself, and the deeper they traveled into the heart of Egypt, she could tell, that seemed to also be making him more introspective, and somehow sadder.

"But I can't fix the sink," she said, smiling up at him and trying desperately to make him focus on the here and now.

"Ahhh, there is that." He turned on the water behind them without even moving or looking at the faucet. "There is that."

*This time when the* porter knocked on the door, they were calmly seated on a single seat. The beds were put up, the ladder stowed, old, soiled clothing was packed away, and they were washed up and refreshed. But they again declined the meal offering, which was little more than a sugary Danish, bad juice, and awful coffee. The only thing they accepted was the water, which of course had a surcharge.

But it was amazing what a little stress relief and rest could do. When they all met in the hall to debark at Qena, even Isda seemed much improved. Word passed down the row quickly that between Isda and Bath Kol, they'd secured another van. The advance ground team of angels from Bath Kol's old barracks and from Isda's old safe house in Brooklyn had boarded the train in the bar, played a few rounds of cards, had a few drinks, and went scouting for resources.

"Some of us got work done, mon," Isda said with a sly smile as Azrael passed him when he jumped down to the train platform.

"I'd say the man got work done. Let's not quibble over semantics," Bath Kol muttered to Isda under his breath, making Isda laugh.

Although the ribald comment made Celeste's face flush, she was glad to see Isda laughing, even at her expense. His dazzling white smile flashed within his dark, handsome face, and his eyes no longer seemed as haunted. That change appeared to boost the morale of the entire group as they trudged toward a beat-up, sky-blue jitney bus.

"Where do you find these vehicles, brother?" Gavreel said, shaking his head and helping to stow luggage in the back.

"It's that or a camel, okay?" Isda said with a shrug. "Count your blessings."

"I hear you," Celeste said, climbing on the bus with Aziza, Melissa, and Maggie. "I'll take a diesel-fuel van any day over a camel funk."

Aziza slapped her five over a seat and laughed. "Want an orange?"

"I do," Melissa said. "I'm starving." She caught it and tore into it as though she hadn't eaten in three days.

"You're supposed to feed your woman, man," Gavreel said under his breath to Paschar as he climbed on.

"Yeah, mon, just can't abuse a mortal and—"

"Oh, my God, Isda!" Melissa said, then looked out the window. "I'm fine."

"My bad, my bad . . . not trying to say anyt'ing untoward, just stating facts as I see dem," Isda said, laughing, starting up the loud, smoking engine. "We'll get some grub on the way to Dendera. I know *all* the brothers are hungry dis morning, too."

*his mission to grab* some grub was to be quick—in and out. No dawdling. They had things to do and places to be, and travel was a process in itself. They covered their heads with the wide scarves that had been provided for them on the bus, as Isda suggested, when they pulled up at a roadside rest stop. Everyone cast concerned glances at each other, but Isda had already jumped out and was walking in.

"You sure about this, man?" Bath Kol called behind Isda as he stared through the dusty windows. "Looks like something out of a spaghetti western, only with camels."

This time Celeste couldn't disagree with Bath Kol's assessment. Camels were tied to posts in front of an adobe-style mud-brick building that had the dome roof blown off it. Buzzards circled above the posts. Flies were everywhere, enjoying camel dung. Men sat in palm-tree shade at scattered wrought-iron and enamel-top tables smoking hookahs and sipping what looked like strong coffee or tea, regarding them with both disdain and suspicion. Again, women were totally absent from the landscape.

Azrael stood and held up a hand, signaling for the others to wait. "Let me double-check with Isda."

"Yeah, you do that, fearless leader, because I really don't think this is a joint where the ladies fit in, you feel me?" Bath Kol stooped down, leaning on seat backs with both forearms.

"Absolutely," Azrael said, moving down the center aisle of the bus.

"But I have to pee," Melissa whispered over the seat to Celeste.

"Aw . . . maaaan," Bath Kol said, then stood. "You ready to do this, brothers?"

Gavreel and Paschar stood.

"I'm sorry," Melissa said, and hugged herself.

"It's all right, baby," Paschar said, and held out his hand to her.

Bath Kol looked at Gavreel with a wide grin and flipped an unlit Camel cigarette into his mouth.

"Whew, what a difference a day makes," Bath Kol said, then began singing the old tune. " 'Twenty-four little hours . . .' "

Paschar shoved him in the back hard as Azrael climbed down.

"Would you guys cut it out," Azrael said, keeping his gaze moving. "Double-escort the ladies to the bathroom, and Isda and I will go in for food . . . one of you stay with the bus."

"Nooo problemmo," Bath Kol said in a merry tone.

He looked at Aziza. "Now, baby, listen to me—when you go back there, don't freak out."

"I'm not gonna freak out," she replied, lifting her chin and frowning.

"Oh, *yes*, you are."

Bath Kol and Paschar moved the group of women forward in what could only be described as a safety huddle toward the bathrooms that were undoubtedly inside, while Gavreel hung back and leaned against the bus, returning wary glares to the men that were eyeing him.

"Do you all know what you want to eat?" Azrael asked as they passed him and Isda.

"No time for democracy," Isda said, walking toward the counter. "Dey got falafel, pita—white and wheat, hummus, grape leaves, dates, olives, figs, lamb, and—"

"No meat," Azrael said.

"In here? Oh, hell, no," Bath Kol muttered.

"Den, like I said. Order for the group and get it quick. We got water on da bus—they got soda and juice in here, and chips and junk. Period. Take it or leave it." Isda folded his arms over his chest.

"I'm good, whatever you decide is fine," Celeste said, trying to not make a face as the odor from the bathrooms drifted on a hot air current to blend with roasting meats.

When they saw the "bathroom," Aziza just turned on her heels and walked back toward the bus, not even waiting for Bath Kol to escort her.

A hole was in the floor and a suspicious-looking, yellowed roll of toilet paper was on a stick poking out of the wall. It looked as if it had rolled across the dirt a few times. A plume of flies took to the air upon the invasion of would-be visitors. This was definitely one of those instant-stress situations that triggered Celeste's old desire for a cigarette. A Newport would have been excellent right now, but she had to quickly jettison the thought before it set in as a real jones for a butt.

"This was obviously contrived by a man!" Maggie announced, folding her arms.

Paschar tried not to laugh as Bath Kol walked back to the bus behind Aziza, calling for her to wait up.

"I knew she was gonna freak—I knew it," Bath Kol fussed, shaking his head.

"I don't have to pee that badly," Melissa said. "I can hold it."

"Only a man," Maggie argued in the center of the group, beginning to lapse into a thickening of her Latina mother tongue as she spoke with her hands, thoroughly indignant. "A woman has to pull down her pants, open her legs over *that* hole? Are they mad! With camel flies diving at your snatch? *Really?* After those flies have walked over camel poop and been down in that human-refuse hole?"

"I can keep the flies back, ladies," Paschar said in a sheepish tone, then looked at Melissa with a pleading expression. "I don't know when the next time will be that we can stop. I really think it's a bad idea to try to hold it . . . as much water as we have to consume out here to stay hydrated."

"Promise you'll keep the flies back?" Melissa asked in a quiet rush.

"Oh, for the love of Pete!" Bath Kol said, pacing back to the group huddle by the bathroom without Aziza. "We'll keep the flies off your butts if you just hurry up."

"See, this is exactly what I'm talking about—no respect for the goddess," Azrael said with a wide grin, coming up to Bath Kol with two hefty bags of food. "What shall we do with this Roman?"

"Hey, hey—we Romans were very respectful of the goddess, I'll have you know," Bath Kol fussed. "But some fancy things we didn't worry about."

"Like flies," Isda said, chuckling as he came up to the group with his bags, chewing a dental stick.

"In the Colosseum, yes, there were flies *and* ladies— and grilled meats, all right," Bath Kol said in a peevish tone. "And what?"

"Work with Paschar, will ya, so they can go?" Isda laughed.

"So, what, I'm now lord of the flies? Gimme a break." Bath Kol pulled out a pack of smokes and tapped the back of it.

"I don't even know why you bother. You know Aziza hates the odor of that nasty habit, and that will not endear you to her after this pit stop," Paschar said with a wide grin.

"Stay in your lane, Paschar, and keep the flies off your lovely lady's rump. Us old heads know how to sling a little ambrosia and desmoke a frickin' T-shirt."

Celeste just laughed as Bath Kol lit a cigarette right in the rest stop while each woman took her turn doing the inevitable.

"You know," Bath Kol said as they filed back to the bus, "groups are a pain in my ass."

Azrael made no comment; his laughter said it all. As each person got settled, he held up two bags. "Pita and hummus or falafel sandwiches on pita. Pass them back."

Celeste watched him navigate down the aisle as Isda pulled out of the parking space, careful to clear the lounging camels that had plopped down beside the bus. That's when she noticed that Azrael had a small, white plastic bag that he'd extracted from the top of one of the larger food bags. He slid into the seat next to her with a smile and handed her the bag.

"What's this?"

"Open it," he said like an excited teenager.

"Chips?"

"Special spicy ones," he said triumphantly. "I knew that you liked them, from before when we first met and you showed me food. When I saw that they had them here . . ."

"That is so sweet!"

"Aw, man, stop trying to make the rest of us look bad, getting your mack on with the chips, dude," Bath Kol said, smiling despite his obvious intent to remain peevish.

Azrael threw an empty water bottle toward him that missed. "Mind your business."

Oddly, that broke the tension and made the entire bus erupt with laughter as food got passed around and shared. A sense of camaraderie took over. Women happily commiserated; the brothers teased each other and talked smack. Everyone marveled at the goatherd roadblock and laughed at Isda's complaining until the slow-moving obstruction passed.

There was no way to remain removed from and impassive to the land or the people as their small jitney wended its way through narrow village streets. In the distance woman worked in green pastures where the Nile had been bountiful as it had for thousands of years, providing rich black silt for farming. Small children ran along the side of the bus waving at the strange foreigners. Women in full garb hung clothes on lines and shooed goats away from their feet. Men walked with cinder blocks and PVC tubing on their shoulders, while others worked on twenty-year-old vehicles or debated in tavern doorways.

This was the Egypt that was hard to see while in Cairo, though no harder than it was hard to see a real neighborhood while standing at the Empire State Building or down by the Liberty Bell. One had to go into the boroughs or the real residential communities to truly see the people and understand what it was all about.

For Celeste, every little upturned face drew her. She watched the angels and their reaction to the children. Even Bath Kol was moved.

"You know," he said quietly as they entered a more industrial area that left the children jogging in the roadside dust waving behind their minibus, "when we would march our legions through small towns . . . man . . . this was the part that would break your heart. The kids would come out and cheer for us. They knew an army, a legion of support, was passing through. But we knew that if the enemy came behind us, our orders were to march forward. We couldn't turn back. So we'd dump our pockets and manifest whatever small treats that we could while conserving energy for the battle ahead." He sat back in his seat and rubbed his palms down his face. "And sometimes, while in a Roman legion, we weren't there to liberate. We were there to kill and conquer . . .

and the children always got trampled first. My men always tried our best to get the civilians out of the way—sometimes we just couldn't."

"Then why did you do it?" Maggie asked softly, no judgment in her tone or her expression. She sat forward, seeming as though she really had to know. "I was one of those children once. In Ecuador . . . when foreign Jeeps would roll through a town, we were excited. It would give us something to talk about for weeks . . . until we learned to fear uniforms."

"Fair question," Bath Kol said. "A lot of us embedded with the crazy side of humanity, those humans bent on war and destruction, to try to get them to turn their course. We weren't allowed to just wholesale slaughter humans because they were doing foul things to each other. Demons, yeah—we could hot those bastards on sight. But bad humans . . . they had the freedom of choice. So, we embedded with human troops, tried to work on people with reason, compassion, blah, blah, blah. If you ask me, that shit is inefficient because some mortals are just stupid. And, since nobody asked me, and I just follow orders from above, for a while they put me in Rome with those crazy sons a bitches. Try working on Roman generals with reason and compassion—ha! Probably where I picked up a lot of my bad habits."

Aziza reached over and stroked the nape of his neck, causing him to look at her. "All of that time wasn't bad, BK. Remember the good in it."

He nodded and took up her other hand and kissed it hard and then fell silent. Witnessing that rare display between the couple sent everyone deeper into his or her own thoughts. Celeste didn't even want to open the bag of chips now, fearing the sound would disturb a moment that needed to be marked by silent reverence. Another brother was purging and healing in their midst.

Looking out the dust-coated window, she stared at single-story, mud-brick, thatched-roof buildings as they passed. Some were painted in bright strips of color with indecipherable Arabic script running the length of the structures. Donkeys and goats were loosely tied to shade trees in front of some, just as one might lock a bike to a pole or park a car in front of one's home. Wooden doors sat ajar; clearly no doors were locked in this countryside community. Some homes she could see into. The foyers had hay covering the dirt floor, and small lambs, goats, and a few chickens pecked around in the enclosure while the family was deeper inside the structure.

But in a bizarre collision of cultures, these rudimentary thatched-roof homes with women washing clothes by hand in huge metal tubs would also have a satellite dish for TV on the straw roof.

Completely amazed, Celeste kept her gaze fastened on the passing scenery, growing ever more thankful with every home she passed for her life in America—for being born a woman in the United States, for clean running water and asphalt and streetlights, and parks and temperate weather without flies, and food and shelter and supermarkets, and everything she'd ever taken for granted in her life.

Azrael slipped his warm palm beneath hers, and their fingers threaded into a perfect fit without their even looking at each other. A sense of anticipation swept through her, although she wasn't sure why as they turned onto a widening boulevard.

"Okay, folks," Isda said. "The lady told us to come to Dendera. This is her. She's forty thousand square kilometers, and she's surrounded by a mud-brick wall that used to make her look like a citadel. Since the beginning of Kemet's history here—"

"The earliest building that's still standing is the Mammisi," Aziza said, standing in the bus with a hand over her heart. Tears filled her large, dark eyes as she clutched the back of a seat to keep her balance. "Nectanebo the Second raised this . . . he was the last of the native pharaohs."

"Yeah, baby," Bath Kol said, standing and hugging her. "C'mon . . . we can do this, right?"

Aziza nodded and held him as Isda brought the bus to a stop. "I'm okay."

Isda turned in his seat and looked at Azrael. "This is all set up according to sacred geometry, mon. That's why I really want you all to pay attention to the layout of the buildings on the complex. It might help us figure out where to begin looking and could save us time."

"Teach," Azrael said with respect. "This is your expedition."

Isda nodded and sat up taller, projecting his voice throughout the van with new authority. "Hathor Temple is the main temple here at Dendera complex. There's also the Temple of the Birth of Isis, Sacred Lake, Sanatorium, Mammisi of Nectanebo the Second—the one Aziza knows . . . plus Christian Basilica, Roman Mammisi—the chapel, a Bark shrine, Gateways of Domitian and Trajan, and the Roman kiosk."

Waiting until he'd received nods from the brothers, Isda began again, "When you roll up on one of dese monuments, mon, it's like a small city within a city. The mortals here had a different viewpoint of time and scale, you know . . . they understood immortality from us. Like you go into one of the huge hypostyle halls with massive columns and—"

Celeste's gasp cut off Isda's words. Knowing slammed into her chest, making it hard for her to breathe. She could almost hear the stones of the monuments whispering to her, calling to her, drawing her to them as a memory so acute that it became an ache overtook her entire body. Her feet yearned to connect with the sand so that she could feel a part of the very earth.

"I have to get out of the bus," she said suddenly, hyperventilating.

She pushed herself down the aisle and exited with another deep gasp, pulling hot, dusty air into her lungs. Coughing and sputtering, she turned around in a disoriented circle as Azrael caught her and thrust a bottle of water into her hands.

"I can cover the Roman-era sections with Aziza," Bath Kol said as Celeste chugged water. "Isda is right—this place is huge and we may have to spread out."

"Me and Paschar can take the outer buildings that BK and 'Ziz aren't covering," Gavreel offered.

"All right," Azrael said, rubbing Celeste's back. "But I need Isda with us when we go into the main temple. I need to know what we're looking at and why." He turned to Isda, gaining his nod. "You have the history, brother, and without that we'll just be searching without purpose."

"Cool, lemme get tickets, all right?"

Celeste stared behind Isda as he took off running fifty yards toward the small exhibit booth. But soon the enormity of the complex stole her attention. Two hundred yards of smooth, polished, perfectly cut stone steps flanked a granite ramp that led to the outer courtyard of the enormous temple. Hathor goddess heads on huge pylons six deep looked back at them in stoic serenity in front of the sandstone-hued, granite structure that had to be five stories high.

Isda came back in a flash and handed out tickets, allowing the group to be processed forward. They were early, and tour buses had yet to arrive. Warriors on a mission waved off eager vendors and children, and if she wasn't mistaken, she could have sworn she'd seen a bit of blue flicker in their hands. The brothers were tense, and she knew they didn't feel like being bothered this morning by petty human concerns such as trading plastic pyramids for a few pieces of silver. When the group split off, that left her and Azrael and Isda.

Enveloped in silence, they climbed the steps, and then stopped in the main courtyard. The building alone was overwhelming, and Isda and Azrael looked at her for answers she didn't have.

"Okay, here's the layout," Isda said, trying to help her, drawing the building's floor plan in the palm of his hand as he spoke.

Celeste watched his palm, intermittently glancing up at him and then behind him toward the building.

"When you enter, dere's a large hypostyle hall, then a small one—columns, okay? Then there's a laboratory, storage magazine, offering entry, treasury, and access to the well and the stairwells." Turning her body by the shoulders, Isda pointed with one hand and spoke to her calmly. "There's an offering hall, Hall of Ennead, the Great Seat and main sanctuary, twelve shrine rooms, the Pure Place . . . Court of the First Feast . . . a passage, and then a staircase to the roof."

Celeste lifted her ponytail off her neck in frustration. Isda might as well have been speaking in Greek because none of what he'd just said had any frame of reference. "Don't say anything else. I just need to go in."

He nodded and lifted his hands in front of his chest.

"No offense, brother, she just needs you to fall back so she can feel whatever it is."

"No offense taken," Isda said, sounding calm. "BK gets like that with his visions, so does Paschar . . . like big ole huntin' dogs."

Celeste took off running, unable to wait. The guards at the door let her pass but held up Isda and Azrael for the tickets. Something was pulling her past thirty-foot columns deeper and deeper into the temple. She spied a room with a metal ladder that went up two stories to another high, open-air room, but kept running. Then she made a hard bank right and ran right into a blue-robed guard.

Seeming amused by the collision, he smiled until he saw Azrael and Isda come around the corner. He held up his hands, clearly not speaking English, but appearing as though he wanted to show the men behind her that there was no attempt to inappropriately touch her. Even though he had an AK-47 draped over his chest, for the guard it appeared to be a matter of good-humored honor.

Celeste dropped to her knees and began touching the floor, ignoring the men as she frantically felt around for a break in the stone seal there. Her fingers caressed the large, carved ankh embedded in a stone disk and surrounded by sunrays and symbols she couldn't understand with her mind, but could comprehend with her being. This was a source of Light and life.

Almost on the verge of tears when the man began to protest, she slapped the floor with her palm and looked up at him, frustrated by the language barrier.

"There's steps!"

The guard shook his head and struggled to find words. "Not for tourists. Dangerous. Is close now."

Celeste scrambled to her feet, and before Azrael could stop her, she thrust her hand in his pocket and pulled out everything in it and shoved it toward the guard. The guard clutched at the falling dollars laughing and looked at Azrael, clearly expecting him to either slap her or protest. But when Azrael shrugged, the man extended his hand.

"Nubian brother!"

"Yeah, yeah, Nubian brother," Isda muttered, picking up $100 bills and handing them off to the ecstatic guard.

The guard looked around, then went up into his sleeve to produce a long brass key shaped like an ankh. He placed his automatic weapon down carefully on the floor and put his finger to his lips. Celeste stooped down beside him and nodded, understanding that, bribe or not, he could get in trouble or possibly lose his job.

Flipping back a small, oval-shaped stone, the guard revealed a lock, inserted the key, and gave it a hard turn.

Then with a grunt he lifted up what looked like the reverse of attic stairs.

Pleased with himself, he smiled a tobacco-colored grin, waved before the steps like a game-show host, then added, looking in Azrael's direction, "Dangerous."

"Cool. Cool," Isda said, talking with his hands.

Unable to wait, Celeste headed down into the darkness on the rickety, sloping steps that were barely Azrael's shoulder width wide. When she got to the bottom, she made the sign of the cross over her chest, sat on the cool stone, and slid beneath the lip of a huge granite block. Thankfully, the guard had flipped on the modern emergency lights that had been added for the convenience of archaeological work.

Regardless, her prayer had been simple: *Please, God, let there be no snakes, scorpions, or anything else really creepy or deadly*. Nothing was between her and the frightening but blind faith as she entered the chamber feetfirst and then drew a breath. Twelve chambers were carved into the stone, connected by a long stone hallway that featured divinely inspired markings of priestly processions bearing offerings of fruit and incense, with celestial patterns covering every conceivable inch of the ceilings, floors, and walls.

After a moment she turned and looked at Isda, who'd been followed in by Azrael, as both men strained to get their bulk through the narrow opening.

"Like coming through the birth canal," Isda said, brushing dust off his arms. "Everyt'ing was symbolic."

Azrael brushed off his jeans and glanced around. "But judging from the size of that opening, Imhotep's sarcophagus couldn't have been hidden down here in the early days or even now."

· Celeste touched the walls and closed her eyes. "Yes, it was, not inside but outside." Her breathing again became shallow as her words stuttered out in short bursts of information. "What you're looking for was inside this whole complex, just not inside this specific building . . . but the walls here somehow . . . I don't know how to describe it . . . the stones are telling me that we should be looking outside, but within the complex itself. The walls say there were a lot of different cultures here."

"What she's saying makes sense," Azrael replied, touching the walls with the tips of his fingers. "This place is a nexus of cultures . . . Nubians, Christians, Romans, Muslims, all built chapels here. There was Hebrew and Coptic influence to the complex as well. There's hallowed ground all around—therefore a perfect hiding place against evil. Father Krespy was here. He was a Christian priest—and if he felt like he was on a divine mission, he would come somewhere he felt he could pray in the way he needed to according to *his* faith, but a place that would also be certain to block out evil. When a person of faith, especially a cleric, prays a prayer of Light—a message sent to On-High—it creates a barrier to darkness. So with all these representative faiths having prayed here, it should have been like a spiritual Fort Knox."

"That's what I'm feeling," Celeste said, taking in a long, slow, deep breath. "The man was here, prayed down here, and then decided where to hide everything next."

"Then why didn't the man just take it to da Vatican, or have Daoud take it to Mecca?"

"These men obviously didn't trust existing power structures and hierarchies or organized bureaucracy. They went directly to ground . . . didn't trust any human in power not to be swayed by corruption. There was something here in the dirt, in the sand." Azrael ran his hand along the length of the wall. "This place is humble, unadorned by comparison to the Vatican and other places . . . therefore would be completely overlooked by humans doing the bidding of the other side. Brilliant."

Celeste opened her eyes and Isda came over to her.

"There's a necropolis on this site that runs along the eastern ridge of the western hill and over the northern plain," Isda said carefully. "The ridge, which is like a little dirt hill, has flat-top, mastaba tombs that go subterranean, sealed in stone. That's definitely in the ground, sis, like you said. Someone could have easily gone to those tombs built into the hills within this complex and stashed a coffin, no problem."

"Twelve tombs . . . twelve crypts," she murmured. "That's what's out there in the hills just beyond this building. That's the ground."

"Sacred number, twelve," Azrael said, becoming absorbed in touching the walls as he pressed both palms flatly against them.

"That sarcophagus was there." Celeste began to walk away from both warriors, but Isda stopped her.

"But before," Isda argued, becoming agitated as she still moved forward, "they were just filled with jewelry and offerings and grain and urns and—"

"Already excavated," she said flatly, looking at him. "It was safe here. People who visit this temple mainly come in here, as opposed to the outer temple grounds and hills, which are closed off to tourists now anyway." She ran her hand along the wall. "Krespy's apprentice knew that . . . had to know that." Celeste stopped walking. "The elderly cleric would definitely say a prayer of Light for protection from On-High here. He would also leave his apprentice a clue or some kind of coded message to follow the Light within the darkness. The only place in this temple that is pitch-black is down here. The rest of the temple gets sunlight because of the way the stone windows are set, the skylights . . . don't you see, he would have led his apprentice to come into this space to receive whatever message he'd left in prayer."

Azrael glanced around. "Without these emergency lights in here, it would be pitch-black."

"The clue is down here somewhere, Isda. Move! I can feel it tingling in the palms of my hands!" Walking quickly along the walls as though reading braille, Celeste kept her eyes closed and then half fell, half stumbled into a new, tiny room covered in reliefs that was adjacent to the one they'd been standing within, then gasped.

"Lights!" she shrieked, then touched the walls in awe.

Azrael and Isda stepped back and stared at the five stone reliefs that depicted a djed pillar and a lotus flower spawning a snake within what appeared to be a giant balloon or bubble. Celeste went to the right side of the small vault where it looked as if two long fluorescent lightbulbs were touching one another.

"Damn if Celeste wasn't right, Az. Okay, I stand corrected." Isda looked at Azrael and traced the fine granite carving with his fingers as he spoke. "Mon . . . this is profound. The snake is kundalini energy," Isda said quietly. "The djed is the spinal column, from which the energy springs forth. With this awakened, there is light. We brought the Light, literally and figuratively. This is one of the few places where that truth was revealed."

"This has to be the place where Krespy's apprentice was sent."

Azrael nodded. "It's the only tomb and crypt complex that depicts the actual makeup of true Light."

"Crazy, mon." Isda just shook his head as he stared at the walls. "And our locator found it."

"But this was done thousands of years ago. They had light down in these crypts, I mean, like, regular electric, back then?" Celeste gaped at Isda and Azrael when they nodded.

"There is no soot on these walls from torches," Isda pointed out. "You cannot clean that off. Look around. There are no windows, and this subterranean chamber, like many of the temples, was carved out of pure granite. How could men get down here and work, huh? How could they see to put such details on eve'y inch of da walls, without light? Slaves did not build this stuff—that is the big lie. Master craftsmen did. Masons from the original Masonic orders that came out of Kemet did. So think about it. Where did the light come from to help humans see?"

"But in school they never taught us about—"

"Of course they didn't teach you about dis!" Isda shouted. "How can you tell people they're subhuman, strip away the true merits of their heritage, and make them accept that for hundreds of years, if you reveal that through deep meditation and awakening they can bring their own Light—that they built a civilization yet to be rivaled? Show her, Az!"

Azrael nodded and closed his eyes and allowed the blue-white spill to spread along the edges of his body and then widen until the small room looked as if it were being flooded by halogen lamps.

"That was the dark side taking hold of the worst in humanity, creating unnecessary prejudice, and corrupting that which was good. Imagine what could have been accomplished everywhere in the world if humans worked together collectively to awaken their spirits, pooled their resources to breakthrough on new discoveries, honored each other's cultures and histories, and harnessed all their knowledge and will for the greater good? Racism, prejudice, false history, just divide and conquer. The dark side loves it, and humans worldwide buy into that lie every time. On our end, it is truly frustrating," Azrael said quietly, then slowly began to allow his light to dim. "This is also part of the inner Light I told you was turned off when they reduced the human DNA strands down from twelve strands of inner Light to a very weakened two."

Even though their words held her rapt, Azrael's brilliant display had hit a speck of something metallic, and that glint had caught in her peripheral vision. Moving toward the far corner of the room where she'd seen the shiny object, she gently swept at a pile of dust, gravel, and sand and came away with a prize.

The men surrounded her as she stood, then opened her palm out flat to reveal what looked like a small, gold wedding band. The center of it was steel and spun on some type of ball bearing in a layered band above the gold. The center steel ring had words written on it in a foreign language that she couldn't make out. Azrael lifted it from her palm and lit it between his fingers. He glanced at her, then turned his attention to Isda.

"It's the Lord's Prayer in Latin."

Isda snatched the ring from Azrael and stared at it in disbelief.

"It was Father Krespy's," Celeste said quietly. "Daoud Salahuddin used it as his ward. As long as he had it on him, it probably kept him safe somehow . . . kept demons from snatching him maybe? What I'm feeling is they definitely kept the remains of Imhotep here and separate from the book, but someone *dropped* this ring here—this was just lying in the corner, not purposefully hidden. With all that was riding on this, it doesn't make sense that Daoud or someone in charge of guarding the sarcophagus and book of tablets would be so careless . . . but it had to be a human, because no demon could get down here."

"Nor could any of the fallen enter here with the protective barriers that have been here for thousands of years," Isda said, glancing around.

"Some human brought him here, threatened him maybe." She felt along the walls. "I don't know. But I can't see or feel that any blood was spilled in here."

"Nor do I," Azrael confirmed. He looked along the wall where Celeste had found the ring and shook his head. "No butchery took place here."

"But how much you wanna bet that the man who last owned this ring, Daoud, lost his life at the site of the tomb that held the sarcophagus somewhere on this campus?"

Isda looked at both of them. "In this land, any land to be fair, money talks and bullshit walks. You can't hear a man scream down in a tomb, mon."

"I don't think we should try to find that desecrated crypt," Celeste said, touching Isda's arm. "We have the ring. Me, BK, Aziza, and Paschar should be able to hold it, maybe all touching it at the same time, and find out where Daoud might have been before he so-called vanished. We might even be able to find where they left his body. I don't think the man survived if they got to the sarcophagus."

"I don't think so either, love. Sad and very fucked up." Isda let out a hard breath. "But you are right. With four strong seers, one of you for each of the cardinal points, we should be able to pick up a direction."

"I think we need to get out of here," Azrael said. "I don't like one-way-in, one-way-out scenarios."

# Chapter 10

*R*ounding up the group took the better part of a half hour, since everyone was spread throughout the vast campus of buildings and ruins, but finally they convened in the parking lot—hot, dirty, irritated, and exhausted.

Aziza looked as if she'd been weeping. Bath Kol was dirty from head to toe. Maggie seemed about to pass out from heat exhaustion, and Melissa was having difficulty breathing.

"We found something," Azrael announced. "Down in the vault rooms, the twelve crypts under the Flame Room floor in the main temple."

Bath Kol nodded and bent to pour a bottle of water over his head, then shook his head, flinging water like a golden retriever just back from a marsh hunt. "Yeah, we found mastaba tombs over on the western hill—the eastern ridge of it."

"We also saw soot on the roofs where temples had burned to the ground," Aziza said, hugging herself and beginning to rock.

Bath Kol nodded and looked away. "And a fresh kill. Not the actual body, but the heavy vibration of blood and death was down there. A man recently lost his life there for sure."

Azrael held out his hand, drawing Bath Kol to the ring without words. Aziza came in closer and then backed away.

"That man's blood spilled on the ground by the tomb I went into with BK," she whispered in horror.

Bath Kol took up the ring. "No . . . this belonged to the priest—and then was passed down to his apprentice, the one man not of his same faith but of his same cause. Daoud."

Paschar nodded as he touched the ring with Bath Kol. "He gave his life in the tomb you entered, brother."

"They tortured him until he begged to die," Aziza said in a quiet rush. "But he was trying to get to a major knowledge center of some sort . . . like a museum or another temple, a huge one, a colossal library or university even, when they abducted him."

"Karnak," Bath Kol said, nodding. He walked in a circle raking his hair. "Damn . . . if that's it, and my sense is that it is, do you know how huge that campus is? It took them like seventeen hundred years to build, through twenty-five or thirty different pharaohs. It's got two hundred buildings on it or more. Shit! Plus that's several hours' drive south of where we are now—through these little streets? Could be longer. You'll have to ask Isda to see how long it'll really take."

"Given the size of that campus, it would make sense, brother," Azrael said, injecting a more positive viewpoint to the group. "Think about it. If you had a tablet, something so magnificent that it would stand out, you'd have to hide it somewhere either massive or remote. Looks like Daoud went for massive."

"But how did they get to Daoud if he had the ward . . . Father Krespy's ring?" Celeste looked around the group and her gaze landed on Aziza.

"He was robbed of the ring," Aziza said, going to it slowly. She reached out to touch it, then retracted her hand, appearing to think better of doing so. "They found him and tortured him until he brought them here."

"We found this down in those chambers under the floors, but there was no blood even in the cracks between the stones in the floors," Celeste said. "So . . . how . . . ?"

"One of the guards," Bath Kol said, nodding to the main temple. "The prayer ring has gold on it, was valuable. Those guys go down in the temple hidden areas and do whatever . . . drink, screw, smoke. Dude probably got drunk and lost part of his prize. A blessed object like this will repel itself away from the unclean, even a human. The fallen can't touch one of these and a demon would burn from it. This was definitely claimed by a human— humans don't fry if they touch holy water or any kind of religious icon, even if they're dark in spirit. The fact that they have a soul and have a choice to change until the bitter end gives them the power to walk through the gauntlet of any barriers. But the man that took this ring off Krespy's apprentice was a very stupid human who couldn't even hold on to it for a night." Bath Kol placed the ring back in Azrael's palm and spat on the ground. "That some sellout even had it in his possession and helped an innocent man die for a few bucks, whoever the ignorant bastard is, makes me sick."

"That part of it is not our fight," Gavreel said, placing a hand on Bath Kol's shoulder. "But you do know the man will have to revisit his actions one day. True?"

Bath Kol nodded and relaxed a bit.

"That's why dere was no blood down dere. A guard got paid with some cash and what he thought was a gold trinket in exchange to turn a blind eye while a man was murdered and a tomb was robbed. Probably took a bottle and a broad down dere and dropped da ring. What difference does it make at this point? Details don't matter, and as they say, the damned devil lives in the details. Point of fact is, the darkness got the sarcophagus, now what?" Isda said, then loped off toward the bus. "And you tell me why we shouldn't beg the Source to leave this entire planet a smoking black hole!"

"Four very good reasons," Azrael said calmly to the others, allowing Isda to walk it off. Azrael let his gaze rove over Celeste, Magdalena, Melissa, and Aziza to make his message sink in for the other brothers. "I want us off the streets and on the water where we have a strategic advantage. Going through these little towns by bus is out. Now that a human has walked over that grave or disturbed the dark site of a murder," he said, pointedly looking at Aziza and Bath Kol, "we're traceable. If we go by rail, that's more risk right now than I'm willing to take. If we go through these streets, we'll be right smack in the middle of an urban combat situation, boxed in and around too many humans if all hell opens up in a ground battle. On the water, on a large vessel with a high deck, we can go airborne and do what we do best, men."

Bath Kol reached into the center of the group as Azrael closed his fingers around the ring and pounded his fist. "Then let's light up the Nile, brothers. Make it flow holy water all the way from Uganda to the Mediterranean."

*Celeste was well past* wondering how Isda was always able to get them last-minute accommodations on various modes of transportation—being an angel definitely had its privileges. But he'd gotten them booked on a Nile cruise headed for Luxor that would continue to Edfu and terminate in Aswan before the mighty river reached the Aswan Dam. The brothers' plan was to use the upper deck of the ship at night like an angel aircraft carrier, where under the cover of the night and with a little cloaking, they could take off and land and do flyovers without causing mortal panic.

As much as she hated to admit it, here in Egypt she felt her mortality in full. Getting used to the extreme temperatures, the concern about drinking water from the tap, the sudden change of diet, and the sheer press of humanity sapped her energy. Then add to that the extremes in emotion, stress, and plain old sleep deprivation, and she was wiped out.

She felt truly ashamed when she stepped onto the ship with her sisters and almost wept at the upgrade in accommodations. Never in her life had she imagined herself as spoiled and soft, not coming from where she came from.

But seeing a little bit of what real poverty was, what really harsh climatic conditions were all about, she would be forever grateful for the small things in life—things that were actually pretty huge. And the sad thing was, what they'd experienced wasn't even the truly rough stuff. She could only imagine what was out there in the so-called bush country.

But as glorious air-conditioning blew through her hair, and plush lobby furnishings and twinkling crystal chandeliers greeted them as they checked in, Aziza squeezed her hand. No conversation was necessary. Every woman's prayer for just a little respite had been answered.

Once they'd gotten the billing and room keys settled and tipped porters, Azrael shut the door and closed his eyes for a moment.

"You okay?"

He nodded, but looked exhausted. That worried her.

"I didn't think angels got tired," she said, trying to cheer him up and make him smile.

He gave her a weak attempt, not his normal radiant one by a long shot.

"You should lie down for a few, you know."

"I can't, Celeste. We've got to secure the ship."

She watched him walk around the room touching the walls, the door, the floor, the bed, and the sliding glass doors that led to the private deck. Everywhere he touched washed blue for a few seconds and then the current disappeared. The black-and-gold rug had looked as if it were a glowing, moving blue river for a moment, and it was so disorienting that she held on to the black lacquer dresser until the vertigo passed. The gold bedspread lit up, just as the king's-chamber-styled appointments had. When Azrael went into the bathroom, the faucets had come on by themselves, running blue water at full blast and turning the gold fixtures glowing white-hot before everything settled down again.

"You can take a shower now," he said, coming to her for a hug. "If anything manages to get in here, it'll fry if it's a demon or a member of the fallen."

"And if it's a human?" she asked in a sober tone.

For a moment Azrael just stared at her. "Then I guess I'll have to mind-stun every passenger on this ship to bypass all our rooms." He frowned and let out a hard breath. "In such a circumstance, it is allowable for self-defense of the innocent."

She didn't answer him, just nodded and relaxed, which seemed to make him relax a bit, too.

"But do me a favor," he said after a moment. "Wait until I'm in the room before you go out on the private balcony. I know watching the Nile go by is seductive. I've placed protection on the windows and the railing, but if you fall over the edge, Celeste, I swear . . ."

"I promise," she said, holding him tightly. "It's hot outside anyway. I'll keep the air in, okay?"

She felt his shoulders relax a little more and he released a long sigh.

"Thank you. I'll only be a little while with the brothers. There are a lot of human passengers on here, just like the train. We need to give them extra protection, too, search the ship to make sure there were no demon stowaways . . . that means charging every floor and pipe, making sure the food isn't poisoned—I'll be back as soon as I can."

"All right," she murmured, and kissed him, tasting so much ambrosia in his mouth that it almost made her squint. "Then when you come back, I'm going to insist you take a hot shower and lie down for a couple of hours."

He touched her face, then slipped out of her embrace and left. She stared at the locked door for several minutes, hugging herself. He'd seen something, had felt something—that and he'd used up a lot of energy not only securing her and their group, but trying to make sure that no harm came to any innocent human. The emotions of his brothers were also taking their toll on him; that was as plain as day. And his worry that something might happen to her had to be the last straw.

*"You look weary, brother,"* Azrael said as he approached Bath Kol at the nearly empty bar on the top deck.

"You look like hell warmed over yourself." Bath Kol turned a beer up to his mouth and winced. "Want one?"

"I'm good," Azrael said, sitting down hard.

"It was warm anyway. Nothing in the country is cold, have ya noticed?"

"Where's Isda?" Azrael rubbed his palms down his face, ignoring the question.

"Going through the ship's bowels with Gavreel and Paschar. You should really have a beer, bro . . . you look stressed."

Azrael stared out at the pool and the honeymooners and the families basking in the sun. Some were sleeping in shade-covered cabanas. Children splashed in the water. Couples nuzzled in double-wide lounge chairs. Top 40 pop tunes blared near the pool bar. Attentive bartenders in white jackets ran drinks to tourists. An older couple played a game of chess with three-foot-high pieces, laughing with each other as they tried to move the oversize plastic pieces along the marked deck surface.

"There's too many of them to save if something goes terribly wrong here," Azrael said somberly, not looking at Bath Kol.

"Bartender, bring this man a beer, please."

Azrael kept his gaze on the mortals before him and accepted the lukewarm beverage.

"There's always too many of them to save," Bath Kol said flatly as he accepted another beer from the bartender. He motioned with a quick nod toward the young man who'd retreated to the other end of the bar. "He doesn't speak English, so, while I pump up the frost on his refrigerator so the next beer is really the way I like it, ass-biting cold, you wanna tell me what's got you all fucked up?"

"She's gonna die," Azrael finally said quietly, then took a long swig of his beer. He looked out at the children and the lovers, and then at the older couple, then took another sip of beer and studied the label. "No matter what I do. She's still part human."

Bath Kol let out a long breath. "That's what they do, man . . . humans die." He polished off his beer and set it down hard and motioned for two more. "Don't look at those little kids playing in the water, man. I saw you on the bus, how your mind was getting twisted around by watching the happy little children who were running along the side of it. Don't go there. You think you're messed up now—ask me how I know. You lose a lover, yeah, you'll grieve, but in time you'll get over it. But you make one of those heart-stoppers and then watch them grow up, get old, and perish . . . and you'll be as crazy as Isda."

When the bartender came, Bath Kol took up both bottles and handed a frosty brew to Azrael, while the confused young man went to go study his refrigerator.

"And stop looking at aging humans. That isn't going to be you guys. You'll look like you look—forever. And she won't. And it's going to make her weep and hurt her soul and make her insecure and damned near suicidal—no matter what you tell her . . . unless you do a little something we're really not supposed to do . . . and kinda allow some of that cosmic juice we've got to make you look like you're aging in her eyes so it's not so hard for her," Bath Kol added more quietly, then took a long guzzle from his beer bottle. "It's in the mercy and peace-of-mind clause. A loophole, but, hey. It's the least you can do."

"I now understand why we were told not to get involved this way with our charges," Azrael admitted in a quiet rumble, rolling his glass bottle slowly between his palms. "It was as much for our benefit as theirs."

"Yeah. I have learned while down here that the Source does have mysterious ways, even for us, but every time I think I might know better—and don't get me wrong, I'm not defecting . . . just talking about using analysis on some of the laws, you know . . . but . . . after I break one, and I get my ass kicked by it and suffer the repercussions, I'm, like, I knew that. I knew better. I was told."

Azrael nodded. "I was indeed told."

"Yeah, man, but being down here is a game changer."

Azrael knocked his bottle against Bath Kol's. "You have never uttered more truth."

"Being incarnate ain't for no punk, bro. This place'll make you bleed. Will put you on your knees and make you sob like a baby. Will make you wish you'd never been created." Bath Kol took another sip of his brew and then turned his head to study Azrael. "Then again, it'll curl your toes." He smiled as Azrael glanced at him and took a long sip of his beer. "It'll put your damned lights on and have you looking like a billboard in Times Square."

Azrael allowed a half smile to tug at his cheek.

Bath Kol bumped Azrael's shoulder with his own. "Am I lying?"

"No," Azrael said, chuckling. "You most assuredly are not lying."

"So, ain't it worth it? Rules broken, wings busted, ass kicked, I'd say on the whole I'd rather be here than up there in the rarefied air where everything is pure and academic. I don't mind getting dirty. I like fighting demons. I love blowing shit up. I make no apologies—like my women wild and crazy. I love being in love." Bath Kol opened his arms wide while clutching a beer. "I like feeling alive. I like good, go-hard, sweaty, ridiculous sex! I love eating food that is bad for my cholesterol! I like . . . what else do I like? Uhm, beer, and bourbon, and barbecue—yeah! I like football and using foul language and dancing. Man, I *love* music, the raunchier the better. I love hanging out with my boys. C'mon, you've gotta lighten up. What do you like? You've been here three months, so if we get called back, what stories are you gonna have to tell the guys who got stuck in administration? Huh? They're waiting for stories from the front!"

"I like potato chips," Azrael said, laughing around his bottle. "The extra-crunchy ones."

"Oh, you are so gonna make me kick your huge ass up on this deck."

"I do. It's my main guilty pleasure. Celeste gave them to me once, and I couldn't eat just one. She told me that I couldn't and she was right."

Bath Kol spun around on his barstool to stare at Azrael with a wide grin. "So, when we go back home, that's what you're gonna tell the guys—you got turned out by Kettle chips."

Azrael laughed hard. "That's all I'm going to admit to."

Bath Kol burst out laughing, spewing beer from his mouth and nose. "See, I knew you had a little rebel in ya! That's my boy—never tell 'em more than they need to know."

Azrael knocked his bottle against Bath Kol's and signaled for another round. "But seriously, man, I respect what you went through for twenty-six thousand. I've only been here three months and I'm worried about her."

Bath Kol landed a hand on Azrael's shoulder. "Look, she's not gonna last twenty-six thousand years. None of them do. That's a fact of life on earth. If you're lucky, since she's Nephilim, you might get a couple hundred together before they call her home. But it's all good. Have you told her yet how long she may live?"

"No," Azrael said, rubbing a palm over the nape of his neck. "There's been so much happening, so much for her to deal with and absorb . . . I was trying to wait for the right time, trying to wait for—"

"Be honest. You haven't had that conversation yet with her because it'll open up the other very real one you're not facing about her eventual mortality."

Azrael nodded, took a swig from his beer, and stared at the deck floor. "More truth, brother."

Bath Kohl sighed. "Think of it this way, man. Now that you've experienced being with her, can you truly say that to avoid the inevitable heartbreak that's gonna come—and, yes, it is gonna come—that you wished you'd never found her?"

Azrael shook his head. "If I had never found her, I cannot imagine who I'd be . . . it's like . . . I see this entire place so differently."

"Oh, shit, you *are* in deep."

Azrael polished off his beer and accepted the new one. "I might have messed up, too," he said quietly when the bartender retreated.

Bath Kol set his beer down very, very slowly. "What?"

"I don't know that to be a fact," Azrael said, then took an extremely long swig of his beer. "But . . . things got out of hand and I don't know. Her intentions are wavering, too. I could feel that on the bus when she looked out at the little ones. You know human contraception doesn't work against our seed; it's all about will, intention, vibrations. And—"

"All right," Bath Kol said, gesturing with his hands and almost sloshing his beer. "First of all, we need to cross that bridge when we get to it—when we have all the facts. Second, you can do one or two things with that information. One, you can let it make you so damned scared about this mission we're on that you're paralyzed, which serves no purpose. Or, because you think that's the case, now you're vested in this planet's surviving. So, if you were crazy before, you ought to be fighting for this joint like you're insane now. Feel me?"

Bath Kol leaned into him, his eyes wide. "I'm serious, man. We need your head on straight for this mission. So, what's it gonna be? Which are you? The warrior who's so worried about what could happen that he's immobilized, or the one who's insane? Tell me now, because I've gotta know who's leading these troops and who's got my six in a firefight. Which warrior, dude?"

Azrael took a slow sip from his bottle and set it down with precision. "The one who's absolutely out of his fucking mind."

Chapter 11

*hy can't we see* this bastard!"

Asmodeus slammed his fist down on the table, splattering the blood contents of Rahab's scrying bowl. She simply stared at the crimson fluid as it webbed across the table like a fast-moving cancer, then dipped her finger into it and calmly tasted it.

"Because he does not *want* to be seen, milord," she said drily.

A serpent-quick backhand struck her cheek, and she smiled as Asmodeus narrowed his gaze and paced away from her.

"It could be a trap," she said, unfazed by his violent outburst.

He spun on her. "How so?"

"You are allowing emotion to cloud your judgment." Unafraid, she walked up to him and stood her ground. "A Sentinel was out there with a human female—the seer . . .

not one of the Remnant. That's who walked over the desecrated area in Dendera, and that was the second time we
picked up on their energy pattern. The first time was out
on the Giza plateau, and they were all there. Now, we only
feel two lesser lights? I say they have used those members
of their team as bait. If we were to rush in and attack what
appear to be two vulnerable members of their unit, that's
when we will be ambushed."

He walked away from her to stare at the setting sun.
"Your point has merit."

"We should send them a lure. Since our search parties
for them have proved fruitless and time is running out,
*make them come to us.* We know they have to be on the
water," she said calmly. "If they were on the ground, we
could track them—the two that stepped on the butchering
site. But even they have vanished. There is no airport in
Qena and I doubt that they have left the area so quickly.
That only means one thing . . . they are on the water—holy
water. The Nile is a death trap. So we must lure them off
that treacherous channel of transportation and get them
to come to us."

*Celeste sighed with contentment.* She had heard Azrael
come into the room; knowing his footfalls anywhere and
able to feel his aura, she didn't even have to open her eyes.
In the far recesses of her mind she heard the shower go on
and then smelled fresh soap drifting on the cool, forced
air. Then she felt his warmth and the bed depress behind
her, and a kiss caress her shoulder as she slipped into the
peaceful abyss of sleep.

Although it felt as if many hours had passed, only a few had. The late-afternoon sun was now an angry orange and painted the lush banks of the Nile in shimmering sienna.

Gently extracting herself from Azrael's hold, she slipped from the bed and went to the sliding-glass doors to stare out at the passing landscape. Tall, robust palms and elephant grasses created a velvety green oasis between the sapphire river and the endless sand dunes beyond it. Cranes and an endless array of waterfowl took off and taxied in for landings as suspicious logs lay in wait for a misstep so they could reveal powerful jaws.

She pressed her palms to the glass and soaked in the majesty before her. A graveyard high on a hill looked as if it had been there since time immemorial. Small village fishing boats carrying the day's haul and hardworking fishermen home added additional color and humanity to the moving landscape. Then peach- and sand-hued buildings slowly came into view, and what was once serenity ebbed into a bustling metropolis again.

The bed sounded but she didn't turn around. Soon she heard Azrael stir and sit up, then heard him pad toward her to wrap her in his arms.

"You look like you're trapped in this room," he said against her hair as she leaned into his warmth.

"It's all so wonderful and crazy at the same time . . . like, we are cruising down the Nile. *The Nile*. I just didn't want to miss any of it."

He pulled the door open and ushered her to the rail, still standing behind her and holding her around her waist. She turned her face to the sun and closed her eyes as the breeze off the water caught in her hair. Now she could smell the water, the river of life that had never stopped flowing, that flowed from south to north. She could now hear the birds, hear the water's gurgle and whispers. Could hear the splashes of predators and the distant babble of workingmen . . . and knew she was home.

"You seem different," he murmured, nuzzling her neck.

"How can one not be transformed here?" she said quietly, leaning back against him with her eyes closed.

*Reluctant warriors gathered in* the ship's ornate lobby awaiting the lowering of the gangplank. But after a couple hours' rest, a decent meal, plus a shower, how could one argue against pressing forward to fulfill the mission? There was no room in the equation for just not feeling like it.

Resigned, they all waited silently without complaint—or enthusiasm—as Isda haggled with a minibus tour driver at the front desk for a private bus, knowing that Isda would ultimately prevail. When the doors finally opened, everyone in their retinue took his or her time, strolling down the narrow, wobbly plank to the street toward the waiting minibus.

"It's not far from Luxor, like a coupla miles," Isda said to no one in particular as he sat down behind the wheel. "Listen, I know everybody has had it already with this expedition, but I don't have to remind you what's at stake."

"We hear you, brother," Azrael said, then glanced around. "I'm as guilty of emotional fatigue as anyone on this bus. But if we're going to find anything out there, we've got to pump up the energy level."

Gaining nods from the group, he passed a fist pound over the seat to Bath Kol, and it lit, then Bath Kol sent it up the row to Gavreel, who sent it forward. When it reached Isda, he nodded.

"Now, *dat's* whot I'm talkin' 'bout."

Bath Kol leaned forward, his eyes slightly glowing blue-white as he pointed at the bus floor. "When we get to this site, we've gotta be extremely cool—as in low-key, people. The temple complex at Karnak is the second-most-visited tourist spot here, second only to the Pyramids." As he spoke a large grid opened out on the floor like an electrified map. "The center is huge." As he gestured with his forefinger, sections of the map brightened. Check it out. The section that all the tourists see is the Great Temple of Amun—that's here when you first walk in—"

"Ramses was a baaad man!" Isda said, laughing and cutting off Bath Kol and beginning to drive faster. "Forty-two wives, a hundred and sixty-five children, and was only half one of us? *And* was married to Nefertari, too? His favorite without question! Have you *seen* her? Aw, maaaan! When he brought her to me, I laughed and tol' 'im, 'You best be glad we're blood,' you know, 'cuz otherwise . . . whew. Dat was a son dat did me proud. You gotta take a look at his joint in Aswan. The man got up one day and said, 'Carve a freakin' mountain out for me and my lady—my favorite wife, yo, den—"

"Can I finish?" Bath Kol said, cocking his head to the side to stare at Isda down the aisle.

"Yeah, yeah, my bad—just some good memories been had here, too, mon."

Bath Kol shook his head and Celeste repressed a smile. The other brothers were chuckling and shaking their heads, while the women in the group smiled hard and shared glances. Nobody wanted to ruin Isda's mood after the pain he'd been through here. Just seeing his perspective shift from the memory of the losses to all the good times he'd obviously had in ancient Kemet made everybody feel good.

"*As* I was saying . . ." Bath Kol returned his focus to the glowing, iridescent lines on the bus floor. "This joint is a campus of buildings. It's like a huge, and I do mean *huge,* open-air museum, but it's also the largest ancient religious site in the world."

"Then that definitely makes sense and syncs up with Aziza's feeling that Daoud was trying to hide the tablets in a knowledge center, one that was also consecrated ground." Azrael leaned forward more to stare at the floor, but Bath Kol held his gaze.

"Here's the thing, brother," Bath Kol said. "There's gonna be tourists climbing all over the place. This campus is set up in four clusters of buildings with a sacred lake in the middle—which we can hot, just do our thing and turn it into holy water, just to be on the safe side. These four areas, or precincts, are spread out and consist of the main one that's open—Amun's, the unseen God's, the one dedicated to the Source. Then there's three that are currently closed to the general public . . . the Precinct of Mut—Amun's wife or, better stated, the yin side of the energy of the Source of All That Is."

Bath Kol looked up. "The ancients got it. The Source is both male and female, whole. Yin and yang, masculine and feminine, balanced."

"I can feel that energy moving all through the grounds," Aziza said, scanning the group and getting nods from the other women.

"But the feminine energy feels weaker here, somewhat constricted for some reason," Melissa said, hugging herself.

"Yeah, like something else happened . . . I don't know." Maggie glanced at Celeste for moral support.

"Like the feminine goddess energy here got shut down somehow." Celeste lifted her ponytail up off her neck. "It makes it harder to intuitively read the site, from our perspective."

"Yeah, well," Bath Kol said with a weary sigh, "unfortunately, when the patriarchies moved in, by the first century the worship of Mut stopped, and humans only started looking at the single aspect of the Source. The male side."

"True dat," Isda said, shaking his head. "It was a crying shame, too. How can you only give praise to one-half of the Source, mon?"

"Right." Bath Kol looked around as though trying to get a layout of the buildings in his mind's eye. "Okay, so they also put up the Precinct of Montu and then there's the Temple of Amenhotep the Fourth—who was otherwise known as Akhenaten—"

"Who got himself in a shitstorm with the priests," Isda excitedly interjected, obviously unable to contain himself. "I told him the politics were dicey. He was going monotheistic on them, and the priests were vested in keeping the temples and energies as separate representations of the Source. So, dat temple you talkin' 'bout, mon, got torn down as soon as the man died. Another crying shame, because dey tried to blot his name out—scratching it off temple walls and razing all he'd built. But his wife was fine, too, mon, Nefertiti . . . what can I say?"

Trying not to laugh and thus encourage Isda, given Bath Kol's serious attempt at keeping the conversation on track, Azrael interjected with logic.

"If I were attempting to hide something," Azrael said calmly, glancing around the bus, "I'd bring it to somewhere that it would seem unlikely—here. It's so open, so accessible, so many unrestricted and unguarded areas, it would seem like putting money in a vault and then never locking it. But I assure you it won't be where normal tourists can trip over it. So, the Temple of Amun is just a place we must pass through to get deeper inside the complex. The Precinct of Montu is a possibility, but we know if the Temple of Amenhotep the Fourth has been reduced to rubble, one might not want to risk something valuable getting damaged there. But the Temple of Mut . . ."

"We're right on the same page, man," Bath Kol replied, nodding. "See, right in the center of her complex is the sacred lake, and the inside bend of that faces her actual temple."

"Water," Celeste said, leaning forward. "Today I was drawn to the water, and so far we know for a fact that the men hiding the sarcophagus initially had it in a place where there was feminine energy . . . back at the Temple of Hathor in Dendera."

"Mut's believed reign was of the earth, creation . . . also

very symbolic for what's being hidden—something that can re-create life to come up from the earth and not down from the heavens," Azrael added, glancing around.

"Not to mention, feminine energy traditionally isn't warlike, but in the case of Mut, she was represented by the lioness head—so that energy is not to be messed with. Just ask any man that has truly pissed off his 'oman," Isda said over his shoulder. "Plus, with a lake, dat's a nice natural barrier for a priest to light up, you know?"

"Same page, yet again, brothers," Bath Kol said, now enlarging the section of the map that dealt with the Precinct of Mut. "All right, here's the challenge. The area is blocked off and this campus is crawling with guards. From the main entrance of where we wanna go, there's a four-hundred-meter-long avenue of ram-headed sphinxes that leads north directly to the tenth pylon of Amun. So if we create a bit of a diversion, we can backtrack from the Temple of Amun right into it. Or, there's another avenue of sphinxes that leads two hundred and fifty meters west to catch the flow into a three-kilometer-long avenue of sphinxes that connects the Precinct of Amun to Luxor Temple."

"Or," Celeste said with a shrug, "rather than going all Green Beret commando, we *could* just walk directly to it like dumb Americans, put up a good-natured pleading fuss, and bribe our way back there."

The brothers looked around at each other and smiled as they realized it had distinct possibilities.

"Feminine energy works like a charm every time," Isda said with a wide grin.

Bath Kol shrugged and turned off the lit floor map. "Works for me."

*Luxor could just as* easily have been any bustling city in
the United States. Congestion was rampant, vibrant shops
crammed themselves into every available inch of real es-
tate. Vendors argued for their fair share of the pavement,
and bodies endlessly milled. Local shoppers and the few
tourists that had braved to come back after the civil unrest
coexisted in an uneasy truce, all made palatable by the almighty dollar. But the thing that most fascinated Celeste
as she stared out of the dingy bus window was how a modern city had imposed itself so thoroughly upon antiquity.

They rode over a busy overpass like one you would
see in any major urban business district; however, beneath
it were cranes, excavation equipment, and construction
workers unearthing a two-mile-long stretch of an ancient
road. Ten-foot-high sphinxes lined the road with one of
the spectacular monuments evenly placed every three feet.
That someone could have ordered such an arduous feat
of building to be done blew her mind. Sphinxes, every
three feet, for two miles, that led from your palace to your
wife's palace? *Dayum*. And it now just so happened to run
through what was like their downtown Manhattan? The
contrast was unbelievable.

She better understood Isda's pride and excitement
as they neared the Karnak complex. Hundreds of buses
packed the lot, and thousands of tourists moved along the
huge granite path, the prior unrest notwithstanding—
people still came to see this world marvel. The crush of
humanity looked pitifully insignificant against the monuments, like swarming ants beneath two-city-block-long

rows of giant stone baboon statues seated in repose as they approached huge obelisks to enter the Temple of Amun.

Everyone looked up the moment they got off the bus. It was impossible not to walk in awe, almost tripping over ground stones. Celeste found herself completely unable to turn away from the enormity of the architecture or the supernatural engineering that could be the only thing that accounted for what they were witnessing. In her heart and soul she knew something beyond human had assisted in creating what she now saw.

As they entered the gigantic Hypostyle Hall, every human in the group gasped. It was like standing in the middle of a fifty-thousand-square-foot redwood forest where the huge trees were man-made of granite.

Isda nodded and turned around slowly with pride, his focus toward the top of the massive pillars. "Check it out . . . one hundred and thirty-four columns set up in sixteen rows. A hundred twenty-two are ten feet tall, the other twelve are twenty-one meters tall, and all are like three meters wide. The architraves on top of the columns are seventy tons each." He folded his arms and looked at the group, even though they were still staring at the structures. "And dey *still* don't know how we did it." He chuckled and began walking with his chest poked out. "We wasn't bullshitting back den."

"Not at all," Celeste said in awe.

What amazed her was that not only were the columns huge, just as the entrance statuary and obelisks had been, but they were also just as detailed, telling a gorgeous story in stone relief on what seemed like every inch of granite.

"In the womb of the Precinct of Mut is da crescent

lake," Isda said, gathering their group in a small huddle. "Now, if we do like da lady says, we may need a coupla brothers to peel off and make sure all these other tourists don't see us get special treatment and then try to use dat as leverage to get in dere, too. If dat happens, da guards won't go for it."

Gavreel and Paschar nodded and broke off from the group.

"Okay, Mut's Precinct has several small buildings in there, but if we focus on the one that has the holy of holies first and then fan out, maybe we can make quick work of this," Bath Kol said, glancing around concerned.

"Holy of holies?" Melissa frowned.

"Main altar. Each temple has one," Aziza said with a nod to the much larger Temple of Amun.

"Okay, you ladies work your magic," Azrael said with a half smile. "My pocket replenishes itself."

Celeste chuckled as she led Melissa, Maggie, and Aziza far away from the brothers toward a group of guards that were gathered by a small barricade outside the Precinct of Mut.

"We heard that Mut was the goddess of fertility and the earth," Celeste said, using her most coy demeanor. "Couldn't we just go in for a quick peek?"

The guards smiled at them as Melissa's voice chimed in with Maggie's to harmonize on, "Please."

"We would be ever so grateful," Aziza said in a sensuous but dignified rush.

The men smiled and took several long drags on their cigarettes, and the leader stepped forward, addressing Celeste.

"Nubian sister, I would like to, and my men would like to accommodate such beautiful women, but . . . it is after all dangerous. Plus, if I allow you—the others will see." He nodded in disdain toward loud-talking tourists that milled past them. "All do not appreciate the *beauty* as you do, but I must disappoint you. Are you married?"

Celeste released a theatrical sigh that the other women in the group also picked up on and mimicked. "No, not yet. That's why we all wanted to go inside."

"None of you are married?" The man looked at his fellow guards as though the concept was impossible.

"No," Celeste said, telling the truth, but pouting for extra emphasis.

"What is wrong in America? This cannot be!" The lead guard turned around and translated for his men, which set off a rapid-fire Arabic conversation that Celeste and the other women didn't need a translator to understand.

"No boyfriend?" The guard smiled a dashing smile and waited.

Again Celeste released a heavy exhale. "Yes, but I don't think he can marry me."

"He has a lot of money, but the man has issues . . . uhm . . . entanglements that prevent that, I think," Melissa offered, smiling at Celeste.

"Yeah—*big* entanglements. Cosmic." Celeste laughed, shaking her head.

"Oh, so sad, a beautiful woman should be married and have lots of children, and, well, if he cannot . . ." The guard shrugged and stepped closer. "I am Hakim. I would like to make you many children."

Celeste laughed hard, for a moment at a loss for words.

African men had a level of forwardness, she'd noticed, that made the average guy on a street corner in Philly look downright timid.

Maggie giggled and filled in the gap. "Hi, Hakim."

Another eager guard stepped up, and although he didn't speak English, he bowed and placed a hand over his chest. "Yusef."

"Hi, Yusef," Magdalena said with a wide smile as another, shier guard approached.

The lead guard named Hakim pointed to the shy man and shoved him forward a bit as the other men laughed. "This is Amir," he exclaimed. But Hakim then walked over to Aziza and took up her hand. "Hakim can have two wives. You and her—one beautiful and young, one beautiful and wise, such makes a man's household rich and peaceful, too. Please say yes, both of you!"

Aziza laughed and withdrew her hand. "You are too kind."

Hakim sighed. "But, I should not allow my wives to go into a dangerous temple area. That would be irresponsible for me."

"Her boyfriend has lots of money," Maggie said with a shrug.

"He is here?" Hakim said, slight disappointment in his voice.

"Yeah," Celeste said, sounding thoroughly disgusted. "Unfortunately."

Her comment seemed to revive the dejected guard. "Well, maybe if he pays for your safe passage, I can call you later . . . since he is so entangled? He should pay for you to be happy now, yes?"

"I agree," Celeste said with a wide grin.

"You are in hotel here?"

Dodging the question, she smiled. "Give me your number. He likes to play cards with his friends."

"Come, come," Hakim said, turning her away from the group to speak privately to her as he dug into his pocket for a pack of matches, and then for a moment closed his hand over hers with a sexy smile. But as he lifted his head, Celeste froze.

The man's eyes were completely black, no whites showing. It happened for the briefest of seconds, and then her mind felt foggy.

"You have something to write down my number?" he said, tearing the matchbook and giving her a tiny slip of paper. "I would be so honored to show you all of Egypt."

Nodding through the disorientation, she dug into her small, black waist bag, which held her ship boarding pass, passport, and a little cash, to find a hotel pen. But as she did so, her fingers felt thick and clumsy, just as her mind had become. Somewhere deep within her a small voice cried out that something was wrong, and just as suddenly as it did, a dark fog choked off the sound of it.

"Tell him he can come, but it will cost him. But don't tell him about this."

"All right," she said slowly, then accepted the hastily scribbled number and put it away with the pen.

"Everything cool?" Melissa murmured, and slung an arm over Celeste's shoulders as she walked back to them.

"Yeah, we're good ta go," Celeste said, lifting her ponytail off her neck again, feeling even warmer than she had before.

"You look flushed, beloved," Aziza said, touching Celeste's forehead with the back of her hand.

"It's got to be the heat," Celeste said, feeling something important dancing at the edges of her mind and then flitting away.

Aziza nodded and motioned toward Hakim with her chin as the man nearly stumbled back to his laughing fellow guards and slumped against a column, wiping his brow. "We need to get some water soon. If the heat is affecting them, then you know we're not used to it."

Maggie placed a hand on Celeste's back. "Come on, let's go break it to the fellas that they've gotta pay another unlisted ticket fee to get into an exhibit."

# Chapter 12

*zrael frowned as he* watched the interaction in the distance, and Isda's and Bath Kol's teasing wasn't helping. Gavreel had his arms folded over his chest, and Paschar was two seconds from crossing the large courtyard. Only Isda's body block prevented it.

"Oh, you haven't run into this emotion yet, huh, bro?" Isda pushed Paschar back by his shoulders, making Paschar shrug him away.

"Don't you know women like men in uniforms, especially ones carrying large weapons?" Bath Kol said, laughing.

Gavreel unfolded his arms and began to cross the yard.

"Yo, yo, yo, yo, yo! Fall back, soldier," Isda said, leaving Paschar to slow down Gavreel.

"I don't like what I'm feeling," Gavreel said, glaring at the guards that were flirting with Maggie.

"Nor do I," Azrael muttered. "It brings violence into

my spirit in a way that I'm unused to. I don't like it at all. It is confounding and irrational and yet impossible to immediately shake."

"Yeah, well, hey—get over it," Bath Kol said with a wide grin, fishing for a pack of Camels in his pocket. "You want to mess up our only chance to get in there?"

"He did not have to touch her," Azrael said, feeling the muscles in his arms contract. "Maybe I should go over there to be sure all is well."

"Man, you *are* violence. The Angel of Death, remember? So don't act like a little negative energy spike is gonna kill you." Bath Kol chuckled and glanced in the direction of the women.

"He put his hands on her," Azrael said, folding his arms. "*That* was unnecessary."

"And she came away unscathed. Relax, man," Bath Kol chided.

"Maybe I should go check that he is aware not to do that again." Azrael set his gaze toward Celeste and lifted his chin, indignant.

"You're about a foot taller than that dude, mon," Isda said, laughing harder and pounding Bath Kol's fist. "Wit dat expression on your face, you might get shot. Chill."

"Chill?"

"Yes, as in be cool and—"

"I know what the damned expression means," Azrael said between his teeth.

"Den beee cooool," Isda said, making Bath Kol laugh harder with him.

Although it only took ten minutes for the women to return, it felt like the better part of an hour. When Celeste came back, Azrael didn't like the semivacant expression on her face, but she perked up the moment he put his arm over her shoulder.

"How much do we need to give these guys?" Gavreel glared over his shoulder at them.

"You sound tight, bro," Bath Kol said, still laughing. "Relax."

"A lot of money," Maggie replied to Gavreel. "We told them that Celeste's boyfriend was rich but didn't want to marry her and—"

"What!" Fury exploded in Azrael's system so quickly that it made his ears ring. "That is not true."

"Whew!" Bath Kol said, walking over to slap Isda five. "Touchy subject."

Ignoring their antics, Azrael turned to Celeste and slapped the center of his chest. "I'm no *boyfriend*. You and I have an eternity bond. And I never said I didn't want to go through the human ceremony of marriage—I . . . I have to ask . . . find out what the rules are—"

"You're stuttering, brother," Isda said, doubling over and laughing so hard that he finally sat on the ground.

"I was not talking to you," Azrael said, pointing at Isda.

That Celeste swallowed a smile didn't help. "It was just for theater, dang," she said, then swallowed another smile.

"I think the larger discussion is for another time or place," Aziza said in an amused tone. "But I got an offer, too."

Bath Kol sobered a little but tried to keep up the banter. "Now everybody's a comedian, sheesh."

"What is that supposed to mean, BK?" Aziza placed her hands on her hips, and Isda whooped and jumped up to jog away a few paces.

"Oh, man, 'Ziza, you know what I meant."

"Make it good, mon," Isda said, wiping his eyes. "You done inserted your big foot in your mouth!"

Aziza lifted her chin, seeming both hurt and indignant. "He said Celeste was young and beautiful, but that I was beautiful and wise—*for your information*."

"You are," Bath Kol said, not looking at Aziza but glaring at the group of guards that seemed to be thoroughly enjoying the argument their group was having. "Did you tell that horny bastard that you were not only beautiful and wise but also very well protected?"

"No," she said, smiling. "I failed to mention that. Didn't think it really mattered that much anymore."

"Yeah, well, it does." Bath Kol spit in the dust. "And I'll make sure I deliver the message when I kick his ass."

"Okay—back up," Isda said, smiling wide and pushing Bath Kol to a halt. "I don't know what's gotten into the group but we are losing focus."

"Yes, well, let me focus on giving this man his entrance fee along with a piece of my mind," Azrael said, and began walking.

But Celeste rounded him. "If you go over there like that, you are gonna really mess up our delicate negotiation."

"Yeah," Melissa said, helping Celeste to body-block Azrael.

Celeste held out her hand. "Empty your pockets if you want in."

"That so didn't sound right," Maggie said, then burst out laughing.

"Don't say a word," Azrael said in a deep rumble to Isda as he gave Celeste a thick roll of bills.

"Let *us* go over there first," Celeste warned with emphasis, "then we'll call you guys over. But like Isda and BK said, be cool."

Azrael folded his arms over his chest and his brothers followed suit. As always, the waiting was the hard part. But after a few more moments of flirting, Celeste waved them over. The guards gave them bemused glances as they passed, and every hair on the nape of Azrael's neck bristled as he passed the leader. It felt as if a hundred tiny spiders had just run up the back of his neck, and fight adrenaline was raging within him so strongly that it took deep concentration not to whirl on the human.

The odd sensations fractured his concentration for a moment, and he jogged to catch up to Celeste, grabbing her by the arm.

"What did he say to you?"

"Huh? Are you serious?"

"Absolutely serious," Azrael replied, completely annoyed when she blew him off and began walking deeper into the courtyard.

"Tell me you're not jealous?"

"No, I'm not!"

"Really, well, you could have fooled me." She walked harder and faster away from him, and he had to widen his strides to keep pace with her. "That emotion doesn't become you, Az—and I for one am not dealing with that shit after all the crap I had to take from Brandon!"

"What?" Azrael said, much louder than intended. "You have compared me to that demon-infested bastard? An ex-lover?"

"Can we look for what we came here for, people? Or is it just me?" Bath Kol caught up to Azrael and Celeste, looking between them and then focusing on Azrael. "Man, if you don't chill out, you're going to block whatever ability to see that she has. I know how the gift works. It's in my province, remember?"

Azrael stopped walking and rubbed his palms down his face, allowing Celeste to continue forward. Bath Kol held him by both biceps as the rest of their group passed them.

"You okay, man—for real?"

"I honestly cannot say that I am." Azrael looked at Bath Kol and then at the human guard. "I suddenly felt murderous, irrationally so."

"Okay, later you and I need to have a very long conversation over some more very cold beer, because if a few of the other things that just happened between you guys isn't enough to get you blasted with white lightning, trust me, smoking a human in a jealous rage about pure bullshit will get you more than banished."

"Forgive me, brother, I literally do not know what just came over me."

"I told you before that I've got your six. And I know I run off the rails a lot, do lots of shit I'm not supposed to down here. But on the fundamentals of *the Law* I'm real clear. *Crystal clear*. Don't get sloppy. You of all of us should know better."

Bath Kol cuffed Azrael's shoulder hard, then grabbed

his forearm in the timeless warrior's embrace. "You good?"

Azrael nodded. "I'm good."

"All right then. Let's go find some history."

As they entered the main round, sandstone-and-granite temple, the thing that bothered Azrael the most was that he'd spent some of his irrational rage toward Celeste in a way that had made her displeased with him. He had never before done such a thing and had no frame of reference for how to resolve the blunder. Yet, as sure as he was standing, he'd felt something that had flooded his system with the desire to fight. Was this the human condition—part of being in a body and being controlled by irrational, territorial instincts? Was this, like the other emotions he'd experienced here, just a part of the package of being in the flesh . . . and was one of the temptations of that state the rush of the fight, of battle, of violence?

Deeply disturbed that he didn't know, and finding that pride was also a part of him now, he didn't want to explore it further with BK or Isda and add to their teasing. Instead he gave Celeste wide berth and studied the walls and floors, trying to see if there was a secret chamber that had been dug out.

"Here," Celeste said quietly as she touched the altar stone and closed her eyes. "This moves."

Immediately the group rushed over, and Azrael and Bath Kol took up the opposite ends of a large granite slab atop a heavy base. Gavreel, Isda, and Paschar added leverage along each side of the length of it.

"It's all one piece," Bath Kol said, straining. "The top doesn't come off."

"But the bottom is over something," Celeste insisted.

Finally the structure gave way and they were able to swing it to the side by a foot. They all stopped and stared at the exposed footprint of the slab, which included a square depression in the sand, one that had been dug to fit something rectangular that was roughly two feet long by a foot wide and several inches thick. But the hole was empty.

"They got it?" Bath Kol walked away and slapped a wall. "Damn!"

"We need to put this back," Isda warned. "Before da guards come, mon."

Azrael nodded, defeated, and walked back to the granite altar to move it back into place with Gavreel and Paschar.

"But even if the dark side has it now, if Daoud was human, as was Father Krespy, how could they have lifted something this heavy?" Gavreel glanced around the group, waiting for an answer.

"Monks could have moved this to place the tablet here originally," Azrael noted. "And they would have sealed it with a prayer."

"But when it was time for Daoud to move it, those old monks from Krespy's time wouldn't have the strength, and in a country that's ninety percent Muslim, the Christian clerics would have to collaborate with whoever was available and reach across faiths to get the job done quickly. But Daoud wouldn't. Maybe he got Muslim clerics to assist?" Aziza offered.

"Or the dark side got a couple of guys just like we did, once they knew the location, and lifted it," Isda said in a weary tone.

"But wouldn't you have felt some bad jolt of energy if the dark side took the tablet out of its hiding place here?" Celeste glanced around the group and her line of vision settled on Azrael's. "And you also said that monks had consecrated this ground, which was already a holy site. Even if they sent in humans to move the slab, wouldn't you guys feel it if dirty energy had entered here?"

Azrael nodded and held her gaze. He liked it so much better when she looked at him as an ally. "Yes, Celeste. You are right. I felt nothing when I opened the small vault."

"Neither did I," Gavreel chimed in.

"Nor I," said Paschar.

"Not a t'ing," Isda said, raking his locks.

Bath Kol shook his head and then looked at Aziza.

"It was here, just as our sister said. But I'm not sensing that distress wrenched it from its resting place. It was purposefully moved." Aziza moved to the altar and allowed her fingertips to gently graze it. "No, it wasn't robbed from here, it was definitely moved."

Celeste placed her hands on top of her head. "Okay, if Daoud moved it, then a couple things. One, he had to have help, benign help. And two, some of those guys who helped him move the stone might still be around."

"If he had help," Azrael said, "that means someone other than him knew that something valuable was stashed here."

"To get in here at night with a bribe means you had to know the local way," Isda said. "People here don't trust foreigners for really big requests, but if you have a brother, cousin . . . you know. And if you say, 'I found an artifact and need to hide it—here's some money to forget that,' because it's blood involved and you were paid well, not to mention it's a high crime that could make you do life in prison for antiquity-black-market dealing—they don't play that shit here, mon . . . then, you would help your family and forget what you knew."

"Especially if that family member suddenly went missing," Bath Kol said. "It would make you afraid, and you definitely wouldn't return to the scene of the crime."

"I still say there's a fifty-fifty chance the other side doesn't have it yet." Azrael dragged his finger through his locks. "If it didn't get removed from here under duress, and the men that helped Daoud move this altar are still out there, then we need to hold out some hope."

"Yeah, but we can't just go around asking if people know this guy." Celeste folded her arms and released a weary breath. "First of all, it's probably a very common name—like asking for John Smith back where we're from. Second, it would raise suspicion. We can—"

"Pssst!" the lead guard said, suddenly entering the temple.

Everyone became stone still, warily watching the man.

"You must go soon. Other tourists are starting to walk by and take notice." Hakim glanced around nervously. "If you are looking for something very old and *very* special, I have a man I know. Nazir. He owns a perfumery, sells top, top oils, in the town. Go see him there and say my name. He will talk to you and make a good deal for you. *Yalla*."

Hakim left, waving them out until the group hurried beyond him and his fellow guards.

"No, no!" he yelled at a group of eager tourists. "They were not authorized to be in that area and we have asked them to leave."

The group shared glances as they headed back toward the bus. Every nerve ending within Azrael tingled with aggression.

"Okay, I think we found the source of the leak," Bath Kol said as they entered the bus. "Dude definitely knew a transaction went down and might have even been the one that allowed Daoud to come in there."

"Ya think?" Celeste said, sitting down hard and accepting a bottle of water from Melissa.

"Twenty bucks says this guy helped sell out Daoud," Isda muttered, gunning the engine as Gavreel passed out more water bottles.

"But he also gave us a great lead," Azrael said. "Men who deal in black-market antiquities here."

⟡

"*Patience always pays off,* milord," Rahab murmured, setting down her scrying bowl. "One of our trackers targeting the human seer's energy let us know where she was next. And playing a fair hunch, an already corrupted soul was the perfect carrier to touch our most wanted, little Miss Celeste, because where she is, Azrael will always be."

"The way your mind works has always delighted me," Asmodeus said, staring across the table at her.

# Chapter 13

*C*eleste *sipped her water* quietly and didn't say a word. The entire ride over to the shopping district to Nazir's Perfume Emporium, the bus had erupted in chaotic speculation about where the tablet could have been stashed, moved, and what the next course of action should be. Everyone's nervous system was fried, and she had a headache that felt as if someone were driving a needle into her eye from inside her brain.

Worst of all, she hated that she'd actually yelled at Azrael. Even given his demon-destroying profession, he was the most peaceable soul she'd ever met. What had come over her to make her lash out at the poor man like that? she wondered. No one was himself. It was as though some crazy new kind of bad energy had settled in among the group, making folks argue and snap at each other and just generally behave miserably. Not all of it could be blamed on fatigue, dehydration, and insufferable heat.

Poor Gavreel, supposedly the angel of peace, looked ready to rumble at the slightest provocation. Something was wrong.

But her two cents didn't need to be added into the layers of conjecture already clouding everyone's judgment. Emotions were running high enough.

She continued to keep her own counsel as they parked and piled out of the hot bus and entered the brightly lit shop. Even getting here had caused drama. The crude directions they were given and Isda's refusal to ask for clarification only added to everyone's exasperation.

A cannon blast of cold air greeted them at the door as they stepped into a place that looked like Aladdin's lair. The walls were covered in red crushed-velvet fabric from the floor to the chair rail, and above it were gold-accented, geometric-design murals painted on every inch. Sumptuous Oriental rugs yawned across hand-laid black, white, and gold marble tiles. Black-lacquer and gold-accented chairs and benches overstuffed with gold-embroidered satin cushions littered the customer seating area. Rich oils blended into a pleasant aroma that wasn't so overpowering that it created nausea.

Lest she accidentally bump into a display, Celeste tried to make herself small as they passed gleaming cases of hand-blown glass vases, perfume bottles, and small jewelry boxes. Each delicate bottle looked as if it had been painstakingly created, and she worried for the shop's treasures as burly angles trudged to the manager's desk, ignoring the salesman's request to assist them.

"Sir, sir," the salesman said, adjusting his poorly fitting, light-blue sports jacket. "May I help you?"

Azrael looked at him with dark clouds of annoyance forming in his expression. "I was told to see Nazir. Hakim sent us."

Several security guards, two salesmen, and a young male cashier stood stock-still for a moment, then the salesman rushed to the back of the store. Celeste glanced around. The air-conditioning was on full blast, the place didn't have a single customer, and it was outfitted like a sultan's boudoir. Staff was standing around doing nothing, but obviously getting paid to hang out. Where she came from, retail operations like this were called a front.

"Yes, may I help you?" an older, balding gentleman said, as he exited the back room. "I am Nazir."

Celeste hung back wondering how many more security guards were in the back and what else beyond hot antiquities the man moved. He had on a short-sleeve, embroidered, Egyptian-cotton shirt, a Rolex, and a heavy gold chain. She noticed that his hands were manicured and he was well barbered. Hmmm . . .

Azrael nodded as the man looked up at him. "I'm told you might be able to help me locate something valuable."

Nazir looked around and gave his guards a meaningful look, then smiled. "I understand you are the American athletes with a lot of money." Nazir smiled and looked at the five warriors. "Basketball or football? Wait, let me guess."

Confident to the point of cocky, the little man walked around Azrael sizing him up, then looked at Bath Kol, Isda, Gavreel, and Paschar. "Although there are five of you, I say football. Am I right?"

Before Azrael could answer with a much too long version of the truth, Celeste jumped in. "Football."

"I knew it!" Nazir exclaimed. "Then we should definitely go into a private salon. I have many deals for men with real money." He smiled at Celeste. "And we will make sure that all the ladies have gorgeous scents . . . my oils are the best in Egypt—there are certain fragrances that can only come from the true fresh-pressed flowers. Maybe the ladies would like a tea or a coffee, and Rahim can let them select beautiful scarves and—"

"She stays with me," Azrael said in a rumble that nearly shook the glass cases.

"Of course, of course, I have three wives and none so beautiful. If I had one like that, I would keep a watchful eye." Nazir smiled and opened his arms with a flourish. "*Yalla, yalla* . . . the salon is this way."

Nazir led them to a room with soft seating, hookahs, and a central oval table where his body language suggested that he'd expect only the men to be seated. Making small talk as he closed the door, Nazir smiled at Azrael, then ushered him to the head of the table. Two silent guards were already in the room standing by the far back wall.

"Hakim said you emptied your pockets for your wife at the temple . . . your team must be going to the Super Bowl." Nazir laughed at his own joke as they all sat, growing nervous as his guests remained stoic. "So, what team?"

The brothers looked at each other for a moment.

"The Eagles," Celeste said quickly, then allowed the brothers to catch her meaningful sidelong glance.

"Yeah, I guess you could call us the Birds," Bath Kol muttered.

The man smiled. "This is Philadelphia, yes? Philly."

"Yeah," Celeste said, concerned that the man had that much knowledge of the sport and could possibly catch them in a bold-faced lie.

"Ah, we have a Philae here. But it is just old temples, no sports team." Nazir smiled broadly and sat down across from Azrael, focused on the man who he'd obviously been told had the wellspring of cash in his pocket.

"So," Nazir said, glancing around but giving his primary attention to Azrael, "this is for your mansion or your office or a gift?"

"I'm looking for ancient tablets," Azrael said, cutting to the chase.

Bath Kol and Isda looked as if they'd stopped breathing when Nazir blanched.

"Something like that, with writing on it—*anything* with writing on it to any significant degree, would cost . . . possibly millions, sir . . . and would be extremely difficult to export, if you understand my meaning." Nazir sat back expectantly with his hands folded in front of him on the table.

"How many millions?" Azrael said casually. "One, two, ten?"

"Ten to fifteen," Nazir said, losing his smile and leaning forward. "At least. Then there would be transportation and security costs."

Azrael nodded. "We can make that happen."

Nazir began to wheeze. "Bring some refreshments for these gentlemen. Top-shelf, and prepare tea and coffee for the ladies." He waited until the men left and had shut the door behind them. "May I ask what has inspired your interest in such an expensive treasure, sir?"

"The man's been retracing his roots," Isda said in a sarcastic tone that went over Nazir's head.

"So you want something that could be representative of your Nubian heritage . . . this to put on your library wall or maybe your living room wall as a gallery piece?"

"Something like that," Azrael replied, and sat back in his chair.

"I ask this because I will endeavor to do all that I can to find a stone with hieroglyphics on it, intact. But those are so rare—wealthy Europeans have taken so much on their so-called expeditions that were really raiding parties . . . Napoléon stole so much that the Louvre has more exhibits than our own Egyptian Museum, as does the British Museum, Germany, Italy, all over the world actually."

Nazir released a dramatic sigh. "You see, I tell you this so that you understand my pricing. Until 1972, all one had to do was set up an expedition, finance it, and take as you pleased if you found a ruin. Before our government, there were fat caliphs who could care less, as long as they were properly compensated, and the wealthy tomb raiders put much in their private collections and gave a pittance to their home government and museums . . . so the collector business, which is still very fertile, had to go underground so to speak—not that I am openly complaining, but with new laws that carry twenty-five years to life for removing even the tiniest item . . . well . . . you understand why this has escalated the cost of doing business. And now after the recent events here with civil unrest . . . a change in the government makes things even more costly."

Azrael stood. "We understand you are unable to help us." He looked at the group. "Let's go."

"Wait, wait, wait, my friend," Nazir said, jumping to his feet. "In Egypt we discuss . . . we negotiate—it is ou way. I did not mean to offend and I can see you are a very direct man indeed. Please sit. Let us work this out."

His expression strained, Nazir coaxed Azrael to si down again and then spoke quickly. "I have a network o people at all the ruin sites, so trust me, for your price, we could move a stone from Ramses's tomb!"

Nazir leaned back and laughed at his own joke and after a moment awkwardly stopped when he realized no one else was laughing with him. "However, it would help me to understand your desire better, because we could have a very long and fruitful relationship. As I see things that fit your taste, I could contact you and send you digital photos and then have anything you decided to buy shipped with you sending me a wire transfer. have many rich clients all over the world, and there i more Egyptian art in rich people's private collection than in the museums."

"Since you are doing custom orders, then," Azrae said, his mood darkening, "I am looking for a very spe cial tablet. It is a single sheet of gold with thirty-six panel on it, approximately one foot wide by two feet long. It' encased entirely in clear quartz crystal and weighs abou fifty to sixty pounds. There was a man who knew where it was—Daoud Salahuddin. But I cannot find him now."

Nazir leaned in quickly. "You were trying to acquire that from Daoud?"

"Yes," Azrael replied flatly.

"Listen to me, my friend. Forget about that tablet I will find you something else very close to it, I assure you . . . but that one must have been stolen from a private collector—a very serious collector who took issue with Daoud's misdeeds. I do not believe anything good came to your courier, which is why you must deal with more established sources like myself."

"Has the other collector recovered the item?" Isda said in an easy manner, then reared back in his chair. "Because if not, a bid war is not out of the question . . . whot, with da way we can make money . . ."

Bath Kol nodded. "Unfortunately Mr. Salahuddin was out of his league. Had we known that . . . hey."

Nazir jumped up. "Let me make some calls. I do not believe the item has been recovered. I have a cousin in Edfu who works with stone and who at times serves as a courier—"

"We can go to Edfu," Isda said, gaining nods from the group. "We like to know who we're dealing with."

*This time when they* boarded the bus, they waited until they pulled away from the curb before erupting into pandemonium.

"Okay, this is taking shape in my mind, folks," Bath Kol said, too wired to sit as Isda drove at breakneck speed to make it back to the ship on time. "You've got these exhibit dudes, like our man back at Karnak, Hakim. They look for wealthy foreigners who look like they could drop some nice coin for original artifacts. With so many people finding their homes have been built on top of ruins and the government only offering them a pittance for whatever's found there, there's a lot of stuff moving illegally across borders. Add in general theft from sacred sites, and you have a nice little cottage industry going."

"So, Hakim sees us poking around and figures a bunch of rich Americans are trying to smuggle home a keepsake," Celeste said. "So he calls his boy, Nazir, and says, 'I've got a hot one for you.'"

"Right," Azrael added, glancing around the group. "And at Nazir's we learn that he'd heard about this tablet someone with a lot of money was searching for and had possibly killed a man over . . . no doubt the enemy was going around saying they needed their tablet returned—which is why Nazir assumed someone had stolen it from whoever was looking for it."

"But I didn't get the feeling that he had actually ever brokered a deal of that magnitude or even had the tablet," Aziza said.

"I'm with you, lady." Celeste shook her head. "No, this guy was about to pee his pants when Az put eight figures on the table. These guys don't have it."

"But they have ears to the ground, and more importantly, if we go talk to this cousin of Nazir's down in Edfu—Omar the stoneworker—then maybe we can find out who helped get poor Daoud into the sanctuary of the Precinct of Mut. It had to be one of the guys he was working with to move the piece."

Celeste stared out the window at the approaching dock. "If I was Daoud and I knew everybody around me was dirty or could possibly be paid off . . . like Hakim . . . dude probably let Daoud in for a price on the side without telling Nazir. Right?"

"I'm right dere wit you, sis," Isda said.

"Okay," she said, turning back to the group, "I would tell them I had found a buyer and would give them a way bigger cut if they didn't tell Nazir. Those guys probably said yes, knowing that if things went south, Daoud could run but he couldn't hide forever, especially with no way to get a passport out of the country without their network knowing about it. So, the deal was, Daoud would go get the cash from some rich guy, split it with them for a hefty cut—higher than what Nazir pays . . . under the table and off Nazir's radar. But then Daoud, an honest man with no buyer, hides the tablet and never brings them their cut."

"So they round him up and take his ass to Nazir and claim that they found him poaching," Bath Kol said.

"And Daoud gets tortured and his family gets threatened, so he gives them one piece. Something bigger than what he so-called stole. Imhotep," Isda said quietly.

Bath Kol released a forlorn sigh as he leaned back against his seat. "But the poor bastard was probably so beat up and had lost so much blood that he expired right out there in the tomb that me and Aziza went down into."

Aziza nodded. "That version of the story resonates with me."

"Me, too," Celeste said, gaining nods from Maggie and Melissa.

"It sits right in my gut as well," Azrael said, standing. "I still want to go to Edfu. This stoneworker concerns me. When they captured Daoud, who knows what information they extracted from him that could be useful to us. This Omar might also lead us to the full group that initially moved that altar."

Isda reached back and slapped Azrael five, but Celeste

leaned forward and rubbed her temples, her head pounding, something pushing at her mind.

"I saw something when we were at the site . . . but it fled my mind and I've felt like I've got something metal stuck in my head ever since." Breathing shallow sips of air, Celeste closed her eyes. "It's getting worse now."

"Give me your hands," Aziza said, and turned around in her seat on her knees.

Weakly, Celeste complied as everyone looked on. But as soon as their hands touched, both women drew back from each other.

"You're carrying something dark on your person," Aziza said in a tight voice.

Celeste stared at her and swallowed hard, paralyzed by Aziza's statement. "Get it off me, sis. I could feel it crawling all over me as soon as you said it."

Azrael got up and grabbed her fanny pack. "What did that guard give you—he handed something to you!"

"A phone number so I could call him back later tonight."

"Why would you do that?" Azrael frowned, unzipping her pack.

"For a booty call," Celeste said, squinting.

"A what?"

"A rendezvous, man," Isda said, frowning.

Azrael extracted the piece of paper, and as soon as he held it between his fingers, it burned. Celeste slumped into a seat and released her breath.

"The headache . . . damn, it's gone," she murmured.

"They tracked her. Sent a black vibration out through the airwaves to cover the mortals in our group at all of the sites where we'd most likely go searching for the tablet and sarcophagus," Bath Kol said, punching a seat. "They can only do that to humans or beings with human DNA in them. Shit!"

"Den they'll let us be their little hunting dogs and go find the tablet for them, and then ambush us," said Isda.

"Did anyone else touch that guard or accept anything from him?" Azrael looked around. "Does anyone else have a headache or feel nauseated?"

Everyone murmured in a confused manner as though they couldn't remember, and Azrael scanned them visually for any signs of additional fatigue.

"You do not break bread or eat with a demon. You do not share water, the most mutable substance on the planet, with a demon. The piece of paper he gave you had numbers on it . . . a dark code containing a scrying spell. And—"

"His eyes turned coal black," Celeste suddenly shouted. "I couldn't remember before! Everything became cloudy."

"And I became irrational . . . and we argued. We don't argue. A demon's foundation is dissension and anger."

"Oh, Az . . . I'm so sorry—I was just trying to run a little game to get us in." She went to him and he hugged her.

"You did the right thing. You were following the plan we'd all agreed upon. I allowed you to be placed in harm's way."

"BK, check your 'oman." Isda looked at Aziza hard. "She walked over desecration, man. She could have been black-tagged, too."

"I haven't felt right since I went to that tomb," Aziza said quietly. "But I've got something for that."

Bath Kol's hands began to glow as his eyes narrowed to a furious glare. "So do I," he said, frowning. "You get a spiritual white bath readied when we get back on that ship—I mean the full monty . . . holy water, frankincense, myrrh, and any herbal medicinals in your bag. If they tried to tag you with anything, we'll get rid of it."

Chapter 14

*I*nstinctively Celeste took Azrael's hand and threaded her fingers through his as they crossed the gangplank back to the ship. His energy was running so high right now that she could tell he was ready to take flight and dive-bomb into a demon battle at any moment. He needed a ground wire. If she could do that for him, so be it.

Dinner wouldn't be served until eight, which gave them a little decompression time. Celeste looked forward to escaping the group dynamics for just a little while.

It was as though everyone was on the same wavelength when they boarded the ship. They didn't even speak to each other; members of the group simply coupled off and headed directly to their rooms. Isda went straight upstairs in the direction of the top-deck bars.

"Hey . . . I'm sorry," Celeste said as she closed the door behind her.

Azrael shook his head so slowly, not even looking at her but contemplating the floor. "It is I who am very sorry, Celeste." When he looked up, his eyes were glowing pure white—which was never a good sign. "They sent a demon to despoil you?" His voice was low and ominous. "And it touched you . . ."

He walked away from her toward the sliding-glass doors and she hugged herself. "I feel so unclean," she said quietly, so upset that she had allowed something like that to happen. What she'd done was something people did every day—exchange a phone number on the back of a matchbook. But common sense should have told her that nothing was normal about normal.

Again he shook his head but didn't turn around. "You will never be unclean to me, Celeste. *Never*. And it would taunt me . . . actually challenge my affection and true intent for you by invoking the subject of marriage?"

"Az—"

With a loud bang, he flung the sliding-glass door open so hard she feared it had come off its hinges. Before she could even yell no, he'd stripped his shirt over his head, had taken two forceful steps, spread his wings, and hurled himself into the air like a rocket.

She ran to the window calling after him, leaning as far over the ship rail as she could. He was climbing in altitude so fast that she had to shield her eyes against the setting sun to watch him.

Panic sent her back into the room to lock the window and bolt from the room. Instead of going deeper into the cabin area, she headed across the lobby at a breakneck speed, hit the steps, and ran four flights up to the rooftop bar. Isda met her with a beer in his hand. The two nearly collided.

"He's so pissed off, I don't know where's he's going," she said, out of breath.

Isda held her by the shoulder. "I saw him battle-rocket out a damned balcony with no shield, no cloak? What happened?"

She shook her head. "He said I would never be unclean and was so upset about the demon tag—even though it's over, it's off me. I don't know what it was that set him off like that . . . he—"

"He took exception to Asmodeus putting that shit on his 'oman, is whot is was. I was gwan get Bath Kol, but he ain't in no better frame of mind." Isda handed her his beer, looked around, then stripped his shirt over his head and gave it to her. "Don't worry. They won't see me." He took a running leap and swan-dived off the star bow.

*Azrael headed toward the* sun, barreling through the sky, fury propelling him faster and faster until he ripped the barrier between time and space in the temporal realm. Gleaming battle-axes filled his fists as he descended into a cave that was deeper than the Great Pyramid was tall.

Bats screeched a sentry warning at his arrival. His feet slammed down upon mudstone and bat guano. Steep, fallen debris cones and outwash fans would have made his footing unsure were it not for his intense outrage. He was not just the Angel of Death, but the *Avenging* Angel.

"Asmodeus!" he shouted into the dark cavern. "I challenge you here in your old lair where we did battle before!

I feel your energy has recently been here—show yourself now! Or do you want to do this like old times, on Mount Hermon, where two hundred thousand of your fallen were sacked to two hundred, and now pitifully twenty-two! Tonight you have gone too far! Thus tonight we shall finish this man-to-man!"

Azrael threw open his arms within the seemingly dead cave, sending a blue-white current of light from his locks to run down his arms and then to blanket the cave floor. Screeching, frying, furious demons lifted from the embers, some popping and burning before they could escape. They came at him from every crevice and from behind huge stalactites and stalagmites, baring fangs and claws.

Using his wings as razor-sharp blades, the delicate plumage turned into twin death dealers as he hacked at the onslaught, his eyes now casting a burning white ray. Demons scrambled to get out of his line of vision and tried to attack from behind, to no avail. Gray-green gargoyle bodies littered the cave floor and acid-slobbering mutations screamed and writhed clutching at severed limbs.

Soon the air filled with gargoyles taking flight trying to escape the cavern. But a huge conventional-weapon blast made Azrael look up as an RPG shell hit the upper cave opening causing a boulder avalanche. Spiraling upward, he was in the air just as the next round connected below him. Two seconds before he threw a death ax, he heard Isda's voice.

"Friend not foe!"

Azrael released his battle-axes in an angry whirl, and they passed Isda by inches and with boomerang accuracy beheaded two gargoyles behind him. Whatever had surfaced in the cave was frying, but Isda went to the opening and sent one more shell down into the abyss for good measure. Anything on the wing was retreating, and Isda held Azrael's biceps before he could throw an ax again.

"You made your point, mon," Isda said, hovering beside Azrael. "You left her back at the boat alone. Blind fury will get you and her fucked up—let's go back."

Azrael nodded, his eyes slowly normalizing.

"You come challenging Asmodeus in his lair . . . alone—here—at the Majlis al Jinn . . . the actual meeting place of the jinn, with no backup?"

Azrael spit into the burning cave opening. "For every one they send after her, they will lose ten thousand. My word as my bond."

*When Azrael came into* the room through the cabin door like a normal person, Celeste sprang up from the chair by the sliding-glass door. He was covered from head to toe with reeking gook and filth. He stopped at the threshold and removed his sneakers, holding them on two fingers. Not sure what to do, she rushed over to him and put a wastebasket in front of him. He took it from her, deposited his soiled footwear, then hurled it at the glass.

She covered her face with a forearm, expecting glass to shatter everywhere, but it didn't. The wastebasket and demon-splattered shoes burned right through it, lighting up the glass in a brilliant blue, then were gone. As she turned back to him, he held up a hand.

"Now I am unclean. Let me wash, then we will talk."

"Okay," she replied quietly, worried out of her mind.

He stripped and purged his clothing the same way he had his sneakers—just balled them up and jettisoned them with a forceful hurl toward the glass and let them burn.

Transfixed, she watched him lope into the bathroom, then heard the water turn on. His back had dried blood on it—his. Against her better judgment she followed him, wanting to help but just not sure how.

"You're injured," she whispered, then sat down on the closed toilet seat as he entered the spray.

He looked so weary that it frightened her. For a moment he didn't answer, just placed both hands on either side of the showerhead and lowered his entire head into the spray. The water crackled over his skin, becoming a blue-white energy wash that made him visibly wince. As his skin smoldered, she bit her lip and stood. But he held up a hand.

"Normally I'd be flying back into the Light, and this filth would strip. On the earth plane, holy water will have to suffice, but it is somewhat less efficient," he said, panting as he turned around and let it hit his back. "You don't need to see this, Celeste."

"Tell me how to help you," she said, tears rising in her eyes as she witnessed his pain.

"You can't," he said, panting. "Go in the other room and turn on the television or some music. I'll have this off of me soon."

"I am here for you," she said, holding her ground. "Who cares for you? Who takes care of you, Az?"

"The Source," he said, hanging on to the top of the glass door and pressing a flat palm against the tiles, and then crying out when he opened his back slits where his wings would normally emerge.

His bluish-red blood fused with demon-black blood as the slit hissed and sizzled and oozed sulfuric stench. Finally the site ran pure red blood, and he slowly opened shaky wings that gleamed pure white again under the spray.

Azrael fell forward and held on to the wall, breathing hard. "Can you hand me the soap."

Anxious for anything she could do to help him, she rushed over and opened the door and, without even thinking about it, stepped in behind him fully dressed. With the gentlest of touches, she lathered her hands and then soaped the tender spot between his wings, then allowed her hands to capture his torso and slide soap down his hips and over the swell of his buttocks. Sending love into her hands, she soaped his thighs and calves, the spray of the shower blinding her as water hit the center of his back and cascaded off his wings in heavy runnels.

Rising, she kissed the small of his back, gently parting his wings, then stood to kiss the center of his back and thoroughly lather his wings and shoulders and arms, hugging him from behind.

"I know the Source of All That Is takes care of you guys, and us, but I can help because I love you so, can't I?"

She put shampoo into his locks and kissed his neck as he sighed and relaxed. "Turn," she ordered softly, and put his soapy back into the spray, then gently washed his face with the tips of her fingers, holding his hair under the water and kissing the bridge of his nose.

"I was so worried," she murmured, lathering his

chest and slowly sliding her hands down his body, washing it in increments and gently kissing his stomach until it trembled. "If I ever lost you, I don't know how I would survive. Please don't frighten me like that again," she murmured in a warm rush against his groin, delicately soaping the area and watching his body answer her despite his fatigue.

Catching clean runoff water from behind him, she rinsed away the suds and kissed along his thickening shaft as she washed the front of his thighs and calves and feet, then abandoned the soap to a corner in the tile and rinsed her hands to capture him.

Every part of him had been embattled, but what was truly injured was his pride. An adversary had caused dissension between them using an unclean thing, had made him taste jealousy, envy, confusion, domestic discord—and in front of his team. Feminine intuition let her know that this also needed to be purged.

She allowed her mouth to slowly sheathe him until he groaned, her suckles intended to siphon away the injury to his pride or any residual doubt in his mind that she accepted his circumstances, accepted him as he was. She sent love into each deepening pull as he flat-palmed the wall and gripped the top of the glass door. He created a small enclosure for her as his passion built, blocking the water's spray with his wings, curtaining her in their protection with his head tipped back and his breaths becoming shallow.

He murmured on a deep exhale, "Celeste . . ."

Yes, she knew how to heal with touch and give quiet reverence to a man who'd gone to hell and back for her honor, a man who'd risked banishment and censure and ridicule just because he loved her. It was such a small thing to give him respite, sanctuary in her touch and her caress, without expecting anything from him but his own indulgence right now. He'd done enough, had given enough, and no one took care of him beyond his spirit, none attend to the very real needs of his flesh, of his heart, of his mind.

But as he heaved against her on an agonized wail and released all that conflicted him, she also knew that maybe he had been provided for in those areas, too, after all.

*He sat on their* private deck in a pair of white linen pants, and an Egyptian-cotton shirt he'd pulled through the ether, handmade sandals from an open-air market on his feet. Celeste was in his arms, sitting on his lap, her white linen dress flowing over her legs and catching warm air currents, as did her hair, off the Nile. She had bathed him and brought him peace. He closed his eyes and allowed the wind to speak to him. There had been no answer yet to his request and there was no rushing such things, as he well knew. For now he was content to just be.

"Are you hungry?" she murmured, still resting her head on his shoulder.

He kissed the top of her head and smiled. "I am, now that you mention it, but I didn't want to break this wondrous contentment."

"We can come back here or sleep out under the stars on the top deck," she murmured, kissing his chest.

He smiled. "Maybe we could rest up there until we got sleepy, but if we stayed all night, there is no guarantee I wouldn't cause a scene."

He laughed softly and lifted her head to look at her. Just seeing her face made him reach out to touch her cheek. "I have never known happiness in this way, or contentment like you have shown me."

She kissed him slowly, then pulled back. "Come on, let's eat. If you keep talking to me like that and looking at me like that, we will never get to dinner."

Again she'd made him smile as she slid off his lap and pulled him up to stand. She gave him a sexy wink over her shoulder, a promise for later, and guided him by the hand back into the room and then out into the hall.

Every muscle in his body felt on the verge of being liquefied, but he just couldn't tell her no or not indulge her desire to join the group for dinner.

Middle Eastern music added to the easy trance Celeste had caused as they descended the stairs to the main dining area. His brothers were there, each of them seeming sated and relaxed. Even Isda was calm with a beer in hand. Bath Kol looked as if he were about to slip into a mild coma.

Azrael stepped around the whirling-dervish floor show as the acrobat wowed ship passengers with fast spins and fabric manipulation at maddening speeds. Azrael's brothers made room for them and greeted them with lazy smiles as they edged by.

"You look a hundred percent more chill, brother," Isda said with a lopsided grin. "And as always the lady is beautiful."

"Thank you," Celeste said, taking a seat.

"It's a buffet," Maggie told her with a smile. "Everything is *so* good. Get some."

Azrael stood, but she rubbed his back. "You don't have to walk me. I'll pick around and will bring you back something good, okay?"

"Are you sure?" He looked at her, confused. Angels were supposed to serve humans, not the other way around.

She kissed him on the cheek. "Positive. I know what you like."

He smiled and sat down. She definitely did.

Bath Kol sat forward and grinned. "*So* . . . uh, how're things?"

"Do not start, BK," Azrael said, laughing.

"Heard you took a little tour of Majlis al Jinn and cleaned out a nest all by yourself. Where's Oman? Like, uh, three countries away, on the other side of the Red Sea and on the other side of Saudi Arabia, dude? By Yemen."

"What can I say? I was very annoyed."

Bath Kol almost spit out his beer as he burst out laughing. "C'mon, son. *Annoyed?*"

"Extremely," Isda said, chuckling. "I was dere. He got a little in for you, me, Gav, and Pasch."

"Well, you look extremely relaxed now," Gavreel said, stabbing into his seasoned rice.

"I believe the lady had everything to do with that," Isda said with a wink as Celeste approached with two plates.

Azrael didn't answer him, just hailed the server. "Two waters?" he asked, glancing at Celeste.

"Water is fine," she said, and sat down beside him, setting his plate down in front of him first.

"Really, man?" Paschar said as Azrael looked toward the waiter that was coming to take his drink order. "Not a beer and some wine for Celeste, after going to *Oman* and back?"

"And almost creating an international incident on Oman," Isda said.

"I was not the one with the rocket-propelled-grenade launcher, Isda. My methods were purely supernatural. You, on the other hand, could have made the humans think a neighboring country bombed one of their caves."

"You took *an RPG* out there, dude? What *is wrong* with you?" Gavreel bent over laughing.

"Bring the man a beer and his lady a zinfandel," Isda said to the server. He waited until the server had retreated to continue teasing Azrael. "See, dat kind of pharaoh-of-old-world-badass-crazy fearlessness will get your plate brought to you and set down *first*, brothers. Dat's whot I'm talking about." Smiling broadly, Isda leaned across the table and pounded Azrael's fist.

Celeste laughed and winked at Isda. "It wasn't just the battle—I assure you, brother."

The women at their table whooped and laughed, causing Azrael's brothers to join in. He felt his face warm. He just chuckled and dug into his plate, shaking his head as the whirling dervish left the floor to applause and a gorgeous belly dancer came in.

Isda's eyes immediately went to the hardwood floor where the beautiful young woman performed a sensual, undulating rhythm. The dancer's glistening cocoa-brown skin moved in a hypnotic, serpentine sway beneath layers of delicate, sheer fabric, while the top of her body jiggled her breasts to a dizzying syncopated beat.

Spinning, her gold-coined, turquoise hip scarf gently chimed as she set her smoky gaze on Isda—the only single man at their table. Bath Kol slapped Isda on the back, making the other brothers laugh.

Men at neighboring tables seemed disappointed, but they were all coupled off with wives and girlfriends and clearly unavailable. The belly dancer inclined her head toward Isda, allowing her long, velvety, black hair to cascade down her back, then she winked at him with a brilliant white smile. He lifted his beer toward her with a gallant nod, and a deal was struck without words or translation.

"You see why I couldn't get enough of being here back in the day? Mon, she's got to be a cross between Ethiopian and Sudanese, have mercy," Isda said. "Don't knock on my door till morning, I'm in love."

"So, okay, call me nosy," Bath Kol said, directing the conversation away from the floor show. The crinkles around his eyes deepened as he smiled around the beer bottle he was sipping. "But what happened? Once you got down there, no jinn? None of the folks that we don't name in polite company showed up?"

"No fallen," Azrael said, then looked up from his plate and frowned. "That is odd—I had expected an onslaught. But only general-regulation demons attacked. Normal hell scum."

"More like defended their hole," Isda said without looking at Azrael. His eyes were glued to the dancer's shimmying behind.

"Gentlemen, can we eat in peace?" Aziza said with a smile. "We had the good fortune of everyone returning safe and sound, and not bringing back anything bad with them. Sometimes you just have to learn to accept the quiet as a gift."

Azrael nodded. It was a gift he was grateful to receive.

Chapter 15

*I*n my house? In my house!" Asmodeus bellowed, then smashed the scrying bowl against the wall. "They blinded me to the woman and then he invaded my eastern lair? I will put his head on a pike!"

Forcas remained on bended knee, his long, flowing, platinum spill of hair shielding his face as he waited for Asmodeus's ire to recede. "Only gargoyles and harpies, some vampire bats and a few serpentines, guard that dark sanctuary, now that the other demons have pulled back. They will no longer defend our strongholds with the same level of alacrity they once did. Their position is, what's in it for them? We have no solid answer at this juncture, milord, beyond what they feel are increasingly hollow promises to deliver. Therefore the normal legions are in hiding and are not ready to come forward to risk extermination at this point, milord. The situation is devolving."

"Hiding? Are they insane! They will die at my hand,

then! Without my direct order, they've had *the gall* to pull back from our strongholds?"

"Yes," Forcas said in a lethal murmur, then looked up and stood. "The demons have pulled back because we have failed to deliver. The only reason they suffer our presence is because we are in legion with the Dark Lord. But he is their father. Never forget that. His spawn from Lilith. Therefore, we are in a precarious position as brothers of the Dark Lord, whereas they feel they are true birthright heirs. Our warriors returning weak and disfigured makes the demons grow bold, milord. They see no reason to be our cannon fodder or to guard our outposts when we cannot even guard them ourselves."

"Then together we shall show *all* of our enemies how much pain we can inflict," Asmodeus said through lengthening fangs.

"Calm yourself, milord," Rahab said in an even croon. "At present we don't have enough of an army to attack the demons. There are millions of them to our thousands. That is a fact, not conjecture. The last thing you want to do is to show Azrael your hand." She circled Asmodeus and Forcas, slowly turning herself into a pillar of black smoke. "You are not prepared to put the Avenging Angel's head on a pike, and the last thing you want to do is to allow Azrael to see that your men have been hobbled."

When Asmodeus roared and grabbed at her disappearing form, she calmly reappeared out of his reach on the other side the room.

"Let them grow confident, let them grow bold," she murmured seductively. "Let them expend their resources to find the tablet. Who cares about the damage that was

done in Oman? It was only demons. Unless he truly beheaded your pride?"

*They woke up in* the small port town of Edfu, and after
hastily dressing and grabbing a quick breakfast of fruit
and sweet breads, they entered the dense fray of humanity. Streets too narrow for multipassenger vehicles greeted
them, and cabs were tiny, honking, flylike cars that drove
at insane speeds over terribly paved roads.

Horse-and-buggy cabs lined the dock waiting on
cruise-ship passengers who wanted the most expedient
mode of transportation to the Temple of Horus. But Celeste and the group only needed a moment to understand
that these were not like the leisurely buggy rides that lined
Central Park or lazily clopped along the cobblestones of
Philadelphia's Independence Mall area. These were more
like *Ben-Hur* chariots, with drivers who raced each other
through the streets and seemed to take great enjoyment in
driving their horses to a froth.

The group watched for a moment as drivers took
off with unsuspecting tourists in their buggies and then
waved Egyptian dollars at each other laughing. It looked
like madcap, unregulated harness racing through the
streets of Edfu. Yet it all made sense. The faster a driver
could get his load of tourists dumped at the monument
and return to collect another fare, the more money he
made in a day. No different from conventional cabs in a
busy city, time was money; the more passengers carried,
the more money the driver made in a day. Simple econom-
ics overruled safety.

"Why do I know you are seriously contemplating this?" Aziza said to Bath Kol.

He shrugged and looked at Azrael. "Because all we have is a name and a business address and all the street signs are written in Arabic, and cabbies always know where things are in a small town."

"You do make a point," Azrael admitted, gaining a nod from Isda.

"It's not like we're going to a monument—I know where those are. Here, we're tryin' to find some dude we got a name of," Isda said, yawning and stretching. "But it is a gorgeous day, the sun is out, a little wake-up wouldn't hurt anyone."

Celeste smiled and shook her head as the brothers chuckled. Melissa just sighed, and Maggie shrugged.

"If I fall, I'm killing you," Melissa said to Paschar.

"Don't worry, I have perfect balance," he replied, laughing and heading toward the lead buggy on the other side of the street.

"You're sure about this?" Maggie asked Gavreel.

He just shrugged and jogged across the street with Paschar, which did not inspire confidence. But in a few moments Gavreel waved them over as four carriages jockeyed for position in the street with agitated, prancing horse chaffing at the bit.

"*Yalla, yalla,*" the driver called out, and jumped down off his carriage platform.

Dodging horse manure and hostile pedestrian traffic, they made their way across and climbed into rickety buggies two by two, with Isda jumping to a top perch with a carriage driver.

"Hold tight," the driver said, beaming, then turned and cracked a whip.

The horse pulling their carriage lifted his tail and leaped out into the street, galloping. Each carriage in the convoy followed suit, and then the drivers began the challenges. In hairpin turns around street corners, sometimes a driver would run alongside another carriage trying to overtake him, playing chicken with an oncoming, speeding mini-Toyota. The winner of the contest would laugh and make a lewd gesture to inspire another challenger. Bath Kol's driver nearly ran their vehicle off the road and overtook another, which resulted in a stream of Arabic curses and much fist waving as their driver stood and urged his horse on.

Potholes nearly sent Isda airborne, but the driver knew the street so intimately, he just leaned into the dip like a race-car driver. It didn't seem to bother him that the wooden wheels smacked the ground with a loud crack and came down in a way that felt as if the vehicle were going over on its side wagon-train-style.

Celeste held on to the side of the carriage as open-air markets, stores with no windows, and multicolored buildings strung with laundry lines blowing fabric went by in a blur. Small children, goats, and chickens seemed to be in imminent peril, but paid the drivers no mind. The haggling at fruit and vegetable stands never missed a beat as their rig whizzed by.

The stop in front of Omar's Stone Works was just as abrupt. With much fanfare and indecipherable trash-talk, the winning driver jumped to the top of his carriage platform laughing as his fellow drivers argued in good nature but paid him.

Isda was the first to dismount. "I'm awake now, mon."

"Ya think?" Bath Kol muttered as he lifted Aziza down.

"A regular cab on the way back, that's all I ask," she said, standing on wobbly legs.

"Not the best idea," Isda warned. "At least out in the open you've got a chance one of us will catch you if you tip over. In one of those little sardine cans . . . hey."

"Point well taken," Maggie said, trying to gain her bearing as Melissa grabbed her arm.

"All right," Azrael said, collecting the group to a safe place on the pavement while Gavreel paid the drivers. "We keep this very short." He looked through the open-air courtyard in front of the carving shop through to the back courtyard.

Celeste allowed her line of vision to track Azrael's. Behind the customer area that displayed items for purchase, dozens of guys were sitting on the ground under the shade of an awning, hacking away at granite with sharp objects. They all wore dusty hospital-blue-colored robes and turbans. From the hungry look in their eyes as they assessed each woman as she came through the door, they could have been working on the chain gang for all she knew.

"Yeah, boss," Isda said with a glance over his shoulder, "you don't have to tell us twice."

Bath Kol pounded his fist. "Let's do this."

Entering as a tourist group on the way to the monument, they entered the non-air-conditioned store. A man behind the front desk slowly swatted flies from his arms with a large goat-hair flange.

"Can I help?" He stood with effort, lifting his bulk and smiling slowly.

"We're looking for Omar," Azrael said. "Nazir in Luxor sent us."

"The American—football!" Omar exclaimed, then ushered the group forward with his flange. "Refreshments?"

"No, we're fine, thank you."

Azrael kept his gaze sweeping as Omar moved the group closer to the back of the store where there was bench seating. Celeste watched tension coil in Azrael's shoulders as the men working in the back began watching them.

"I understand you're looking for something very special?"

"I am," Azrael said, glancing past Omar to his workers, who had stopped carving.

Between the time it took her lashes to touch and open in a blink, Azrael had jumped up, drawn a weapon she hadn't even realized he was carrying, and pointed it to Omar's temple. The other brothers were on their feet, with barrels pointed toward the courtyard.

"So, Nazir's into taking hostages, too?" Azrael said calmly. "Figured a wealthy American on vacation with his friends, women along with him, might get lost in a back alley of Edfu—or his woman might, and she'd be worth far more than the piece of stone you bastards couldn't steal. What's a little ransom between friends, right?"

Omar held up his hands in front of his rotund body, his expression holding both fear and shock. "No, no, sir, I assure you, everyone should relax so we can have a conversation about your needs."

"Then tell the son of a bitch that's hiding with a weapon behind door number three to put down the AK-47," Bath Kol said, spitting on the floor. "I'm feeling kinda reckless here this morning. Haven't had my coffee yet."

Omar nodded and Bath Kol relaxed, pulling back his weapon and pointing it to the ceiling.

"You are military as well as football?" Omar glanced around the group.

"No, just from Philly," Azrael said, still pointing the gun at Omar. "What happened to my friend Daoud Salahuddin?"

Several men in the yard stood up.

"Easy," Isda warned, causing Omar to nervously nod again.

"I have nothing to do with anything," Omar said, holding up his hands in front of his jiggling breasts. "My men make *figurines* to sell to tourists, that is all. We may know the guards there and have some cousins so that we can get the best spots and sell more of our wares than others can, but we do not do bad things to people. We see things, we provide information."

"And you transport things out of this little port town," Azrael said.

"A few pieces of art, here and there . . . the laws have changed. It's not fair. After 1972—"

"Blah, blah, blah, a man's gotta make a living," Bath Kol said. "So we heard from Nazir."

"Then you must ask *him* about Daoud. I don't know why he wanted him. That was not my business."

The brothers passed glances among each other, and Azrael pulled back his weapon.

"But you threatened his family," Celeste said, touching the wall and moving closer to Omar.

Aziza nodded. "You handed him over to Nazir."

"It was not my business!" Omar shouted. "He stole something from a big client of Nazir's, and all anyone was trying to do was get that back. What happened in the north country, I do not know. I mind my business here. That is all I do."

"So you weren't given orders to find anything special for me?" Azrael asked in a low, threatening tone. "Nothing at all?"

"No, just to give you something from the shop if you wanted something."

"You lying piece of shit," Bath Kol said, lunging, but Isda caught him. "You were either gonna give us a fake piece of antiquity using your bootleg-copy scribes in the back, or do what my man here said and try to shake us down."

"Picked the wrong fight on the wrong day, *my Nubian brother*." Isda glared at the man and then his henchmen in the back. "We need to get out before we violate the prime edict of not snuffing a human in a rage."

"I feel you, man," Bath Kol said, then spit on the floor. "I am so ready to kill this fat bastard where he stands, you have no idea."

Glancing around nervously and feeling every hair-trigger nerve fraying and popping in the men around her, Celeste looked at Azrael. That Isda had slipped and called Omar a human, which could have revealed to a demon that they were angels, was the tip-off that he was too close to the edge. If they didn't leave soon, the room might explode in sudden violence.

"We'd better get the guys out of here before it gets really messy," Celeste said quietly, keeping her gaze on Azrael. "Even though they are as dirty as sin, there are still a *lot* of *people* in here."

"You tell Nazir I'll see him," Azrael said grimly, as the group backed out of the store.

Once on the pavement, the group jogged a few blocks, trying to get out to a main thoroughfare, which was almost impossible to find among the tightly packed, winding labyrinth of alleys.

"Eyes," Bath Kol said, turning around in a full circle, watching their backs.

Warriors surrounded their female human charges, moving the group forward and trying to stay away from going deeper into blind alleys, which was also next to impossible.

But a small boy zigzagged through their huddle and grabbed the loop in Celeste's jeans.

"Miss, miss, you have to hurry. Come this way to the boats before big man comes."

Warriors stared down at the dirty-faced child. Azrael placed a hand on his head, leaning down with a frown. "Who sent you?"

"Daoud," the child whined, his large, luminous eyes filling with tears. "He still comes to me and my family in my dreams—he is so sad. He said the nice lady who glows inside like an angel would be there and he showed her to me," the boy whispered, and pointed to Celeste. Then he took off running. "*Yalla*. They are bad men. Hurry!"

The child ran like one of the carriage horses unbridled.

His skinny, brown body wended its way through human traffic, dodged cars, and sped down treacherous alleys at a breakneck pace. Every few minutes he'd glance over his shoulder to be sure the group of warriors and women were still behind him. His panic grew more palpable the deeper they got into the residential neighborhoods. Then he made a wrong turn and skidded into a hard body. But like a fleet-footed mountain goat, the child scrambled back, pushed off a wall, dodged the grab of the man—whose eyes were all-black—and zigzagged back behind Azrael, panting.

Instantly the alley filled in around them with human bodies that had black eyes and no souls. The rooftops darkened with predators in human shells. Demons had found them.

"Get down," Azrael shouted, and then flung out his arms, calling his blades in his hands to release in opposite directions, clearing a path. In one swoosh, his blades sliced through chests, viscera, and sent demon screams and black smoke to rent the air. "Wings up!"

A hail of bullets rained down, but every angel trapped in the alley had formed what looked like a Spartan phalanx, covering the women and the small boy. Advancing in slow lockstep, they moved to the edge of the alley, and as soon as they were in the open, Azrael called his blades back, sending them hurling through the air to clear the roof.

Embers burst everywhere. Just then three carriages pulled up to the end of the block and waved them forward. In a mad dash the group hurtled toward them, climbing on as the carriages took off.

"My nephew," their driver from before explained, lifting a rifle off the carriage floor.

He turned the reins over to the child and fired several warning shots from behind Azrael's wings. Every brother was now standing on a carriage roof, balancing and shooting, picking demons off one at a time in awful explosions, while Azrael's blades left scorched earth and cinders. At the water's edge locals screamed and fled as the carriage drivers dismounted and rushed to the small, unofficial dock and climbed onto a motorized fishing boat.

"Yalla, yalla," the lead driver called out, urging the group forward.

One of the other drivers slapped the horses on the haunches to send them dashing in runaway carriages, then ran to help the boat shove off. Half-falling, half-thrown, Celeste hit the deck with the others as they pulled away from the dock.

"Light this water up, gentlemen," Azrael said, breathing hard and scanning the shoreline.

Immediately, Isda, Bath Kol, and Gavreel stood wing to wing facing the water while Azrael and the others watched their backs. Bowing their heads, the angels that faced the water began to get a blue-white glow along the edges of their bodies and wings. Soon that eerie light spilled down onto the ground and into the water, sending a blanket of what seemed like a glowing current over it, which just as suddenly disappeared.

Bath Kol turned with Isda and Gavreel and nodded at Azrael. "Done. It's hot."

"Thank you, now let's move this team," Azrael said, staring at the frightened but willing men in the small craft.

"It's all right," the boy said, watching the panic and fear in his uncle's eyes. "We should go now."

The boy's uncle only mutely nodded, clearly too overwhelmed to protest or ask questions at the moment. But the second the boy's uncle stepped back, the warriors advanced and boarded his vessel. Time was of the essence. They couldn't wait until the frightened men adjusted to what was going on—they had to move.

After quickly jockeying themselves into position, the brothers huddled in the center of the boat, creating a safety ring around the women and the boy.

"My uncle, he sees. He knows," the boy said. "I told him the Mu'aqqibat, the protector angels, would avenge my older brother's death."

The brothers retracted their wings to the wonder of the men driving the boat. The child was in awe, but his uncles were completely freaked out. One man was on his knees weeping, the other was prostrate. Only the boat driver kept his hands on the wheel and his eyes on the rushing current, too overwhelmed to speak. The boy went to Azrael and hugged him tightly around the waist.

"These bad men hurt everybody. My uncles must pay so much to them to drive—now they will have no work and must hide because they helped you. They could do nothing when they took Daoud but beat their chests and hide their wives and anyone that big man might take to make Daoud talk. But Daoud told no one where he hid the gold and glass."

"You saw it?" Azrael said, stooping down to look into the child's eager eyes.

The boy nodded. "Yes, he showed it to me in the water

and said the lady who glows within can see it, too, if she holds my hand."

Celeste moved to the child and squatted in front of him, then looked up at Azrael. "From the mouths of babes . . ."

"And with the innocence of a child." Azrael stood and addressed the weeping men. "Please, stand. You bow only to the Source of All That Is. But I will help you for you have surely come to our aid." He reached into his pocket and gave the men each a large handful of cash. "Keep one bill off this and it will always multiply for you. You family will know vast abundance; your wives, children, and parents will be safe always."

"You must come to the village in Aswan," the boat driver said. "You must please come to bless our houses there, the Nubian village is so poor and the people there are so good. We need protection. This place were we are is just sixty miles from Sudan—you know what has happened there?"

"Az," Bath Kol warned, "we are getting off mission, bro."

"No, it is all part of the mission," Azrael said calmly.

The child nodded. "You can meet your boat tomorrow when it arrives in Aswan. But you come now to the village where the old grandmother who sees is. Daoud came to her and to me. I know what the gold book looks like, she knows where it is. Then tomorrow you get back on the big, big boat. But no demons come into the village because she puts down many prayers. Not even big man comes there because the people there fight fiercely . . . it is our home. In Edfu, it is different. We are overrun."

"The boy speaks the truth," the boat driver said, wiping tears from his face. "Come, please, this is an opportunity of a lifetime for us to serve you; the thing of legends. Let us offer angels our hospitality and a meal and a place to sleep for one night among us."

# Chapter 16

Celeste sat with her arm around the solemn young boy who'd identified himself as Abdullah while the small fishing craft plowed through the water en route to Aswan. Deep melancholy filled her with every one of the child's breaths. Soon she found herself stroking his thick, dusty hair as he snuggled against her for human touch, clearly starved for that, too. The others on the boat watched the dynamic, then allowed their gazes to drift along the distant shoreline, as though watching her and the boy dredged too much emotion from their souls.

"I wish you had come before," the child said suddenly, looking up at her with wide eyes. "My father, he had the sickness, my mother, too. They died. But Daoud took good care of me and my sister—he was studying to be an imam. He was friends with the priest who had come to help people who were sick."

Celeste nodded, unable to speak for a moment past the lump in her throat. She knew the child was referring to the ravages of AIDS, which had left entire villages devastated and so many children orphaned. Just looking into his small face, she remembered losing her own mother at a tender age. But then she'd had Aunt Niecey until she was well grown. This poor child didn't even have that secondary mother figure. Only his uncle.

She hugged him harder, knowing her arms weren't wide enough to circle the globe and to heal all the tragedy within it. But she wished with all her might that she could do something about the one happening to this one small boy and his family.

"The boy is sick, too," the boat's driver said in a weary voice. "The priest came to our village with people and medicine—this is why my brother Daoud worked side by side with him across beliefs. The old man was a Christian, we are Muslims, but we are all human."

"My uncle Kadeem is good to me," the child said. "We are still family."

Celeste could feel her heart pounding harder within her chest as she turned to Azrael and stared up at him. The other brothers and the women in their group looked at Azrael and their sad eyes asked the same question: Could he do it?

The women sitting beside Celeste slid down the white wooden seating so that Azrael could sit next to the boy.

"You are very brave and very strong, even at your age, Abdullah," Azrael said, landing a hand on the boy's back.

"I am not afraid to die," he replied proudly, and sat up straighter. "I have seen others die before me. I will see my parents and my brother and all of the ancestors, if that is Allah's will. So the bad men cannot make me afraid."

Azrael nodded. "You have the spirit of a warrior." He closed his eyes for a moment and slowly his hand began to glow blue, then that light covered the small boy's back. "Only if it is Allah's will can we help people, Abdullah. Do you understand?"

Abdullah nodded. "Yes," he said solemnly. "Daoud told me that we cannot know the mysteries sometimes."

"No, we cannot," Azrael gently. "Even I have difficulty accepting that sometimes."

Azrael shared a look with Celeste, then turned away. In that moment she knew he couldn't heal the boy, and her heart quietly shattered for them both.

"But we all live forever anyway," Abdullah said with a calm shrug. "In heaven it is much better than where I live now, so I am still happy. We do live forever, right?"

"Yes," Azrael said. "You will live forever."

Maggie stood up and walked to the edge of the boat, turning away from them; Gavreel went to her and put an arm around her and looked back at Azrael with a silent plea in his eyes. When Azrael removed his hand from the child's back, the emotions strained to a breaking point on the boat. Aziza closed her eyes as Bath Kol turned away toward the water. Melissa slowly laid her head down against Paschar's chest, while Isda jumped up on the bow and gave everyone his back.

Azrael stood slowly and went to the side of the boat alone. Gazing out over the water, his serious profile reminded Celeste of the ancient pharaoh carvings in black granite. The muscle in his jaw pulsed as he stared at the other passing vessels, then turned slowly to look past the shoulder of the demoralized boat driver, who seemed to understand that Azrael had done all that he could do.

But when a battle-ax slowly materialized in Azrael's fist, the brothers sprang into action, rimming the boat, trying to see what he saw.

A fast-approaching military vessel sped toward them with several men aboard, yelling at the smaller boat. Kadeem released a curse, but then stopped the engine.

"These are Egyptian police," Kadeem said, then spit. "They are Arab, not Nubian, and this is apartheid here that people don't know. This was part of why people gathered in Tahrir Square! Even after the protests, old ways die hard, and the corruption goes on! This is what you don't see on the American news. But we all have lived this for years."

"Put the ax away, brother," Bath Kol warned quietly, going to Azrael's side. "This is just some human bullshit. Do *not* smoke a mortal by accident."

Azrael opened his hand and the ax disappeared.

"We have to pay," Kadeem fumed. "They see Americans on my boat or heard of such on my fishing boat, and they think I am poaching tourist business. I don't have a license to ferry tourists to the monuments or even to my own village! I can only fish. I cannot have friends. I must pay these bribes they will ask. This just lines their pockets and not a penny goes to the actual government. They have moved my people farther and farther south, flooded us when they built the dam and made us move without a care about our lands—now these bribes! Nothing is free—not the land, not the water . . . soon not the air!"

"Rest easy, brother," Azrael said with a frown. "Some things I *can* fix. This is one of them."

"Stop, stop!" an officer yelled, pulling his military speedboat up beside Kadeem's fishing trawler. "You have no authorization to carry commercial passengers!"

*"Asalamu alaikum,"* Azrael said, looking at the lead officer hard. "I'm not a commercial passenger. I'm here visiting my family. I am Daoud's brother from far away, and these are all my family. We are here because we heard he died."

The officer glared at him. "Daoud had no rich American family."

"Solve his murder and you might find out what resources the man had that you don't know about," Azrael said in a booming voice as he leaned into the officer. "Extort my brother Kadeem here, and you will see just how unhappy we all are that Daoud lost his life in an untimely matter."

"We had nothing to do with any of this unfortunate business," the officer said, backing up.

"No, but you turned a blind fucking eye to it," Isda yelled from his position up on the bow. "A lot of t'ings can happen in the dark, bro—police officers go missing sometimes, too, mon."

"Have you threatened me? I am the law!"

"No!" Azrael shouted, his eyes turning blue-white as he pointed upward toward the sky. "The Source is *the Law*! Be gone and never bother my brother or his family again!"

Terrified officers bumped into each other as they stared into Azrael's supernatural gaze. They pushed down on their vessel's throttle full force, speeding away, leaving Kadeem's boat bouncing in their wake.

"What did you show them?" Kadeem said, laughing and amazed. He glanced around at the group, not having seen Azrael's eyes from his position behind the tall warrior's back.

"I showed them their own mortality and what hell looked like from the inside out," Azrael said.

Isda jumped down off the bow. "It's just a little something that he does."

———&diams;———

*Forcas entered the perfume* shop and glanced around. The salesman immediately ran to the back to summon Nazir. An unnatural wind lifted Forcas's long, silken tresses and full-length, black leather coat, so out of place in the arid Egyptian heat. Guards and customers alike stopped and stared as Forcas proceeded to the back of the shop without waiting for an invitation or escort.

Nazir ran out of his back salon, trying to block Forcas from barging in on his most recent customer. "Wait, wait, come to my private office."

Forcas grabbed Nazir by the front of his cotton shirt and slowly closed his fist, then held up his hand to paralyze the approaching guards.

"You did not follow my instructions," Forcas murmured through lengthening fangs. "You were to be our eyes and ears and to simply watch them. But you got greedy and allowed that *fat fuck*, Omar, to try to abduct them? What was your petty little scheme—to shake them down and to get paid twice? Watch them as well as extort one of them for a hefty ransom?"

"No, no, I assure you—"

"*Cease* to speak before I rip out your tongue." Forcas leaned in closer. "Did you invoke the demons for such a task or did they simply seek an opening in your loyalty and seize the opportunity?"

"Demons?" Nazir wheezed, his eyes bulging as he gazed at Forcas's extended incisors. "I do not do sorcery! I am a businessman."

Forcas smiled and released the man. "Of course you don't, but you've already made a deal with the devil nonetheless."

——◆——

*The tables blew over* in Omar's Stone Works as Forcas walked through the front door. Gale-force wind knocked icons off the shelves, scattered receipts and papers off Omar's desk, and made the men working in the stone quarry yard cover their faces with their forearms.

"Emerge, demons!" Forcas ordered, and waited as Omar's body began to tremble and then convulse.

After vomiting green bile all over himself and the floor, Omar threw his head back, and the veins in his thick, meaty neck, temples, and eyes bulged as he opened his mouth and a large, slimy figure the color of bog silt climbed out of his mouth. His human shell dropped to the floor like a discarded skin sack in a grisly pool of blubber and blood. The faceless, slimy entity that had abandoned Omar's body then slowly began to take shape from its previous sluglike form. Gnarled teeth and claws appeared first, then a sunken face and red-glowing eyes emerged from the darkness of its hunched and twisted form.

The entity sneered as others climbed out of the bodies around it, leaving the humans unconscious.

"You summoned?"

Forcas thrust a dripping burlap rice bag forward. "A message from Asmodeus."

The entity cautiously accepted the bag and dumped the contents on the floor. He hissed and the others joined him as Nazir's head hit the floor with a thud and rolled to a stop at his feet.

"Attempt an abduction of our property and my orders will be to replace this bastard's head with yours. As a general warning, and just in case anyone gets any insane ideas or has any delusions of grandeur—do not even *think* about using the tablet for your own legions. The sarcophagus is ours—the body within it is Nephilim. Any attempt to get the tablet to raise your own armies or to negotiate with us because you have acquired the tablet before us will result in war. You may have the numbers, but never forget that we have a nuclear device on our side—the Dark Lord."

*Three hours into the* voyage, Kadeem slowed his engines and began navigating his boat toward a small, dilapidated dock. Immediately children rushed over with vendors and camel drivers, but he and his brothers shooed them away in an agitated flurry of Arabic.

Standing off a bit and watching the strange foreigners with wary curiosity, men in long, one-piece, loosely fitting cotton *didasha* robes seemed dejected that no wares would be sold. Women scowled at Kadeem, holding handmade beads and bracelets that could have been sold to the many foreign females on his boat. But the children giggled and smiled, peeking around the backs of every angel brother and then running away.

The brothers passed uneasy glances among themselves.

"Is something wrong?" Bath Kol asked Isda under his breath as they climbed off the boat and jumped onto the wooden dock.

"I don't know, but it's like they can see our wings," Isda replied quietly.

"I thought we were cloaked, even back in the recent firefight. Normal mortals shouldn't have seen that," Azrael said in a low murmur as the children oohed and aahed. "Only Kadeem, and his brothers and the boy."

"Pure innocence will see the unseen," Gavreel said quietly. "These children haven't been exposed to anything beyond their village, and they obviously believe in us."

"They want you to put your wings out for them," Abdullah said with a wide smile. "They know you have them, they want to see how they come out of your backs."

Azrael stooped down. "That might give their fathers and mothers heart attacks. Not such a good idea."

"No, it won't. It will make the people fight harder to keep your secret and to help them have courage." The child looked up into Azrael's face and touched his cheek. "You worry so much."

Azrael stood, visibly shaken by the child's words, and went to stand with the brothers as the last member of their group debarked from the vessel.

"Messages and signs are coming from this child. Abdullah says we should show the people in the Nubian village our wings so they'll not only help us on our quest, but also protect our secrets and fight our enemies if their village is laid siege to by forces of evil."

The brothers stepped in closer, conferring, and Celeste elbowed her way into the center of their all-male group with the other women.

"I think you guys should do it," she said, challenging their stony gazes. "These people need hope, and their faith is so strong. They *believe* and they would rather die than betray the Light. That's something the darkness didn't count on. The dark side looks at people like this as weak and frail, but their spirits are unwavering. They're literally dirt-poor and still can't be swayed by bribes or loss of life. How else would Daoud have kept his secret here so long? They literally had to drag him away from his people and threaten to raze the entire village if he didn't tell, but they would never give him up."

"What do you think, brothers?" Azrael glanced around the group.

Isda shrugged. "Hey, this is definitely biblical country, settings for the Torah and Quran, mon. If you gwan show the feathers, I think dey could take it better than if you broke 'em out in midtown Manhattan."

"Hey," Bath Kol said with a sigh. "Just prepare the folks, though. I don't want a medical emergency that will require a Lazarus-type resuscitation."

"I feel you," Gavreel said, dragging his fingers through his hair.

"This could be really dicey," Paschar warned. "But if you guys are in, I'm in."

An odd sense of knowing filled Celeste as she listened to the brothers' debate the merits of revealing themselves before more humans, and that knowing encompassed an eerie sense of remembrance. Not in a bad way, but as though she'd walked back in time and was experiencing déjà vu.

"Can I try?" Celeste said, stepping up as the group's spokesperson. "We don't want to invoke terror, but rather inspiration and hope."

"I cannot think of a better person to do that, Celeste." Azrael brushed a wisp of her hair behind her ear. "You will not only be speaking to the hearts and minds of mortals, but to us as well."

She nodded, knowing how much he needed hope after his failed attempt at healing the boy. Glancing at the waiting locals, she walked over to Abdullah and Kadeem.

"Can you gentlemen translate a message for me? We don't want to make people flee or become afraid."

"Yes! Yes!" Abdullah said, about to take off running toward the crowd, but his uncle placed a hand on his shoulder.

"As Daoud's next-oldest brother, and head of our household, I should speak for the main lady who travels with the angels."

Disappointed but understanding, the boy capitulated to his uncle with a hug. "But can I stand at your side when you speak?"

Kadeem lifted the boy and walked forward. "Yes, little man. You will always be at my side."

Celeste followed them, feeling emotion bloom so fast and hard within her chest that tears spilled as she walked forward. Expectant faces quickly gathered at the edge of the dock, and she looked out over a sea of desert-weathered gazes. In them she saw her mother, her grandmother, and her aunts and uncles, father, cousins.

Their eyes held the eyes of generations of people she'd known. Their silent yearning as their bodies leaned forward straining to hear news of another world, another land, another life, shrouded her like another layer of desert heat until she suddenly realized that she'd been in this village before. That knowing slammed into her core and ignited her DNA. Suddenly she felt fused to the people, to the land, to the history, all in one fell swoop of awareness that left her reeling. They were her; she was them. It was all an unbroken chain of lifetimes, and she was *home*.

Brothers walked behind her and she closed her eyes for a moment, saying a quiet prayer that she would speak the right words, then nodded at Kadeem.

"I was born far away from this land, but I am one of you," she said in a reverent tone. "Just as I was taken away by water, I return that way to bring you news that all you've heard is true. There is more to this life than what we see."

Kadeem set the boy down beside him and, in a strong voice, repeated Celeste's words, gaining nods from the crowd. Yet she doubted they fully understood where she was headed with her speech.

"Strong men of war have abused this land and its people for a very long time. Many have suffered and died."

Murmurs of assent and nods rippled through the crowd as some beat their chests and moved closer.

"But a child has seen that there are angels who walk among us. Abdullah came with an open heart and was the first to see . . . then his uncle Kadeem, he and his brothers also saw, and they ferried the angels across the water to visit you."

Kadeem repeated her words with passion, gesturing wildly with his hands. For a moment no one spoke but simply shared confused glances, then laughter rang out.

Crestfallen, Kadeem looked back at Celeste for support, and she looked at the brothers.

"You think now would be the time for a little burlesque?" Bath Kol muttered, stripping off his shirt.

"Wait, wait, wait," Isda said, stopping him with a flat palm to the chest. "These people are very conservative. They may get the wrong idea. Put your shirt on, man."

Celeste went to the edge of the dock when several men scowled and a few women turned away at the sight of Bath Kol's bare chest.

"You all have seen demons, fallen angels—the jinn?"

As soon as what she'd said was translated, the fervor died down and people stood rapt but looking afraid. It was as though something were speaking through her, as if she were channeling the words from something much larger and way more important than herself. But the rightness of the feel of those words as they exited her mouth told her it was coming from a place of Light that she could trust.

Nodding, Celeste walked along the edge of the small dock. "They cause great suffering and destruction, and sickness and corruption. But you have prayed for a sign, just as Daoud prayed for a sign, that there are Allah's Light bearers. His protectors, the Mu'aqqibat, or in Hebrew the *malakhav*, or in my language, just *angels*—all cultures have the winged ones. On the pyramids and in the temples, how many beings with celestial powers are shown with wings? It doesn't matter what you call the Ultimate Source of good or what gender you claim that Source to be, it is the Most High, and that Source is very displeased with the abuse happening to its good creation."

Fervent agreement in tones and words and hands clapping followed Kadeem's translation.

"We bring you a sign to hold on to your Light and your truth," she said, walking over to the brothers and speaking to them privately. "Now would be a good time to lose the shirts, backs to the crowd, and just bust 'em."

Isda laughed and whipped his shirt off over his head. "Maybe this is burlesque after all, BK. But guaranteed, the nine-millimeters in our waistbands are gonna be a problem."

Amid angry jeers and a light pelting of small stones from offended religious men in the crowd, everyone immediately fell silent as each brother's back expanded and then burst forth with pristine white plumage.

Several women fainted. Children shrieked and clapped and rushed the dock. Men fell down on their knees and wept, slapping the sandy shore.

"Having humans bow down is way beyond the rules, Celeste," Azrael said to her over his shoulder in a quiet rumble. "Please make them get up!"

"Yeah, sis," Bath Kol said, joking in a nervous tone, "so what do we do for an encore?"

She held up a finger. "Give me a minute." Then she walked to the edge of the dock again, where mesmerized children stared up as their parents wept. "These angels are a little different from others you may have heard about. Most of them, except a couple, have been here a long time.

They have helped throughout the ages and weep with you. They understand our plight and our weaknesses as humans. They certainly understand mine. So these guys aren't here to judge you—they're here to help you, and all they ask is that you be honest with them and do the right thing by them and others. In fact, you're making them uncomfortable by bowing. They say you should only bow to Allah, the Most High, no one else—no man, no angel, just the Source. So, please get up."

As people stood and slowly realized that a vast terror of judgment hadn't been brought to wipe them out, rapt awe filled their eyes. Celeste took little Abdullah's hand and walked him back to Azrael. She placed the boy's tiny hand in Azrael's, and a few women shrieked, but then calmed when they saw that the child didn't fall away dead from touching an angel.

"Abdullah, take him off the docks with his wings spread and let the children touch them." She looked up at Azrael. "I don't mean to make you feel like you're in some kind of petting zoo, but you guys are like big, scary lions. People have heard so much about the horrors you inflict when vexed or the harsh judgments you cast down, and each person here knows their own imperfection."

She pointed out to the crowd. "That's why they were screaming and covering their faces. You guys have to go down there and walk amongst them, let each person touch you to be able to say, 'Yes, I, too, remember the day when I walked with angels of the Light . . . and they were good and kind and funny and loving, and they didn't beat me down or strike me dead or cast me into the fires of hell for being a flawed human being.' Let the little boy lead you among them. If you walk forward without a child escort, these folks are gonna freak. They'll think you're coming toward them to strike them dead or something, most likely. The kid kinda takes the edge off of that fear and shows you guys came in peace . . . and are gentle giants." She touched Azrael's face. "Please do that for these people, baby."

"How a man gwan say no to somet'ing like dat?" Isda said on a sigh.

Azrael nodded and kissed Celeste's forehead. "There's nothing in heaven or earth I can deny her."

# Chapter 17

*They rode into the* gates of Nubia on camel back across a vast stretch of sienna. Here the Nile narrowed and left no space for cultivation. High dune walls flanked the river with only a thin strip of green contrast like a living ribbon to provide a colorful fringe of life against the endless golden-brown sand.

As they entered the small village, vendors immediately bombarded them, but the people who'd been at the docks shooed them away—telling relatives and friends to put away their wares. Confusion created chaos until the mini camel caravan came to a halt in the middle of an adobe-brick courtyard. Kadeem sent Abdullah to run and fetch the village elders. Spice suppliers looked on with curiosity as the foreign riders dismounted. People created a semicircle as Kadeem breathlessly explained to the elders when they arrived, every adult who had been at the dock providing corroboration.

When the old men and women tried to fall to their knees, others lifted them up and tried to keep them from beating their chests. Then the children surrounded the brothers, urging them to open their wings and show their grandparents the miracle they'd witnessed. Reluctantly the brothers complied.

People wept and made prayer hand gestures toward the sky. But slowly, as the children showed the adults that the angels were safe, the adults timidly came up and touched the brothers' arms and hands and wings.

Bath Kol and Isda were in tears, then just started turning out their pockets, giving money away.

"It feels like the old days," Isda said in a hoarse tone, looking at Bath Kol. "The Most High never said we couldn't, but after twenty-six thousand years, we just stopped. Mon, why did we stop?"

"Because we got tired and people stopped believing in miracles," Bath Kol replied, wiping his face. "We left it to Guardian Angels to do the one-on-one stuff, but I forgot how good this felt."

Gavreel touched vendors' tables, making goods and inventory instantly multiply, and Azrael and Paschar went through trying to heal as much as they could. Then the people did the strangest thing. They sat down on the ground, waiting.

"Teach," one man with sketchy English said, then bowed as he plopped down in the dirt.

Azrael looked at Celeste. "That's not exactly in my gift set, Celeste. What can I teach them? I'm a destroyer."

"Hey," Bath Kol said, holding his hands up, "don't look at me. I never did lessons well, not even in Heaven."

Glancing at the crowd over her shoulder, Celeste looked back up at Azrael as Abdullah came between them.

"Teach them that it's okay to be imperfect, as long as your heart is golden," she said quietly. "Teach them that it's all right not to know all the answers, or to be able to fix everything, even when you really want to with everything within you, and teach them how much the Source loves them no matter what."

"I'm not so good with words, Celeste, you should tell them these things."

She sighed. "Only if you two come with me."

Abdullah took up both of their hands and led them before the waiting people. Everything Celeste said, he repeated, then the little boy stared at her with a serene, open gaze.

"Can I tell them something, too?"

"Of course," Celeste murmured, stooping down to hug him.

The child had never let go of Azrael's hand, and to her surprise, when she let Abdullah go, he tugged Azrael forward.

"This one is big," Abdullah said, then repeated his words in his mother tongue so both groups could understand.

The people watching the boy nodded and some even smiled.

"His heart is so big, he is a champion defender. That was the gift he was given by the Most High Beneficent One." The child paused and stared up at Azrael, having to actually lean back to take him all in. "But even he could not heal me, and this broke his heart. He weeps inside his chest, even though I know I will see Daoud and my mother and father one day soon."

The crowd blurred before Celeste and she watched as Azrael's Adam's apple bobbed in his throat. People who knew the boy's plight began openly weeping, but hung on his every word. Those in the crowd who had been healed looked at the child with empathy and confusion; it was all over their faces—why me and not the boy? I am less deserving.

"It's okay, it's all right," the child said, hugging Azrael around his waist as Azrael lifted his chin to hold back his tears. "This one knows there is Heaven, he comes from there. That is why I am happy now, no matter what. But he also knows now that being alive is a gift, and he grieves for one little boy that he does not know, me, because for one moment, all he wanted to do was to let me see how magnificent this world is. I felt this when he tried to heal me. He tried to give me everything there was inside him. He wanted me to grow up big and tall and proud like him, but he couldn't do it. And this has injured his soul, even though he is loyal to the Most High to the death. But he taught me that even angels weep. So do not be ashamed of your tears. They cry for us and cannot fix all, unless it is supposed to be fixed, and there is a reason. So if you are not as big and strong as the one they call Azrael is, and you have fallen short, you can weep because you are disappointed, but do not weep because you think you have failed. You have not, if you tried your best."

Azrael slowly dropped to his knees and hugged the child to him, his tears spilling over the bridge of his nose onto the child's shoulders. "I tried, Abdullah, I really tried."

"Wrap the kid up," Isda said, his voice breaking as he went to kneel beside Azrael. "C'mon, mon, if we all put in?"

Bath Kol came behind the child and knelt. "You know, old school—one mind, one body, one spirit. Trinity never fails, right?"

"You need female energy for that," Aziza said, wiping her face, and calling over Celeste, Maggie, and Melissa to ring the three angels that touched the boy.

Gavreel surrounded half of the circle, and Paschar surrounded the other half, with open wings.

"Lead the prayer, Azrael," Celeste said through a sniff. "I know he's just one small boy, but we were told that the last will be first and the first will be last and we should all care for the least of us, and all we're asking is for one little boy to get to grow up. Is that so impossible? He could be a doctor, an engineer, a teacher, or a cleric. That's just it—he should have a chance to find out. And God knows this child's heart is pure, even after all he's seen. We're just begging for a little mercy, a little Light to come through the darkness of the badlands down here. His mama is gone, his daddy is gone, his big brother is gone, what more?"

Celeste's voice broke with a sob and then she quickly apologized, "I'm sorry, say the prayer. I just—"

"That *was* the prayer, Celeste," Azrael said quietly. "Amen."

A rumble of amens traveled through the small circle, and as everyone pulled back, Celeste hugged Abdullah and patted his back.

"You are so loved, sweetheart, and you have taught us far more than we could have ever taught you."

An elderly woman in the back of the crowd stood and made her way to the front of it as each angel stood up. She spoke in a flurry with tears streaming down her weathered cheeks, gesturing with her hands.

Kadeem wiped his cheeks with rough, broad palms. "She says the boy has brought the angels to their knees. He has humbled them on their journey, which is the lesson for us, too. None of us is too great to be humbled. If the angels can bow to the innocence of a child, then we should, too. The children are the future. Women and men together working for the good of the future, like the one crying woman who speaks with the voice of an angel said to us. We have just witnessed a miracle."

The elderly woman closed her eyes and turned her face up to the sky and beat her chest with her gnarled fists. "My great-grandson is no longer sick. He has the white light around him now. There is no black spot in it. The power was in you all working together, not one trying alone. A bundle of many sticks is not easily broken. We must stand together as people against evil!"

A loud murmur broke out in the crowd as Kadeem swiftly turned to the brothers and then crushed his nephew to his side.

"Grandmother has visions. Everyone here knows her word is truth. Please, look at the boy and tell me—we must be realistic and not have false hopes. I don't want to not have him treated and then—"

"Wait," Azrael said, pulling the child away from Kadeem's side to inspect him. After a moment, two huge tears rose in Azrael's eyes. "I can't feel any sickness in him, nor can I see it." He reached out to Bath Kol. "Look at him, all brothers. Hope can sometimes make one's eyes see what we wish for, not what is."

"Den we're all going blind," Isda said on a ragged whisper, and shook his head. "I don't see it no more."

"Me either." Celeste shook her head with Aziza.

Kadeem raised the child's arm, then lifted him up and yelled out, "The boy is healed!"

Pandemonium broke out in the crowd; Kadeem didn't even need to translate.

Celeste watched the brothers weakly smile and then let their bodies slump with relief. Jubilant voices rang out and people rushed to go to their homes to bring a spontaneous potluck feast together. Vendors closed their stands. A miracle transcended money as everyone headed to Kadeem's compound.

Threading her arms around Azrael's waist, Celeste leaned against him beneath a wing, walking down the dirt path with a hundred festive people skipping beside him. He looked down at her at the same time she looked up.

"I know," she said quietly.

"If we couldn't have . . ."

"I know. But you guys did."

"We all did, you leading us. . . . But maybe we should pull in our wings now?"

"Uh-uh, they make the people happy to see them. Leave them out for a little while."

He released a sigh. "I'm not used to this kind of attention, the indulgence makes me uncomfortable."

"What have we learned today?" She smiled up at him,

wanting so badly to kiss him, but she would never do that in public among people where such a PDA might deeply offend.

"A lot," he admitted as they entered the enclosed mud-brick courtyard of Kadeem's home.

"Then you should also know that people get joy out of giving to others and seeing that they've made the receiver happy. Azrael, you all have made these people's lifetime. They just want to offer you some bread and wine and water to say thank you for touching their lives. *Let them* do that and be a gracious receiver."

He stopped walking and turned to her, letting the throng pass into the space around them. "Celeste, that's it. You know how you've kept asking me how does one voice, your voice, turn on the lights at the end of days?"

"Yeah . . ."

"Well, look what you just did." He glanced around. "It was your understanding of how we should approach these good people and make ourselves known. *You* were the one who had the wisdom to usher us in with the boy. *You* were the one who wept for him first. You were the one who said we had to teach, and then insisted that I try—but the child became the professor and I became the student before an entire village . . . and that became the lesson for me, for them, for my brothers. And then we had to learn that it was about pooling our gifts, the synergy of combined effort . . . something over the years we'd slowly forgotten."

He let out a deep sigh as he touched her face and let his hand fall away for the sake of propriety. "The layers of this are profound, Celeste. It was your prayer, your out-loud, heartfelt request that Heaven hear you that made her open her gates to the boy and rain down mercy on him. I felt it as you were speaking. Ask any of the brothers, we are attuned to that vibration. And it was the boy's very simple acceptance of his circumstance, without anger or self-pity, that made the lesson even deeper for us, and that child's transcendence—"

"It wasn't me," she murmured, then bit her lip as she thought about it. "He came to you wide-open, unafraid, and *knowing* there was something else out there."

"Yes, there was that, as with all the children, which is why we are told to come to the Light as a little child, trusting," Azrael said. "But it was *you* who saw all the elements of this lesson unfolding and knew how to blend them together across cultures and across varying levels of understanding—without judgment . . . and the people felt that. Even as they laughed at you, you stood your ground, and you did not judge them. Just as when we first met, you did not judge me."

"How could I judge you, Az? With my past, I definitely can't cast the first stone."

"You could have, but you didn't, and more than that, you accepted me and my difference. Even today, when I so bitterly disappointed your hopes to heal that child on the boat, I didn't feel judged or that your disappointment was aimed at my failure. You were disappointed for the sake of the child alone. That is a pure emotion. A selfless one. I now better understand your gift, Celeste. You convert the darkness into the Light . . . even I cannot do that."

"C'mon, you guys," Bath Kol said with a wide grin as he bound toward them, "you're missing the party!"

Pushing them forward, Bath Kol entered the wide

mud-brick room with them and the space had become an instant house party. Sky-blue and white paint made the small, lantern-lit area bright. Murals of pastoral scenes and butterflies added to the gaiety indoors. Wrought-iron chairs, wooden benches, and rusty three-legged stools balanced precariously on the uneven dirt floor. A large steel washtub rested under a well-pump spigot by the door so people could take off their shoes and wash their feet upon entry.

Every age range of women brought food to the tables—fruit, honey, warm whole-wheat pita bread, dried dates, olives—and the buffet just kept coming. Spice vendors left fragrant fresh-ground peppers and herbs in small stone cups, then backed away from the table and the angels with a deep bow. Men brought over bottles of homemade beer and wine and shyly left them for the brothers. Aromatic tea and strong coffee were offered in a way that made it impossible to say no. Incense was left in bundles, some set to burn around the room. Fabrics got left on the chairs, and even small children brought beaded goods and candles to leave on the buffet, which was quickly turning into a makeshift altar. People had emptied their homes and their larders.

Then Kadeem bowed and yielded the floor to Azrael to bless the meal. Each person who was crammed into the room seemed as if he or she were holding his or her breath in case Azrael made another miracle occur while their eyes were closed.

Then the music played.

With eating and dancing and clapping, a celebration of life was in full swing. Finally the old seer came to

Kadeem and whispered something in his ear, and he came to Azrael and Celeste to murmur confidentially.

"She wants to speak to you alone in the back. Is that all right?"

"Of course," Celeste said, standing quickly with Azrael.

"Good, then come this way."

Following Kadeem past the partying throng, they left Abdullah to translate for the group. In a small courtyard behind the main building was a little mud home with a piece of red fabric serving as a front door.

Gesturing with her hands, the old woman smiled a toothless grin and sat her bent frame down on a hard wooden stool with a grunt. She smoothed her gnarled hands across the white, embroidered tablecloth, then held both Celeste and Azrael in a cataract-impaired gaze.

As she spoke slowly, Kadeem interpreted, glancing between the old woman and Azrael and Celeste.

"She says you are the ones Daoud had prayed for, but never lived to see. My grandson was a good man and he said the angels would protect what he has guarded."

The old woman wiped her eyes with trembling hands and let out a soft sigh.

"Grandmother says . . . there is a guard at Abu Simbel, not far from here—an honest man that Daoud once helped. She says my brother helped bring in the doctors through the priest when his wife was very sick. She almost died and could have taken the unborn child with her when trying to give birth to his first son. This man had Daoud say a prayer and his wife got better. This man swore allegiance to Daoud, if he ever needed help. On the life of his firstborn son, this man would never betray Daoud. He is the keeper of the key."

Celeste and Azrael shared a look. The old woman nodded.

"She says Daoud wouldn't tell her exactly, for fear bad men or demons might try to come and wrest it out of her. She says, 'I am old and weak, they are big and strong. My great-grandson didn't want me to be in jeopardy. So he told none of us where this thing is that you seek. He didn't tell the boy, either, but the boy knows what it looks like.'" She waited until Kadeem nodded. "It is an alphabet—words, carved in gold inside thick, thick, clear stone. This is what Abdullah says to her when he dreams and cries for Daoud. Then because of the child's constant lament, she dreamt of this thing, too. It was down deep in the Nile and in a locked chest. A man with a key opened it using a life symbol. That is what she saw in her dreams."

"A life symbol would make sense as a dream interpretation," Azrael said, glancing at Celeste.

But the old woman shook her head and frowned when Kadeem translated Azrael's statement. In a flurry of Arabic she called for a pencil and paper. Once Kadeem had produced it from a kitchen cupboard, she leaned over the paper closely and painstakingly drew the symbol of an ankh.

Pointing at the paper, she stared deeply into Azrael's eyes and spoke in a firm, confident tone.

"She says this is what the key itself looks like. A man has this key for his job and also around his neck in metal. He works at Abu Simbel. Take Daoud's prayer cloth to him and show him your wings. That is the only way he

will take you to the place in the water where he dropped
the chest that holds the glass and golden book."

"How far is Abu Simbel from where we are jus
outside of Aswan?" Celeste looked between Azrael and
Kadeem.

"Two hundred and seventy kilometers, roughly," Kadeem said.

"I'm not good on the conversion." Celeste looked a
Azrael.

"That would be about one hundred and sixty-eigh
miles, give or take," Azrael said. "About three and a hal
hours, based on the state of the roads and assuming Isda
can get us reliable transportation in short order."

"I know people who have vans and minibuses. They
make money from tours. I can ask them for a family emergency," Kadeem said.

"We would compensate you and your friend if you
could make that happen quickly," Azrael said. "Plus i
you could provide a map."

"No compensation will be accepted," Kadeem said
slicing his hand through the air. "No. Your money is no
good. I am in the presence of the divine who has come to
avenge my brother's death."

"You saw in the market back at Edfu, we have people
and demons, chasing us." Celeste reached out and hel
Kadeem's arm. "You have a family, and you have Abdul
lah, and—"

"And you saw that I am not afraid to fight or die, yes?"

Neither Celeste nor Azrael answered, not wanting to
be responsible for the injury or death of an innocent mar
who'd so quickly come to be their friend.

"You are very brave," Celeste hedged.

"I am a believer. My little nephew says to me, the good people in the carriages are in danger to bad men and demons, and without a thought I run to not allow this. I know what they did to Daoud—they spilled his blood for money and make my family weep. I know these roads, and the guards at Abu Simbel know me. They will be wary of you but I can get to Daoud's friend to coax him somewhere private so he can see the truth. I can come up with excuses and speak in Arabic to the guards so he can slip away to take you where you must go. I am useful to you, and if I die or get hurt, it is my honor to die for the cause of angels . . . and for my brother."

# Chapter 18

*N*ubian villagers sent them off as if they were
soldiers going off to war. Tears and hugs, food
and back pats, everyone touched them, sending
love and energy that needed no translation. One could feel
their hope for success through every gentle and not so gentle hug. Village women bitterly wept, loudly so, as a purge
for everyone's soul, while men echoed their well-wishing
by loading the vehicle with supplies that they'd never use,
and children jogged beside the bus waving good-bye.

For the better part of the three-and-a-half-hour drive,
no one spoke, their emotions still raw and the revelations
at the village from simple, good-hearted people still unfolding within them.

One thing was clear, even though it went unstated:
they didn't want Kadeem there. It had nothing to do with
his bravery or skills or his integrity, but everything to do
with vulnerability. If something happened to him, no one

on that bus would be right with it—just as if anything happened to the village, there'd be no way to accept it.

Celeste kept her gaze focused out the window, quietly processing all that she'd seen and learned in such a short time. Azrael had told her that more would be revealed as the great cosmic clock wound down to the planetary alignment of 12/21/12. Time would change as the veil began to open, as planets shifted into place to line up to the galactic center. A day would pass in a flash; hours would zoom by like minutes . . . she was definitely experiencing that weirdness in sped-up time as new experiences were crammed into her life. How could she absorb and make sense of it all? The only way she could cope was to surrender, to float on the essence of just being.

That's what she did now, casting her gaze out over the dark-gold landscape on her west side with the Nile on her east as they headed south, and simply let her thoughts flow free like the river.

Slowly impressions flitted through her mind. Memories just outside her grasp teased the edges of it in a game of hide-and-seek. The landscape, as old as time itself, hadn't been too dramatically changed, except for the modern road. But all around it were markers of civilizations gone by.

Fatigue from the heat and emotional duress tugged at her eyelids and made her head heavy, until she finally surrendered into a nap. Images continued to pass through her mind as the bus struggled and whined in and out of gears.

Then she knew why she'd disliked the camel ride so much. Miles and miles of caravan had brought her from Nubia on an annual family trek to trade in the west.

Celeste felt her body stiffen as the thunder of a thousand horse hooves pounded the earth. Men in blue turbans attacked the caravan—Berbers trading slaves . . . and she was no longer with her mother or father. Blood soaked the ground. Then everything went dark until the next image entered her mind. She was weeping and standing in Independence Mall? The mental switch was so jarring that it shook her out of her sleep.

Celeste awakened with a start, causing Azrael to turn toward her and take up her hand.

"Are you all right?"

"My mother was from Philae and my father from the village we just left . . . and only nine of us were in a house in Philae. I was there with people I didn't know and very powerful men. They didn't hurt me, just ignored me, and I worked there my entire life. Sometimes I would hear them talk about ideals that didn't apply to me." She pulled back her hands and rubbed her palms down her face.

Slow awareness filtered through her bloodstream until the emotions caught up with her colliding thoughts. She'd been sold into slavery. The pain that surrounded her spirit stole her breath for a moment, physically made her slump. To be a human being but not to be treated as human, to have one's life only considered for the service of others and to be so disregarded as a domestic stock animal . . .

"Celeste, talk to me," Azrael whispered, monitoring her body language.

"I was a slave. In Philadelphia."

He closed his eyes and kissed her forehead. "I know, beloved."

Tears filled her eyes as outrage filled her heart. "I wish

I had never remembered that part, that incarnation or whatever the hell it is. That era was so . . ."

"Dark and brutal," Azrael said, holding her hand.

"Then why did it come back? Why was it necessary to pollute my mind?"

"Because there's a link. The word *Philae* or *Philly* and *Philadelphia* have been mentioned too many times before we came and once we got here not to take note. Now you are remembering, now that we are near Philae." He stroked her hair and gently pulled her against him. "I'm sorry you experienced that abomination in one of your soul's lifetimes."

She nodded and kept her gaze out the window as she leaned against him. "But if I hadn't, maybe I wouldn't have known the people in the village so well."

"Perhaps . . . or been received like a returning daughter," Azrael murmured into her hair. "But there are also gentler ways to learn lessons, Celeste. That is my prayer for you until the end of time—that all your lessons be visited upon you as gently as the ones you've taught me. The universe can sometimes be a very hard taskmaster. I don't want that for you."

"We have to park and get tickets and walk from here," Kadeem announced, going into his pocket to pay for the entire bus. When Bath Kol leaned forward with a fan of bills, Kadeem waved him off. "My pocket keeps refilling," Kadeem said, laughing. "The big man, Azrael—thank you!"

Azrael chuckled and stretched. "You're welcome."

"Man, this is no time to be moving like you're ready to take a nap—we've gotta hustle," Isda said, standing. He paced two steps in one direction, then paced two back like a caged panther. "I cannot wait until you see this, man!"

Azrael just shook his head as passengers on the bus came out of their own thoughts to mentally rejoin the group. After a bit of jockeying, Kadeem found a spot, then jumped down from the bus quickly to lend a hand and urge the group forward.

"*Yalla, yalla* . . . the park will close soon, so we have to hurry to find Daoud's friend."

The warning got people moving, and they jogged and power-walked a half mile down a steep asphalt road that plunged into a valley behind a mountain on their left and the jewel-green Nile on their right. Running ahead of them, Isda stood in the middle of the road and held out his hands.

"Do not look to your left until I tell you, all right?"

Laughing, the group grudgingly agreed as they kept their gazes on to the ground.

"Come on, brother, we don't have time for . . ." Azrael's words trailed off as he looked up.

For a few seconds the group came to a complete halt. An entire mountain had been turned into a living temple. Carved into solid granite were four colossal statues of a seated pharaoh. Blazing orange-gold sun painted the sandstone-hued temple in metallic splendor. People looked like ants at the footstones of kings, and adjacent to that temple was a smaller but no less spectacular one with feminine flourishes on it for a queen.

"*Dat* is Ramses the second," Isda said, taking a bow. "Wait till you see inside the Hypostyle Hall—every room carved from the rock where it stood—they went in there and carved because what's inside is bigger than the doors . . . and they followed such strict mathematics that on his birthday the sun rises on his face! Without fail! Every equinox the sun rises on a different aspect of him when it comes up over the horizon, through the front doors, down the long corridor to the holy of holies, and *bam*."

"Oh, yeah," Bath Kol said, nodding as the group pressed on. "Angels definitely had a hand in that."

"You think?" Aziza said, completely awestruck like everyone else.

"But we must hurry," Kadeem said, beginning to run.

Following him to the front doors was like running the length of two football stadiums. The ancients definitely did things on a grand scale, and the more Celeste thought about it as she ran, everything they'd built seemed as though it was designed to be seen from an aerial view. Now it was all beginning to make sense. What if a bunch of fallen angels clashing with angels of the Light had been the ancient extraterrestrials the hard-boiled alien-conspiracy theorists were trying to prove existed?

But the stitch in her side and the unrelenting heat made her abandon random musing. By the time they'd reached the massive thirty-foot-high front doors of the temple, she was gulping air to catch her breath.

"Where is the normal key keeper?" Kadeem said, panicking.

A suspicious guard frowned and then regarded the group. Kadeem thrust tickets into his hand with a sizable tip. The guard smiled and produced a two-foot-long brass key in the shape of an ankh and handed it to Celeste with a smile.

The two men exchanged a flurry of Arabic, then the man seemed to recognize that they didn't want a picture taken at this late hour with the temple's main-door key, but were looking for the man who normally stood there.

"He is smoking. We must find him and hope he doesn't leave to go home early," Kadeem said, jostling them forward past the last of the tourists.

Quickly passing the massive interior columns, Kadeem became frantic, circled a corridor twice, then dashed back out in the opposite direction.

"He is a good man, a religious man, and respects the temples of the ancestors. If he is smoking, it would not be inside, where the other guards like to take their breaks."

Crossing the massive courtyard in the opposite direction, Kadeem headed toward the Nile, and a white, hot concrete meditation deck with a series of benches. The small lunch area was fenced in so one could overlook the water without falling in. A lone guard sat in the waning sun with his back toward them staring out at the water. No tourists seemed ready to brave the unshaded Egyptian sun when a naturally stone-cooled temple was just a couple of football-field lengths away.

Kadeem stopped for a second, placed a hand over his heart, then resumed running as he called out, "Muneer! Muneer! It is Kadeem—Daoud's brother!"

"Kadeem?" The man named Muneer turned, stood, abandoned his weapon on the bench, and flung down his cigarette butt to embrace Kadeem.

After a warm reunion with Muneer in their mother tongue, Kadeem turned to the group behind him and spoke to Muneer in English. "So that my friends understand . . .

and they are also friends to Daoud. Do not be worried, I was not tricked. These are not bad men. They are angels."

An expression between pity and despair crossed Muneer's sad, dark expression. "I miss him, too, Kadeem, but we must not allow wishes to replace reality." Muneer sighed, then regarded the group with a hard frown. "It is not right to trick a grieving man. Have you no heart?"

"Block me, so we don't panic this whole complex of tourists," Azrael said to Isda, and stripped off his shirt. Azrael then looked at Kadeem as Muneer moved for his AK-47. The guard had spotted the nine-millimeter Azrael was carrying and had obviously jumped to conclusions. "I hope your man has a strong heart, because we obviously do not have time for Celeste's gentle preamble. I would just appreciate not getting shot right now."

Kadeem held his friend's arm gently to lower it. "Trust me, what you will see is Daoud's dream. Do not harm these beings sent from Allah."

Azrael spread his wings. "Yeah . . . Allah, Yahweh, Jehovah, God, the Source of All That Is, Buddha . . . the Most High has a lot of names, and we don't have time to go into all of that at the moment. What we need and would appreciate is your cooperation."

Kadeem caught his friend as the man covered his heart and his legs gave out. Azrael walked over to him and turned around, giving Muneer a full, close-up view of his wings.

"They're real."

Celeste went to Azrael as Isda helped Kadeem sit Muneer down easy on a bench.

"Baby, back off," she said, touching Azrael's shoulder.

"I knew we should have brought some water off the bus."

"Here," Aziza said, digging in her large, tie-dyed shoulder satchel and producing an unopened bottle of water for Muneer. Who was clearly too terrified to accept it.

The poor man just sat there, looking shell-shocked. His jaw was slack, his limbs floppy, and he seemed to be on the verge of actually passing out.

Azrael retracted his wings and yanked his shirt over his head. "So, are we good?"

"Man, you don't do subtle, do you?" Bath Kol said with a half smile.

"Not when the sun will set soon," Azrael replied, glancing at the horizon.

"Our brother's got a point," Gavreel said, then sat down beside Muneer, who looked to be on the verge of both weeping and running screaming across the courtyard. "Let me conduct a little peace into his spirit."

"Make it do what it do, mon," Isda said as he held Muneer still long enough for Gavreel to grasp his head between his palms.

Slowly but surely Muneer relaxed, then looked up at all the brothers and nodded. He pulled a long metal dog-tag chain up and out of his guard's uniform, and on the end of it was a heavy, beautifully engraved sterling-silver key in the shape of an ankh.

"Daoud saved my son," Muneer said in a rasp, and finally accepted Aziza's water. He opened it and took a deep sip, never loosing eye contact with the group. "I promised him that I would never tell where he'd dropped the chest. I don't know what's in it. That never mattered to me. I told him that, just as I am the key keeper for Ramses's temple, I will be the keeper of the key for him and will guard his treasure—whatever it is—just as well. I never broke my word to my friend. He was like my brother, and I fear the bad men took him and harmed him. Now, seeing an angel, I know this is so."

Tears wet Muneer's handsome brown face, and he turned the ornate key over and over in his fingers as though it were a worry bead. "They killed him for what was in there, yes?"

Both Kadeem and Azrael nodded sadly.

Muneer quickly took off the chain and held it out to Kadeem. "Then this was no treasure; it was a curse if it took a good man's life. I want no more to do with it. I sadly give you, as his next-oldest brother, your inheritance."

Kadeem closed his fist around the key and briefly shut his eyes. "I don't fully understand what's in there, either. But I know it belongs to the angels, not to me. Evil tried to find this and rob this from their temples." He opened his eyes and Muneer nodded to him, then Kadeem handed Azrael the key. "I don't know where it is in the Nile. The river runs from Uganda where it begins and flows up the continent all the way to the Mediterranean."

"I was there with him that day," Muneer said quietly. "The chest was too heavy to lift alone. We went by sailboat to Philae Island and dropped it in the sacred waters by the restored Temple of Isis. Then he prayed over the water that demons would be blinded to its location forever." Muneer looked up. "When he said demons, I thought he meant just bad men. When he said angels, I thought he spoke in . . . just hopes for goodness and protection to come from above. I never . . . I . . ."

"It's all right," Celeste said, placing a hand on Muneer's shoulder. "Neither did I when I first saw one."

*To the dismay of* everyone on the bus except Kadeem and Muneer, their party had increased by another mortal man. But Kadeem's and Muneer's argument held weight. Muneer had a weapon, a pretty good one, which could be retrofitted with angel-blessed shells on the way. His AK-47 added to the arsenal of nine-millimeters the brothers carried in their waistbands. Every woman was packing now, too, just in case. Kadeem knew the driving terrain and could get to the small port quickly, plus the man was an expert at navigating the dangerous cataracts and eddies should they encounter any, in the Nile. Muneer, quite simply, knew where the treasure was dropped. That settled it.

But two and a half hours to get to a place where they could acquire a vessel, a half hour of haggling and finding the right craft for the job—one that the owner would not come along on, with at least another hour on the water, put them at the very vulnerable hour past sunset. The brothers would have to go trawling for the chest in near blue-black river water.

"It was right here," Muneer said as Kadeem maneuvered the craft into position.

Celeste's gaze followed Muneer's outstretched arm. Daoud couldn't have picked a more beautiful resting place for the sacred tablet. Breathtaking temples nestled high on the steep banks of Syenite stone and kept watch over the Nile with graceful colonnades and tall pylons.

With a weary sigh, Bath Kol started taking off his Timberlands, then stripped his shirt off and placed his gun on the boat bench. The other brothers followed suit, studying the ripples on the water and dark shoreline like Navy SEALs.

"Be sure to light it up when we go down there," Azrael warned, then slapped Paschar in the center of his chest with a broad palm. "You and Gav are boat security." He gave the key that was on a long metal dog-tag chain back to Kadeem, looping it over his head, then pointed with two fingers toward Bath Kol and Isda. "You take port side, I'll take starboard."

"And you ladies can hold it down with some serious prayer," Bath Kol said, looking back at the darkening sky.

"Done," Aziza murmured, then slipped one hand into Celeste's palm and another into Maggie's. Maggie in turn grabbed Melissa's hand.

The three divers sat on the edge of opposite sides of the boat for a moment, then inhaled deeply and went over the side backward.

"They don't need oxygen?" Muneer said, amazed.

"They're angels," Kadeem replied with confidence, but still peered over the side in awe.

Balancing out their weight after their prayer, the women split into two groups to watch over the side of the vessel. Soon Celeste could see a blue-white glow moving under the water. The eerie light looked thoroughly extraterrestrial from where she stood, and she doubted any Nile crocs would go near the strange beings that had invaded their habitat.

Bath Kol came up and sucked in a huge inhale but shook his head.

"Told you to stop smoking," Gavreel said, smiling.

Bath Kol gave him the finger and went down again. Muneer stared at Kadeem, clearly shocked.

"These angels aren't the ones with harps and cherub's cheeks," Paschar said through a chuckle. "They may be colorful, but they get the job done."

More than forty-five minutes went by with the brothers intermittently surfacing for air, shaking their heads no, and diving again. Silent worry began to set in, and night rolled a blanket of dark-blue velvet over the sky, then punctuated the late hour with moonlight and twinkling stars.

"Water can make things drift—" Kadeem said, accepting one of Muneer's cigarettes.

Nerves on end, Celeste looked at Kadeem's cigarette as he took a drag, almost needing one herself. Three months clean felt like a lifetime.

"I've got almonds in my bag," Aziza said calmly, giving Celeste a meaningful look.

"You wouldn't happen to have a flask in there, too, would you?" Melissa said, lifting her hair off her neck.

Maggie dropped forward to lean on her knees. "What if they can't find it?"

"Plan B, I guess," Celeste said, staring at the lights in the water.

"What's Plan B?" Maggie looked up.

"Armageddon," Paschar said flatly.

"Would you allow *me* to dispense the peace on the ship?" Gavreel said, punching Paschar in the arm.

"Ow! Well, it's the truth." Paschar rubbed his arm.

"Truth doesn't always inspire peace, dude. So, if you can't say something positive, just chill."

But as three lights flowed together under the surface of the water on Celeste's side of the boat, she stood. "They're coming up!"

Chapter 19

**B**ent over the side of the boat, her heart beating a mile a minute, expectation mixed with adrenaline, Celeste held her breath. The wind had kicked up, blowing the first cool breeze she'd felt since they'd arrived in Egypt. But the hair also stood up on the back of her neck.

As the wind kicked up behind her, she glanced over her shoulder at the same time Gavreel, Paschar, and Aziza turned. In the distance small sand dervishes had begun to form on the steps of the temple, and an unnatural wind moved the lush palms and thick green foliage on the bank.

Gavreel and Paschar went to the opposite side of the boat, straining to see, causing the others to divide their attention between the brothers coming up from beneath the water's surface and the riverbank.

"This happens all the time," Muneer assured them.

"Small sandstorms. This is the *holy* island of Philae, the Pearl of Egypt, and it is why Daoud chose this place."

"But the original island is the one that was holy. That one was flooded when they put in Aswan Dam. This one wasn't the site of thousands of years of sacred prayers, so they must have had to put down prayers to protect it," Kadeem said quickly, glancing between the angel brothers and his friend Muneer. "The government dismantled the entire temple and rebuilt it here. If my brother dropped his chest here because he thought prayer of the land and water protected it, that barrier had been disturbed years ago. Tell me he consecrated the grounds again."

Gavreel and Paschar took one look at each other and then shouted in unison, "Incoming!"

"Down, down, everybody get down!" Gavreel shouted, taking to the air with his nine-millimeter drawn.

Paschar went up on the top of the boat's pilothouse roof, guarding the human passengers with his gun and Bath Kol's in his hands. But as soon as he had, a huge tail slammed against the side of the vessel and sent everyone sprawling.

A massive croc with red, gleaming eyes and twice the size of the boat disappeared under the surface as Muneer scrambled to his feet and grabbed his weapon to begin squeezing off rounds. Suddenly the air was filled with leather-winged gargoyles that screeched and dove at Gavreel as he fired at them, using two hands, to blow them out of the air.

Beasts with clenched, yellowed teeth swooped down, eyes gleaming red in contorted, flesh-ravaged faces. The smell of sulfur polluted the air in their wake, as gray-green bodies tried to slash and grab at the boat's inhabitants with razor-sharp claws and bull-whipping spaded tails.

Using both hands, Celeste, Maggie, and Aziza popped off rounds, splattering demon gook everywhere and making it rain black and green.

"That thing in the water!" Melissa screamed, then blindly squeezed off rounds at it over the side of the vessel. "How can that be? It's holy water!"

"Natural beast with something inside it," Paschar said, then looked at Muneer. "It can die from normal bullets—stay on it!" Then he joined Gavreel in the aerial offensive, trying to keep the mass of gargoyles from reaching the boat.

An army of hooded demons bearing scythes and blades erupted from the sand and shore. Nothing was in the hoods but dark, skeletal faces and red, gleaming eyes. Their haggard hands were weathered gray-green skin that peeled away to expose claws and bones. Kadeem pushed Muneer down just in time to miss a whirling scythe that would have taken both of their heads, as Celeste and her sisters flattened themselves to the deck and kept their heads down.

To Celeste's horror, she saw a chest rise to the edge of the boat above her. She would know the hands that held it anywhere. Risking it all, she lifted her head and scrambled toward the surfacing Azrael and leaned over the side. He came up with Bath'Kol and Isda and sucked in a huge inhale.

"We're under attack!" she shouted, trying to help drag

the chest over the edge of the boat so they could get out of the water to fight.

It only took a second, and with a powerful upward thrust, all three brothers were out of the water and standing on the deck, wings spread, water cascading from their hair and over their heaving chests. Azrael dropped the heavy metal box that was crusted with river sediment and took three running steps to go airborne, battle-axes in his fists. Isda swooped in, relieving Muneer of his AK-47, and was right behind Bath Kol, who'd picked up Azrael's nine-millimeter on the run.

But the huge beast in the water slammed the vessel again, sending the passengers sprawling and the chest sliding. Up and running toward it, Celeste went after the box, grabbed one of the heavy metal handles, then felt something slam into her back with such force her vision went black.

Agonizing current traveled swiftly up her spine and terminated at the top of her skull, making it feel as if the top of her head would explode. Something icy had wrapped around her entire body, burning her and freezing her at the same time. It was as though she'd been lassoed by a dark-energy current that had a paralyzing effect. No matter how hard she fought against it, she couldn't move—just felt the painful electric shock convulsing her body and limbs. Then she was moving so fast that it stripped the air from her lungs. In the distance reaches of her mind she heard her sisters screaming *no*. Could see Azrael turn in the air in the midst of battle and throw a battle-ax while yelling her name.

She hit a hardwood floor with a thud, coughing and

sputtering and trying to stand up. But something held her that felt as if a thousand ants were eating her skin. As soon as she drew in a good enough inhale, she screamed and forced her eyes open. Hooded, scythe-clutching demons surrounded her. She covered her head with her arms, balling up to keep them from tearing at her stomach.

They didn't attack her, just smiled and hissed, their decomposing, skeletal faces oozing with gore and maggots as they slowly parted. The handsome dark angel that she'd seen before stood over her with his raven-hued wings extended. Instinctively she knew he was the leader. She remembered him in her mind as the Roman with his once-flawless features and dark-olive complexion and thicket of dark-brown, wavy hair.

But after the battle in Philadelphia, he was marred, and that gave her some small measure of satisfaction. They could be hurt and had been hurt. The side of his face was badly burned, and he smiled at her as his demons cut open with their scythes the chest she'd been trying to save.

A blond fallen angel, the one that had first attacked Azrael in Philadelphia at the library, was there, too. The tall, platinum blond with a husky's eyes walked closer to her. She'd know him anywhere; would never forget his cruel grin. What looked like a female vampire laughed at her when she tried to scramble backward to get away from them, but hit a wall instead.

"Thank you," the dark one she remembered was named Asmodeus crooned. "You've brought me what I've been looking for."

Confusion tore at her mind as she stared at Asmodeus's pitch-black eyes.

The blond laughed without sound, just baring razor-sharp fangs. "You touched the brass key at the monument t Abu Simbel . . . you knew we had guards posted every-vhere. All we needed was one more tracker to bring us o this."

Asmodeus backed up and lifted a linen-covered, quare object from the heavy metal chest as the woman vho'd taunted her drew in close to him while he un-wrapped it. The blond stood off a bit, his eyes suddenly urning black and hungry as he craned his neck to see.

Despite her terror, the book made Celeste gape. Asmo-leus gloated over his find as iridescent colors swirled over he surface crystal. Even from where she sat on the floor, he could see the heavily inscribed gold shining through he thick crystal enclosure.

"Bring me the key," Asmodeus ordered, stroking the neavy tome as one would caress a lover.

A demon behind him hissed, "There is no key, milord."

Asmodeus spun around and looked at the blond war-rior. "What do you mean there is no key? This sacred book cannot be accessed through the crystal without the blessed key!" Suddenly he whirled on Celeste as the female fallen and blond fallen warriors backed up. "Where is my key?"

Celeste lifted her chin, suddenly understanding that the key wasn't for the metal box. That was sealed and the key to that discarded. What Muneer had worn around his neck was the key to the actual book itself. A slow, angry smile tugged at Celeste's cheek as she looked up at both fallen angels that were surrounded by hooded demons. The lie formed in her mind quickly, to her great satisfaction.

"The last time I saw it, the key was around *Azrael's* neck."

*"She's not here!" Isda* shouted, grabbing Azrael by both shoulders. "We have to evacuate these other mortals before the next onslaught."

Azrael pushed Isda off him so hard that he fell into Bath Kol. "I am not leaving without her! Tonight I will open a chasm to hell and see Lucifer himself!"

Terrified glances passed between the other mortals on the boat. Blue-white light sparked from the edges of Azrael's shoulder blades, turned his eyes glowing white, and lifted his locks off his shoulders with crackling energy.

"They will not kill her—they can't kill her," Bath Kol said, staying out of Azrael's swing range. "If they do, everything they raise during a reanimation ceremony will fight for our side. They *cannot* kill her, Az. You know the Law from before—if the dark side directly kills a member of the Remnant, then the power reverts to our side. It has always been that way."

"They can make her kill herself! Just like they did to countless others! How long do you think she can last if they torture her? They are allowed to torture her, BK!"

Bath Kohl looked away. "We *have* to get these people out of here."

"They don't have to kill her to make her suffer," Azrael bellowed, causing small fissures in the structure of the boat. Soon the seams of the vessel began to snap and crack as white light raced along them with crackling sounds of fury. Water began to leak in as the wood in the hull began to expand and groan. "I want her back and I want Asmodeus's head rolling at my feet!"

"First order of business is saving the lives we can, mon." Isda looked at Azrael hard, not backing down. "Aswan is about twenty miles from here. On a cloaked carry we can airlift Kadeem and Muneer back to the Nubian village. Same with the ladies. The cruise ship has docked in Aswan by now, which means we get 'Ziza, Mel, and Maggie back there safe. That's real talk, Az. We don't need no more hostages taken or God forbid any casualties. That ship is prayer tight, and they can stay on it all the way back to Cairo while we search for Celeste. There, in Cairo, we can get 'em on a protected flight. But what is crazy talk is being out here on a compromised vessel with mortals aboard and calling out the fallen for an air strike. For you and me, mon, that's a brawl—for dese people, that's suicide and irresponsible. I'm not down wit dat, even for our beloved Celeste—she wouldn't want that and you know it!"

Azrael walked away, seething with frustration. He stood at the bow of the ship for a moment. "Fine. I surrender the search until we ensure the safety of the group."

"But they cannot open the book without the key," Kadeem said, looping the chain over his head and timidly offering it to Azrael. "This is what Daoud said. He locked the box and threw that in the Nile. Then he turned and put this valuable one over my head and said the prayer. He said only the righteous can hold the key; only the righteous can make it open the book that gives life."

Azrael took the key and looped it over his head. "I thought you said you didn't know what this was."

"I didn't. I thought it was superstition by a man studying to be a holy man. I never actually saw the book. But
after tonight . . ." Muneer shook his head.

"They have to bargain for that key," Gavreel said, trying to break through Azrael's rage. "She could have been
demon-snatched into a million caves and caverns in this
region. You have the key; that means we have something
to bargain with."

*"Bargain with him!" Rahab* shouted, walking in
a smoking path in front of his desk in the villa's study.
She looked at Asmodeus and then stared at Celeste, who
was sitting smugly in a high-back leather chair across the
room.

She was on Celeste in a blur and slapped her so hard
that blood and spittle flew out of her mouth. Out of the
chair in a shot, Celeste jumped up to punch her, but Rahab
grabbed her by her throat and hissed, strangling Celeste
until she sat down again.

"Think about it," Rahab threatened.

"No, you think about it," Forcas said, making Rahab
leave Celeste to approach the desk. "We cannot outright
kill her or anything we raise from the pit will fight for
them in the final days."

Asmodeus nodded. "This does pose a slight but not
insurmountable dilemma. If I call out Azrael now, he is
insane with fury and fear about what we might do to her.
Therefore, we need to allow that worry to strangle him
and calm him down so that we can better bargain with
the man. If I call him into a duel at present, he will come

through the ether like a bolt of lightning to find her. He needs to think about this awhile . . . call it a cooling-off period to twist in the agony of not knowing."

Asmodeus stood and went to Celeste, caressing her face as she shoved him away to no avail. "He needs to wonder what sweet torture I've visited upon his beloved." Holding her jaw, he kissed Celeste's temple, then laughed when she tried to punch and slap him away.

The kiss there created a dull ache as though something were trying to enter her mind. She squeezed her eyes to fight it, praying with all her might to back it up off her until Asmodeus laughed out loud.

"I like her," he said. "I do see why Azrael is so smitten." He turned to Celeste. "Won't you consider joining our side? Even for a little while? I bet you'd be killer sexy with fangs."

Celeste leaned away from him as far as she could in her chair and turned her head.

"No matter. I am going to kill your boyfriend . . . then I'll make my offer again. We have time."

"We need to be where we will be strong when we do the double cross," Rahab said, her eyes beginning to glow as they became narrow slits. "In order to get the maximum benefit from the incantation, we must open the dark gateway in the pearl city of the strongest nation."

"Philae? But it is so small an island." Forcas looked between Rahab and Asmodeus.

Rahab shook her head and dropped her voice to a sexy, sinister murmur. "No. When this book was crafted, Philae was the center of commerce in the region and Egypt was the strongest nation. Now the strongest nation is the United States and the original seat of power was Philadelphia. It is also a port city."

"But it requires the power of the ancient temples." Asmodeus paced away from Celeste and stared out the balcony window with his hands behind his back.

"The founders of modern Philadelphia were Masons. They laid a power grid there by setting up all their monuments in the exact formation as the ancient, sacred temples. It's called sacred geometry, gentlemen, and the Masons and original builders of the West's new empire lifted the technique from Egypt to ensure its power. Very convenient for us."

Asmodeus turned and stared at Rahab. Forcas looked at her with a sly smile.

She nodded. "The power grid, based on how the modern buildings and monuments are set up, is laid out in the city according to the kabbalistic tree-of-life grid. Every symbol has a reference to ancient Egypt in it. You will get the maximum effect from doing the ceremony there, and I have found a dark portal that is perfect. Within the grid is a place where something very dark against humanity happened—that creates a portal to our side that we can use."

"Talk to me, Rahab. Quickly. I'm not in the mood to be played with." Asmodeus leveled a pure black gaze at her and she walked away from him, unfazed by the threat.

"Did it ever occur to you to wonder why Azrael had to go to Philadelphia to find this scrawny little bitch?" Rahab folded her arms over her chest as Forcas chuckled.

Celeste glared at Rahab, promising in her mind to kick her evil ass somehow, someday—and *knowing* that Azrael was going to take that other foul bastard's head.

"We were advised, as you recall, by the Dark Lord's messengers that her DNA recurred in Philadelphia, and so Azrael came to that location to recover one of theirs before we broke her. Your point?" Asmodeus folded his arms over his chest. "How does this resurrect my army?"

"Because if you do the ceremony anywhere else, you will get weak results—just like when you brought back Malpas and the others. Everything points to Philadelphia. The Remnant was there. The first battle with Azrael was there. Trust me, milord, the energy needed for the ceremony is there, and the power grid set up by the founding fathers is there."

Rahab approached Asmodeus's desk and leaned on it to stare over it at him. "Here are the elements involved in your not-so-simple demand to raise your army, milord. I am good, the best, but even I must combine the resources just so."

"Then beyond what I have already provided, what *specifically* do you require to make this happen?" He leaned over his desk and said in a low warning, "Make this your last request on this subject. I need results."

Rahab released a frustrated sigh. "First of all, they do things in trinities. A book, a key, a sarcophagus. I've got two out of three; I should have known there'd be a third element, but until I saw the book there was no way to know that."

"A little research might have given you a clue," Forcas said through his teeth. "My ass has been on the line acquiring your spell elements."

She narrowed her gaze on him. "My research is impeccable. This is what you would never learn from extorting demons and humans. . . . The book is gold, symbolic of male energy—thus the key we seek must be silver, feminine energy. This is why the crystal book of tablets was hidden in waters near a feminine energy site, the Temple of Isis. Just like a very strong male Remnant, Imhotep, was buried on the site of a female temple, the Temple of Hathor, to balance out the male energy. To create or re-create life you must have balance *and* female energy."

Rahab walked away. "Normally, the book would be silver and the key gold—the male key inserting into the feminine lock. But the creator of the book reversed it, meaning the female energy of life or birth must come into the male bringing it to life . . . the warriors we want to raise. Feminine ground on the site of the Temple of Hathor hid Imhotep, and when we dug up his crystal sarcophagus, symbolically the feminine earth gave birth to man. He came out of the earth. Now the male book will *take in* the female key to create life. Don't you see, the two processes are mirror images of one another."

Asmodeus ran his palms down his face. "I hate this complicated bullshit! I just want to raise my army!" He pounded his desk, then swept everything off it. "Why couldn't they just have made it a basic spell?"

"Because then any general-regulation demon would have had access to reanimating their fallen." Ignoring his outburst, Rahab pressed on, "So, if we have the three elements, then with this fortuitous acquisition of Azrael's Remnant bitch, we have the three life-forms needed from three Remnants . . . Imhotep's male DNA by way of his golden-dipped bones . . . this female creature," Rahab said, waving a dismissive hand toward Celeste, "who, by the way, is probably what we need to open the book, given that they've no doubt booby-trapped it with a blessed key made of altar silver—of course they would make it so that if we touched the key, we'd fry, so we need a human who can actually touch the key . . . and immortal cells."

Both Asmodeus and Forcas frowned but remained silent.

"*HeLa* cells," Rahab murmured with triumph. "Henrietta Lacks . . . a poor black woman who got cervical cancer and is buried to this day in an unmarked grave. Because she was placed in a segregated ward that was not up to standard, she got uremic poisoning." Rahab stopped and smiled as Asmodeus slowly clapped.

"One for our side," Rahab said, widening her evil grin. "It wasn't a direct kill of a Remnant, so the powers that be couldn't blame us. Her family remains indigent to this day, even though the biological research industry has made billions off this woman's immortal T cells. They do not die, even though she's been dead for *sixty years*. Her cells were the first biological property sold in the United States and have been used ever since her cells were studied at Johns Hopkins. Easy to acquire. I always keep some for anything like this that might come up."

Rahab laughed at her own joke and crossed the room gaily. "So, we have a dead Remnant male, Imhotep; a living Remnant female, *her;* and one in the spirit with immortal cells, in a petri dish. The living blood, of course, will come from that one," Rahab said, glancing at Celeste with a cruel smile. "The other elements get mixed into the center of the ritual pentagram. We have the sarcophagus, the book . . . and only need the key."

"But you mentioned the portal?" Forcas glanced around. "This dark portal that exists on a kabbalistic tree of life . . . how so?"

"If you look at the city's grid," she said, drawing with her finger in the air and allowing black, sulfuric smoke to follow where it traced to linger there, "Independence Mall has that nation's first president's house, which could be likened to the first pharaoh's palace." She glanced over her shoulder at Forcas. "You gentlemen must be creative. But George Washington was a Mason. His first home was on Sixth and Market—our number, six, plus the word meaning 'commerce' or 'trade.' Where this location resides, if you go down that long boulevard called Market Street, is at the very termination point from all the monuments down a straight axis to their metaphor for a pyramid and temple—the Art Museum."

"The energy creates a portal? But how is this dark?" Asmodeus said, beginning to pace.

Rahab threw her head back and cackled and pointed at Celeste. "*She* is the dark portal, where dark energy came in."

"She's a Remnant," Forcas said in a flat tone, studying his manicure. "Get serious. This one didn't break."

"The *pharaoh* broke, making his house or his palace—chose your words, it doesn't matter—unholy ground." Rahab crossed her arms and smiled. "He espoused freedom and had *nine slaves* . . . in that house, on that mall, in that power grid of Light where the founding fathers prepared to go to war over freedom. On December fifteenth, 2010, they even put a memorial for the nine there because it was a dark secret and finally people found out and demanded justice, posthumous." She looked at Forcas with triumph blazing in her eyes. "I *did* my research. I *read* the newspapers—internationally. I *scour* the Internet looking for portals. Don't *ever* doubt me in the research department."

She then returned her attention to Asmodeus. "All around that mall area, slaves were sold and brought to market. *That* is an energy breech. Nine is an end number, a number of termination. *She* was one of the nine in her last life. *That* is a conflict in ideology, wouldn't you say? Where there is hypocrisy, we can come in . . . true or false?"

"Rahab," Asmodeus said with a slow smile, "this is why you always make my dick hard."

Chapter 20

*M*ortals had been deposited safely, a village had been doubly secured, women in Azrael's care were out of harm's way . . . all except Celeste.

The fury radiating from his presence alone cleared the top deck of the small cruise ship. Whether it was free will or some instinctual reservoir of self-preservation, mere mortals found a reason to enjoy another area of the ship when Azrael and his men took over the stern.

Nearly blind with rage, Azrael leaned on the railing with both forearms, trying to see beyond the horizon into the next dimension until the rail glowed white-hot.

"You're going to cause a deck fire if you don't channel this properly, mon," Isda said calmly.

Bath Kol was on Azrael's flank. "Listen, as long as you've got that key—"

"You told me that already," Azrael yelled, pushing

away from the rail. "But standing around and doing nothing doesn't help her!"

"Burning yourself out doesn't either, brother," Gavreel suggested soothingly. "Let's think this through strategically."

"Think, wait . . . what *the hell!*" Azrael said now, pacing.

"That is exactly where Asmodeus wants you to be," Paschar said calmly. "In hell. In your mind. So you can't think."

Aziza walked up to the gathering of men with Melissa and Maggie and stood in front of Azrael. "You're connected to her, you know."

Tempering his response out of respect, even though the words wouldn't form, he nodded.

"May I see the key?" Aziza held out her hand. It wasn't a request.

Azrael looped the chain over his head and gave it to her, watching her study it.

"The book was gold, right? Quartz crystal around it and gold?" She looked up at Azrael but Bath Kol nodded.

"Yeah," Bath Kol said, and took out a cigarette.

"A key is usually symbolic of male energy, yet this silver key, silver being the feminine principle, is going into a male book." She stood on the deck holding the key, absorbing from it as the chain dangled between her graceful fingers and Azrael's nerves frayed down to a nub. "You've been trying to locate her, right?"

"C'mon, 'Ziza," Bath Kol said, lighting up. "What kinda question is that? The man here is losing his freakin' mind and—"

"You've been trying to go into her mind for knowledge, trying to locate her by forcible entry, and the people who have her aren't worried about her—they're worried about you. So, fall back. Surrender."

"What?" Azrael walked in a small circle, trying to keep his voice modulated when responding to Aziza.

"Let her come into you," Aziza said quietly, then closed her eyes. "In fact, there are three sisters here. She can come to us, rather than us trying to chase her down."

No one spoke for a few minutes as Aziza scanned the environment for impressions with her mind.

"Paschar, that's why your visions aren't connecting with her, either. You aren't allowing her impressions to come into you . . . you are chasing her, running her down to capture her thoughts. All with good intent, of course, but it doesn't work that way under these circumstances. Old paradigms are falling away. It is a return of the feminine principle."

Aziza opened her eyes and laid a hand on Azrael's arm. "Come. Sit. You need to be healed before you can complete this mission."

"No offense, Aziza, but I need to kill something. When I'm done, you can heal me."

Steadfast, she blocked his attempt to step around her. "No. In order to find her, you have to use the lessons we learned in the village. At every turn, we've been given signs. What did we learn there? That we cannot do it alone—you cannot do it alone."

Azrael let out a hard breath, uncomfortable with the reminder.

"Pride goeth before a fall, man," Aziza said, frowning. "You of all people know that."

"Wow . . . she went there," Bath Kol said with a low whistle.

"Dat's cold, ma," Isda said in a dejected murmur.

"It's the truth," she said, folding her arms over her petite breasts with the key firmly clutched in her hand. "Tell him, BK. I can turn his chakras inside out, and he needs that right now. In fact, didn't that little boy teach your big, burly ass *anything* about surrender in order to conquer the dark?"

"Surrender is my Achilles' heel, I admit," Azrael said in a low rumble.

Aziza sucked her teeth and then pointed to a chair. "Go, sit!" She spun on the group as Azrael moved to a deck chair and plopped down in it. "This man is the one among us who is most injured, but unlike the child, not only doesn't he accept that he's been mortally wounded by the abduction of Celeste, he rejects a collective effort to try to take this pain from him. Pain is sickness, dis-ease of the mind, body, and spirit. So, we are going to surround him like we did for that child and we are going to send so much love, so much Light, so much hope, into him that his spirit will be bright enough for Celeste to see through the darkness clouding her head. And, then, he is going to be receptive—open—yielding to accept in her transmissions to him so he can see *her* . . . and we're gonna get on our knees beside him and be his training wheels until he gets this receiving thing down cold. *Then* he can go kill something. Agreed?"

"Yes," Azrael said as others joined in. He stared up

at the petite women who stood before him with her arms folded looking as though she were ready to have a street fight. "I'm sorry. You're right. This thing is tearing me up, Aziza."

"Ashé," she murmured, getting down on her knees in front of him and taking up his hands.

Hers were so small within his as she pressed the key between their palms and she kissed the backs of his hands. "We're gonna get her back, honey. I know this to be true, but you've gotta believe."

His brothers and sisters in battle slid beside Aziza and fit in all around him. She bowed her head and led the prayer, pelting stanzas with "Ashé, amen, and so it is!" Her fervent energy channeled in from all the others' energy took hold of his spinal column, layering Light and current where trauma had blacked out sections. Then she placed her hand over his chest, pressing the key to his heart chakra, making warmth bloom within the once-heavy cavity. Soon that warmth spread to his lungs and through his torso and down his limbs. Peace was there but so was determination.

"Feel her," Aziza murmured, now placing both hands on his chest with her eyes closed. "Remember everything you love about her and invite her into this space of Light within you and then be still . . . suspend all thought. Just feel her warmth coming into you."

Azrael could feel his brothers' wings gently brushing his shoulders and arms as they surrounded him, then they faded like the breeze. Melissa's and Maggie's slow, easy breaths melted into the night. Aziza's hands, like hot stones, disappeared into the heat that became Celeste's

mile . . . and her laugh . . . and her sigh . . . and her warm
embrace. Her sad, sad smile and distant gaze out of a window drifted on a tear that ran down his cheek. Then her
eyes became his eyes as he looked out from them from a
villa on the Red Sea.

"Baby . . . where did they take you?" he murmured,
feeling her breaths become his breaths.

*I don't know . . . but they are taking me home. Go home.*

"To heaven . . . or to our home?" he said on a quiet
exhale of her breath.

*Philly.*

"Are you hurt?" he said, tracing his bottom lip and
tasting blood. "Who struck you?"

*Rahab,* the wind told him as the Nile lapped against
the ship's hull.

"I love you so much, baby. I'm coming for you."

*No . . . let me show you what they have planned. Then
come to me. I love you.*

Images poured into his mind, reverberating against
the darkness of his worst fears and deepest rage, and soon
the images rippled through the group, entering each person who touched him until it was over and they were left
spent.

Azrael sat up, then stood up and rubbed both palms
down his face. "Thank you, Aziza. I am forever in your
debt."

"You all have to leave us; we'll just slow you down,"
Aziza said quietly, and looked at Bath Kol. "We can catch
a flight out of Luxor so we don't have to go all the way
back to Cairo, if Isda can arrange it. But we'll be protected. They don't want us and don't want to jeopardize

you giving them the key. Some of the brothers that es
corted us over can escort us back, but you have to go an
warn the others."

Bath Kol came to her and held her hands and then
suddenly hugged her. "Didn't we do this before, Aziza
You told me that before and they burned the temple to th
ground with you in it. You didn't come back for *lifetime.*
We'll figure out—"

"Shhhh," she whispered, and kissed him gently. "Yo
have to go. I eventually came back when it was time, and
it's probably far more dangerous what you're about t
walk into than me catching a flight with the girls home."

"You are minimizing, woman, I know you," he said
dropping his head against her shoulder.

She rubbed the broad expanse of his shoulders by hug
ging him tightly and reaching up and under his wings
"Walk through the ether and don't look back."

Gavreel folded Maggie into a winged embrace, and
Paschar took Melissa into his arms and shielded their dee
kiss with his plumage.

"We're gonna get her back, mon, seriously," Isda said
landing a hand on Azrael's shoulder. "And all in on
piece."

Azrael looped the key over his neck and rubbed i
"Absolutely."

*Take a memo," Asmodeus* said, staring at a hooded mes
senger demon as its eyes began to glow. "Go find Azrae
and tell him that I have something of his of value and h
has something of mine, and I'd like to do an exchange."

The demon nodded and lowered his scythe. "I will need protection, given his state. And how will I find him?"

Asmodeus stood and went to Celeste. He stroked her cheek, then slapped her, opening up the cut on her lip. He tore a bit of fabric from his sleeve as she angrily glared at him while straining against the nylon ties that held her. When he wiped her lip with the fabric, she spit in his face.

"Perfect," he murmured, and wiped his face with the bloody fabric, then handed it to the demon. "This is bait. He was last seen around Philae but is probably heading back toward Aswan where he came down from this afternoon. He has to have made camp somewhere. Put this cloth out there in the desert and come to him as a swarm. Become many insects with very tiny heads or I assure you he will take yours."

*Blood on the wind* made Azrael lift his head from his top-deck meditation and push away from the rail. Total panic electrified his limbs. The sense of complete powerlessness made him grind his teeth. He'd been waiting for Isda to secure the women's safe passage back to the United States, then the brothers would walk through the ether as a unit to return early to Philadelphia. But now Celeste's blood was in the air? Intolerable.

Wings spread, he ran across the deck and launched himself into the air. Moonlight turned the golden desert sand an eerie blue-gray, and he spotted a piece of cloth that had her signature on it . . . her blood, her sweat, the sweet saliva from her mouth. Panic made him hit the sand in a one-knee crouch. But as soon as he pulled the strip of fabric out of the ground, it was as though he'd detonated a grenade, and he knew he'd been set up.

Thousands of vicious, biting scarabs frothed from the sand, tearing at his skin, infesting his wings, burrowing into his skin, and trying to enter his nose and mouth. He stood up like a burning force of nature, jettisoning the refuse from him by going still for two seconds, then glowing blue-white hot, causing the evil little beetles to scream and crackle-fry. Then off in the distance the insects converged into a tall black pillar that soon resolved into the injured body of a hooded messenger demon.

The wicked creature stared at him with a sinister grin, maggots crawling through the putrefied skin of its skeletal face. Its eyes gleamed red and cruel as it gripped its scythe with rotting, skeletal hands. "The master says you have something of his, avenger! He will make a trade."

"Tell him yes," Azrael shouted. "Tell him to meet me in Philadelphia—where I can return her safely to her home and her people."

"You are in no position to bargain," the demon said smugly, then hissed.

"Nor are you," Azrael said calmly, then with lightning speed threw his blue-white battle-ax.

❖

*Asmodeus smiled as a* demon head burst through the air with a sizzling battle-ax and cleaved into his floor.

"He homed it to the demon's energy, which brought it back to us. Very dangerous that he's aware we are so near.

Our only saving grace, not that we have such a thing anymore, is that he's showing amazing restraint because of the girl," Rahab said calmly, kicking the smoldering head away and making the ax clatter to the floor.

She waited until the weapon slowly disappeared into the ether before going to retrieve the head. Picking it up by its bloody hood, she brought it to her scrying table in Asmodeus's office.

"Hmmm, so what did the avenger say? How did he take the threat?" Forcas smiled and placed a finger to his lips. "From the looks of things he didn't take it well and definitely killed the messenger. Just a guess, but I don't think he's in a hostage-bargaining mood, milord."

"Stop toying with that disgusting thing and read the response," Asmodeus snapped, then eyed Forces with a warning when he smiled.

After a moment Rahab looked up. "You broke him." She stared at Celeste and smirked at Celeste's horrified expression. "An angel violating the ultimate rule, and he'll trade the lives of humanity all for her. Really? Do you know how many angelic Laws that violates—to turn away from one's mission to be concerned about all of humanity to only care about one mere mortal . . . if you are not a Guardian Angel? This is so rich!"

"You must have interpreted incorrectly," Asmodeus said, walking up to the table and shoving her aside.

"Feel for yourself," Rahab said, folding her arms. "He's panicked and worried and will do a trade in her hometown *tonight*." She threw back her head and laughed. "The man is totally smitten by her. Oh, you should feel this, and so naive that he thinks if he gives us the key, she can just go back to West Philly like none of this ever happened. How cute."

"Do you know how many wars in antiquity began because of a woman? How many betrayals and poor strategic moves were made because a man or a general was blinded by emotion? I never thought that I would live to see the day that the Angel of Death was so moved." Asmodeus shook his head. "Pull her through a demon door and set up the ritual elements on the Philadelphia site. We raise an army tonight!"

*"It's awfully quiet, mon,"* Isda said in a low mutter as they crept around the building that was only five hundred feet north of Independence Hall.

Bath Kol nodded. "Too quiet. The Liberty Bell Pavilion sits just east of the mansion in what was the president's garden, according to the map. We need to get an aerial view—but if they've got gargoyles on patrol in the building rafters, not good."

"You think they took the bait?" Paschar glanced at Gavreel.

"We'll know soon enough," Gavreel whispered, then made a fist.

They all looked at Azrael.

"I don't like you going into that center alone, mon."

"Either I walk in there alone or they send her out in pieces," Azrael said, keeping his eyes on the building. "And she can still live so they wouldn't be violating the Law. They can chop off her fingers, her ears, her toes, shear sections of flesh off her body, or send me her beautiful eyes in a bag, and leave her alive for a human ambulance. She would survive, but I would not."

He stood and walked across the wide street. There was nothing left to discuss. Asmodeus's demons were already here. He could smell their sulfur. Bodies moved within the glass-enclosed structure. They'd defiled the building and, deep within it, had set up for a ritual—he could see that right through the glass.

His old nemeses stood back by the wall as he took in the horror of what they'd done to Celeste and what they were about to visit upon the world. A glass sarcophagus with ancient gold bones was in the center of a pentagram with Celeste also tied to a chair, the tablet in her lap, waiting on the key, blood dripping from her arm into a chalice set on the floor. Black candle flames licked the air and added tallow to the sulfuric sick stench wafting off the demons.

Eyes filled the ceiling rafters. A carpet of insects waited for the order to devour. Snarling beasts haunted the shadows. Asmodeus's inner circle of fallen brandished weapons, remembering their deaths at his hands. Malpas, Appollyon, Bune, Onoskelis, and Pharzuh, killed by Celeste, all wounded and rotting and seething for their chance to exact revenge. Forcas bowed and smiled a vicious grin. Celeste looked so weak that she could barely lift her head. The sight of that alone was enough to make his eyes glow white-hot with pure warrior-angel rage.

Asmodeus stepped out of a fold of darkness with Rahab. She left his side and went to the pentagram and dipped her finger into Celeste's blood.

"You are the Angel of Death and yet you have a problem with death," Asmodeus said, smiling. "Ahhh, just like the self-righteous, you talk a good game, but when it comes to you following the same rules..." Asmodeus wagged his finger at Azrael. "Are you sure you can still go home? Or are you banished, like us? What other bad things have you done while here?" Asmodeus turned and laughed with his demons, but his inner circle of fallen didn't even smile. "You are standing on very shaky ground, Azrael. Why not join us? The pay is excellent, the benefits are Cadillac... you can even have her back when we're done."

"Our deal was that I get her now and walk out of here with her unharmed." Azrael looped the key over his head and dangled it in front of Asmodeus, allowing a battle-ax to fill his other hand. "All I want is her."

"You would allow me to raise an army that could wipe out half of humanity, for her?"

"We're early. Twelve twenty-one twelve is a couple of weeks away yet. Much can happen in that time." Azrael swung the key back and forth like a taunting pendulum. "We conquered the army of darkness before when it was full strength; I have no problem doing so again. So we will meet on the battlefield soon enough, but she is not a part of our conflict. Take it or leave it."

"You're surrounded," Asmodeus said calmly. "Look around."

"Do you know that you are not?" Azrael said, arching an eyebrow. "The one thing you do know from the old days in the Light is that I cannot lie. If I say that I will give you this key for Celeste, then my word is bond. I want her away from this."

"We *need her* to open the book," Rahab hissed. "The key is made of silver."

"You already have her precious blood in the chalice," Azrael said in an unwavering tone. "*I* will put the key in the book. But she comes with me before you turn the key—I want her away from here! Sacrifice a demon to turn it to open it. That is my final offer."

Tense quiet strangled the room as Celeste's head lolled back.

"Put the key in the book," Asmodeus murmured, his eyes glowing black.

Azrael nodded and crossed the symbol that was drawn on the floor. Celeste looked up at him bleary-eyed and shook her head.

"No," she whispered weakly when he thrust the key into the crystal opening.

Wary and watching the evil entities that surrounded them and the pentagram that was in the center of the room, he placed an arm at her back and under her legs, dissolving the twist ties, and stood slowly, then instantly spun into the nothingness with her in his arms and the book on her lap.

The glass blew out of the Liberty Bell Center. Asphalt rippled and stacked slab against slab against itself, tossing cars, setting off alarms as black-winged fallen burst forth from the building. Gargoyles screamed their discontent, drowning out Asmodeus's roar. The grassy knoll in front of the Constitution Center erupted with demon warriors on nightmare horsebacks.

Celeste lifted her head and clutched the book to her chest, letting the fake key that was silversmithed in

Aswan fall to the ground as Azrael flew up Market Street toward City Hall—the goal to reach the cathedral on the Parkway.

Isda's hands shook as he gave her the true key from around his neck midair. He looped the chain around her neck, then somersaulted back in the air to add cover, sending an RPG shell into the dark flock. But expert fliers veered off and the shell took out a section of the Constitution Center without slowing down the pursuit.

Gavreel, Bath Kol, and Paschar formed a protective barrier between Azrael and the mob of mutant ravens that split off from Malpas's twisted body. But Onoskelis and Rahab flew up parallel streets, sending from between buildings black-energy charges toward them that looked like black lightning-bolt strikes.

"Do it now!" Azrael shouted. "We may not get to hallowed ground!"

Working quickly, Celeste opened the book. The moment she did, the radiant light pouring from it scorched demons that were dive-bombing at their flanks.

"I call the ancestors, the warriors of Light from the pharaoh's armies, the Nubian armies, the armies of antiquity . . . chariots, palace guards, cavalry, infantry! I call the men of this land that had good ideals but did not live up to them then—here is your chance now to bring your armies forward against the darkness! Rectify the wrongs of the past with this right! We fight together against that which divided us. I forgive you; forgive yourselves and change the future!"

The book slammed itself shut. A concussive blast blew Azrael and Celeste five blocks against the top clock of City

Hall. Bath Kol hurled into a glass office building. Gavreel hit a hotel with Paschar. Isda went into the plate-glass window of a restaurant.

Suddenly a massive blue-white orb swept out from the book, like a fast-moving carpet of energy, and stopped everything and everyone, demons included, from falling, stopping time, soaking up sound, freezing their motion as Celeste's eyes fluttered blue-white. It was as though time stopped, motion stopped, sound evaporated, in a blue-white miasma. Everything she witnessed connected psychically to Melissa, Maggie, and Aziza as it coursed through Azrael. Knowing slammed into Azrael as the contents of the book filled Celeste's mind and then fused with his.

Then suspended time snapped back to real time. Demons and the fallen crashed to the ground. Warriors of Light slowly stood. Azrael caught Celeste in the air, still clutching the book, her body convulsing in a frightening seizure as the asphalt turned to desert sand. Mighty armies parted the ocean of sand; soldiers raised gleaming blades. Desert warriors released high-pitched battle cries and took off toward the Liberty Bell. Warriors from different eras emerged from beneath paved streets, running in the same direction like a bizarre tapestry of uniforms and weapons not in correct time sequence. Cannon fire from Revolutionary infantries punched the air. Demon bodies exploded in cinders as expert fighters hacked and cut back the darkness.

Shoppers and pedestrians, businesspeople and tourists, screamed and tried to take cover as their world and minds shattered from witnessing the incomprehensible.

Angels swept them aside to safety as much as was possible, while cars and gas mains exploded, blowing out the glass fronts of buildings. Chaos reigned; humans bled and were healed on the fly. War was what it was and took no prisoners.

But Azrael's goal was hallowed ground. Celeste was still in seizure. As he carried her as fast as he could, death went by in a blur. Isda took Rahab's head with a pharaoh's razor-sharp flail, as Gavreel caught Forcas with a shell to the back of the head. A cannon blast crushed what was left of Malpas's destroyed chest. Appollyon and Pharzup went down under horse hooves and desert blades. Lahash was stunned right between the eyes with a hallowed-earth-packed shell from Bath Kol, who then swung around and squeezed off three more to blow away each of Bune's snapping dragon heads.

Demons on the ground retreated. As soon as the army of darkness opened a crater in the asphalt, the sand sucked itself back into the earth with it. Glass snapped back into building windows, asphalt smoothed out, cars righted themselves, and monuments belched out any desecration to again be pristine tourist attractions. But totally traumatized humans remained. The people who'd been on the streets dashed about waving their arms in panic. Screams could still be heard behind Azrael like a Doppler effect. His brothers would have to quell their minds; there was no time and his focus was singular—Celeste.

Celeste's body calmed and then she went limp in his arms with her eyes open, not breathing.

He hit the steps of the basilica, moved the book off her

chest, and laid her on the ground trying to resuscitate her with CPR. The variable none of them had considered was that her human heart might not be able to withstand the supernatural power unleashed by the book.

Frantic, he worked harder, sent more healing toward her through his hands, then suddenly the key chain was strangling him.

Azrael fell backward into the force that had lifted him off Celeste's body. Attacked from behind, his preoccupation with healing Celeste had left him vulnerable. A hard crack stunned him and sent blinding pain into the back of his skull as his body lifted off the ground. The black-energy charge came with such force that it temporarily blinded him. Then he heard a whoosh, ducked, but was now strangling. Metal was wrapped around his throat, and a giant mace had missed his skull by only millimeters.

Grabbing the chain that was cutting into his throat, he flipped the body that was behind him, and Asmodeus hit the church steps for a second, sizzled, and flew up in a rage, billowing black smoke.

He flung another dark-energy ball at Azrael, who deflected it off his wings. The translucent black orb hit the ground and exploded like thunder. Then in a rage, Asmodeus hurled one at Celeste.

In an aerial slide, Azrael took the charge in the chest. It blew him back so hard that it singed his entire abdomen and made his back slam again the building brick, toppling masonry. Dazed, he shook his head, just in time to see Asmodeus reaching for Celeste and the book.

With his arms crossed over his chest, a fresh blade

filled each fist. In a snap motion with all the force within him, Azrael uncrossed his arms, hurling the axes forward in fury. Half a block away, the blades clanged against the side of brick buildings. Asmodeus froze as his torso slid apart in opposite directions.

Azrael touched down and watched black blood ooze across the concrete. "Go to hell," he said in a low command, then watched the pit open up to take a new body.

Concrete crumbled and gave way to a demon-rimmed abyss belching molten lava. Asmodeus's hands scrabbled at the cement, creating deep, black gashes in it as gale-force winds pulled him to the edge. He stared up at Azrael for a second, halved, his grimace in an asymmetrical Picasso slide. Shock soon became an agonized wail that turned into the word *"No!"* as his dark spirit went up in a plume of sizzling black smoke and was gone.

Instantly the sidewalk repaired itself. Azrael turned back to the steps and dropped to his knees. The victory was so hollow he could have wept, but he didn't even have that left in him. It was what it was. She had sacrificed herself for the whole. He now fully understood Bath Kol's pain.

Leaning down, he brushed her mouth with a kiss and closed her eyes with the gentle sweep of the palm of his hand. Then he lifted her to leave her body on the altar in complete surrender.

But as soon as they crossed the threshold, she gasped. Just hearing the breath of life in her body made him tremble. Mercy had been visited upon him, upon them. The Most High had heard his prayers and had not forsaken him. As he rocked her against his body, tears flowed down the bridge of his nose. He couldn't even speak around the thickness that had taken over his throat. There were no words, he could only hope she could feel his heart and spirit as he dropped to his knees and buried his face in her hair and wept.

# Epilogue

*You ready?" Azrael said* quietly, reaching through the ether to push a stray wisp of hair behind Celeste's ear.

She smiled up at him and spoke confidentially, turning away from the tense Secret Service detail that guarded them. "I wish you didn't have to stay hidden until the very end, but—"

"It's best this way. Me and the guys do not have the time to be lab rats, and if they try to incarcerate you . . . well, you know how long that'll last, right?"

Her smile broadened as she changed the subject and whispered to him quickly, "How do I look?"

"Beautiful and incredible . . . and just as important, *credible*," he said, wanting to kiss her but knowing that messing up her lipstick would only make her more nervous than she already was.

"Wish me luck?" she said, then joined Melissa, Maggie, and Aziza by the stage entrance.

"You ready for dis, mon?" Isda stared at the backstage monitor watching as the women took a seat at the UN press conference.

"Man, I never expected it to go down like this," Pasmar murmured, raking his fingers through his hair.

"You know, the Most High works in mysterious ways," Gavreel murmured, his eyes glued to the monitors.

"Yes, and she was always worried about having her voice heard, or being able to do anything that could influence people to turn their personal Lights on," Azrael said in amazement. "One can never predict how they will be used."

"Yeah, well, her mind was obviously like a giant transmitter while she was seizing. At least now we know what *the living key* was supposed to do—use the Light frequency of the twelve DNA strands within her to spread the word. That's probably what almost took her from us, man. Had to be hard on the human part of her body. She was transmitting everything that happened while she was in a seizure to the top twelve TV and radio outlets in Philly like a live feed, and having that go viral from them to blow up within thirty minutes to hit a hundred and forty-four thousand stations worldwide, not to mention going viral on the Internet, was so not what I expected." Bath Kol shook his head. "But I think your lady definitely lit the mortal community up."

"They think it was extraterrestrials, though, mon."

"What*ever*," Bath Kol said, shrugging. "A visitation

from the stars, E.T., Heaven's gate . . . it got a cease-fire t
a war in the freakin' Middle East because all sides want t
conserve arms in case a UFO lands in Times Square. Te
rorists are chilling out now that there's truth to the rumo
that the real Mu'aqqibat blew up a cave in Oman and vis
ited the desert and disclaimed any crap about a hundre
virgins for blowing up innocent people—kinda hard t
sell that rhetoric under the circumstances."

Gavreel pounded his fist. "It got people of all ethni
groups and religions talking about life beyond this bullsh
here . . . which is not necessarily a bad thing."

"This is my point," Bath Kol said, opening his arm
"So, the prophecy said, three Remnants are to stand at
sacred place on twelve twenty-one twelve in Philadelphi
to light up one hundred and forty-four thousand. Okay, s
we were a little early—but consciousness is shifting. I wa
just off by like a week, gimme a break." Bath Kol leane
in to Azrael and smiled sheepishly. "So, uh, you give an
more thought about that marriage petition? Any word o
the outcome of that little situation that you were worrie
about in Cairo?"

Azrael stepped away from the others, pulling Bat
Kohl in close by his elbow. "Michael brought me word tha
I almost got smoked for that," Azrael whispered quickly

"She's pregnant?" Bath Kol whispered in awe, eye
wide.

Azrael nodded and held Bath Kol's gaze.

"Oh, shit, man . . . are you trapped . . . like a Sentine
now—the only one on the team that can't go home again
That is so screwed—"

"No. I'm not trapped." Again, Azrael looked over h

shoulder, then leaned in close to Bath Kol's ear. "This child factors into the Armageddon, BK. They wouldn't give me more than that, but I got a pass. However, it means that the moment this pregnancy registers with the dark side, all hell is *really* gonna break loose."

Bath Kol held Azrael by his upper arms and stared into his eyes. "You know this is right up Lucifer's alley, bro. He sent his top lieutenant, who failed. This is gonna be insane."

"Yeah, I know." Azrael briefly closed his eyes. "Maybe that's why Michael didn't bother to do the honors himself."

"Yo, man, none of us are going home unless we all go home together. We've got your back. We've got Celeste's back."

Azrael pulled Bath Kol into a warrior's embrace. "Thank you."

"Hey, what are you talking about? This is how we roll, right? Been that way since the dawn of time."

"Truth."

Bath Kol held Azrael away from him, then gave him a lopsided grin. "Man, you look so freaked out that I don't know whether to say congratulations or to—"

"Shhhh," Azrael warned, looking around again. "She doesn't know yet."

"Holy moley. And when are you planning to tell her?"

"I'm working on it, but I definitely didn't want to do it before her big press conference. Work with me."

Bath Kol ran his fingers through his hair. "I guess I'll know from the glass-shattering shriek we'll hear one day soon? Okay, suit yourself, but I can tell you from experience this is not a casual conversation to be had with a human female. You, my friend, are in for the ride of your ever-living life."

Azrael nodded chuckling. "Yeah, but . . . I'm gonna be a dad."

"Yeah, man, and that's pretty cool. Three-quarters angel, too—now *that's* deep."

Azrael released a long, satisfied breath as he and Bath Kol rejoined the waiting group of fellow warriors. Azrael didn't care about the battle ahead. What he cared about was that he was allowed to love Celeste; love her until she'd filled with life and then love the life that filled her beyond the both of them. The sense of thrill mixed with peace was almost disorienting. And one thing was for sure: if the dark side wanted a fight, if he had to protect Celeste and his child, they hadn't seen anything yet.

Steadying himself so as not to give away anything to the other brothers, Azrael squared his shoulders and addressed them as though nothing out of the norm had occurred. "You ready to walk out of the ether onto the stage and spread 'em, gentlemen? I advise you to also be ready to get the ladies out of there in case the CIA or military wants more information . . . and we don't have time to indulge that. Plus, there is still the Armageddon."

"Yeah, but not today—and you're changing the subject, man." Bath Kol laughed with a wink. "Besides . . . *dude*, the Armageddon is like a border skirmish after this bull."

"You say that so casually, brother," Azrael replied, sounding concerned, but the real warning in his tone was to let Bath Kol know if he spilled the beans, Azrael would kick his ass. "That's nothing to joke about. We won yet another battle, but that's not the ultimate war."

"Battlefield humor. Relax," Bath Kol said, letting Azrael know he was just yanking his chain. "It keeps my sanity to joke about things I can't change or that might really twist my head, so allow me that one indulgence until we have to do the big campaign, will ya? You might want to do the same—appreciate every moment we're not battling all of hell. What's that thing they say? Take it one day at a time. Feel me?"

Azrael nodded, mollified. "I see the wisdom in that. I'll stand down."

"Thank you," Bath Kol muttered with a sly smile.

Isda smiled and then took off his shirt. "Well, den, let's go do some fan-dancin' burlesque with da wings."

Azrael looked at the monitor one last time, then at Celeste's smiling face as they began walking. She knew he was coming toward her, even while he was invisible. All he could do was quietly chuckle. *Man*, the things this half-mortal woman made him do.

# Fantasy.
# Temptation.
# Adventure.

## Visit PocketAfterDark.com, an all-new website just for Urban Fantasy and Romance Readers!

- Exclusive access to the hottest urban fantasy and romance titles!

- Read and share reviews on the latest books!

- Live chats with your favorite romance authors!

- Vote in online polls!

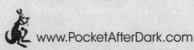

www.PocketAfterDark.com